ICE
FIRE

ICE
FIRE

A Thriller

DAVID LYONS

EMILY BESTLER BOOKS

—

ATRIA

NEW YORK   LONDON   TORONTO   SYDNEY   NEW DELHI

ATRIA BOOKS

EMILY
BESTLER
BOOKS

A Division of Simon & Schuster, Inc.
1230 Avenue of the Americas
New York, NY 10020

First Atria Books hardcover edition May 2012

EMILY BESTLER BOOKS / ATRIA BOOKS and colophon are trademarks
of Simon & Schuster, Inc.

For information about special discounts for bulk purchases,
please contact Simon & Schuster Special Sales at
1-866-506-1949 or business@simonandschuster.com.

The Simon & Schuster Speakers Bureau can bring authors
to your live event. For more information or to book an event,
contact the Simon & Schuster Speakers Bureau at
1-866-248-3049 or visit our website at www.simonspeakers.com.

Designed by Dana Sloan

Manufactured in the United States of America

10   9   8   7   6   5   4   3   2   1

Library of Congress Cataloging-in-Publication Data

Lyons, David.
  Ice fire : a thriller / by David Lyons.
        p.   cm.
  1. Political fiction. I. Title.
  PS3612.Y5745I27   2012
  813'.6—dc23   2011028535

ISBN 978-1-4516-2929-3
ISBN 978-1-4516-2931-6 (ebook)

ACKNOWLEDGMENTS

I THANK THE GEOPHYSICIST WHOSE name I never knew, who told me one night in whispered tones of his work on a secret government research project involving a new fuel source called methane hydrate. He said that energy companies were beating down his door. He told me nothing more than that, but the idea of such an exotic source of energy at the bottom of the ocean fueled my imagination, and the premise for *Ice Fire* was born. I would like to acknowledge the Woods Hole Oceanographic Institution, which has done significant research on methane hydrate found on the deep seabed, and inspired the fictional organization mentioned in the novel. I want to thank my friend Adene Corns, whose advice and guidance have been invaluable. Finally, I wish to thank the people of New Orleans and especially the French Quarter, the home of my protagonist, Jock Boucher. Your magical city will always have a home in my heart.

To Sherri

ICE
FIRE

PROLOGUE

ONE OF THE TWO men would die within the hour: the one who should have known better.

They sat in a small office, identifiable as such only by the cheap desk in the middle of the room. There was no sign outside to indicate what purpose this anonymous space served. Bob Palmetto sat behind the desk. Unruly wisps of sparse blond hair fell down his forehead, but received no attention. An occasional toss of his head kept the errant strands out of his eyes. He was extremely thin, as if eating were a routine largely ignored. His closely set eyes darted from the man sitting across from him to the tinted floor-to-ceiling glass wall, all that separated the room from the sidewalk and parking lot of a dingy strip mall. A frayed pea-green shag carpet sported coffee stains. In an old wooden chair across from the desk, lawyer Dexter Jessup sat in sport coat and tie, the tie loosened, a Windsor knot hanging at his throat.

"Why'd you set that damn meeting for tomorrow afternoon? I need you in court with me," Palmetto said.

"An attorney from my office will meet you in front of the Federal Building," Jessup said. "Her name is Ruth Kalin. Don't worry, she knows what to do."

"I'm supposed to produce more documents," Palmetto told him. "Last time the judge said he'd throw me in jail if I didn't turn them over. He had two federal marshals just standing—"

"I was there, Bob, remember?"

"Sorry." Bob Palmetto looked down, studying the bony fingers splayed across his desktop as if seeing them for the first time. "I wish I'd never started fighting this thing. They're too powerful." He looked up. "And what you're doing scares the hell out of me. What good is a dead lawyer to me?"

"I'm going to talk to the FBI, Bob, not the Mafia. I have proof of a federal judge accepting bribes, stealing your intellectual property. The bastard belongs in jail, not on the bench. I'm going to see he gets what he deserves, and you can finish what you've started. You're going to be a rich man."

Palmetto waved away this last remark.

"My discovery is dangerous. If it gets in the wrong hands, the damage could be irreversible. I've got to make sure that doesn't happen."

Dexter looked away from his client to the parking area outside. The afternoon sun hung low in the sky and was reflected in the windshields of less than a dozen cars, one of them his, casting blinding flashes of light. It was so incongruous. In a two-room office in a failed strip mall sat a man who had invented a process that could double the world's available fossil fuel deposits by withdrawing methane gas from the frozen subsea surface. A leading energy company was stealing from him, and using a federal court to do it. There was no doubt. Photos of surreptitious meetings with the judge, documents stolen from court files; Dexter had found this and more. Tomorrow he would share his findings with the only people who could do something about it, the FBI.

"I've got to go," Dexter said. He stood and extended a hand over the desk. "I might be late, but I'll see you in court tomorrow."

Palmetto clasped the lawyer's hand, staring at it, speaking to it, not raising his eyes. "Be careful," he said. "Be damned careful."

The lawyer's route from Palmetto's office took him due east, toward downtown New Orleans. He knew the direction he was traveling because the sunset was in his rearview mirror. He adjusted it, rendering it useless for its intended purpose, but at least keeping the reflected sun from blinding him. Five minutes later, the sun had dropped and he readjusted his mirror. That's when he spotted the car behind him, a black Jeep Cherokee. He knew that car and its driver. What did he want now? Dexter slowed down. There was no other traffic on this little-used secondary road. The Jeep flashed its lights. It pulled up right on his tail and flashed again. He could see the driver waving one arm out the window, motioning him to pull over. He pulled over onto the shoulder and got out of his car, leaving the door open and the motor running. The driver of the Jeep also got out and moved toward him, a little too fast. There were less than ten feet separating them.

"What do you . . ."

Dexter saw the gun in the man's hand. He turned and jumped toward his car's open door but slipped on the loose gravel of the shoulder, falling painfully to one knee. His pursuer was on him in an instant. He felt the metal against the back of his head. He did not feel the bullet that blew out his brain.

The body was left next to the car with the motor running, the radio playing the nation's number one pop single, "Ice Ice Baby."

It was October 1990.

For more than two decades, Dexter Jessup's death would be all but forgotten. Not by Bob Palmetto.

CHAPTER 1

JOCK BOUCHER SANG "ORANGE Colored Sky" in the shower. For a federal district judge, he could do a pretty good imitation of Nat King Cole, his father's favorite singer. He'd done a fair share of singing, humming, even whistling over the past two weeks since his swearing-in. It had been a long year with the congressional vetting process, but now it was over. His life's work lay ahead of him, and it was his dream job. He smiled at the recollection that his first act as a member of the federal judiciary had probably been illegal as hell. He had recorded the President calling him at home to extend his congratulations. He'd been informed of the call in advance, of course. You don't want the leader of the free world calling and getting a busy signal or no one at home. The President had pronounced his name correctly: *boo-SHAY*. Most people seeing before hearing it mispronounced it *butcher*. The President said he knew that the judge's nickname, Jock, was bestowed after lettering in basketball, football, and track in college. The two spoke as if they knew each other, which in many ways they did: two men whose love of country could not be challenged. Judge Boucher did not correct the President's error. He would have loved to have told him the true origins of his name:

that his father, a black Cajun from the bayous of Louisiana, had named his son Jacques. The French pronunciation sounded almost like *shock*, but with accents of the Deep South and demonstration of athletic ability at an early age, *Jock* it became and Jock it was to this day.

The Senate confirmation process had gone smoothly; his credentials were lauded and deemed more than adequate to assume the lifetime post of federal district judge, one of the most powerful positions in the land. "Slam, bam, alakazam," he sang. He stopped and listened. Had he ever taken a shower and *not* thought he'd heard the phone ringing? No, there it was. Who could be calling him at this hour of the morning? He cursed, turned off the water, and dried himself in the shower stall. He was not about to track water from the bathroom across his polished hardwood bedroom floor or his mid-nineteenth-century Oriental rugs. The phone rang and rang as he toweled himself dry. *I'm a federal judge and you'd better have a damn good reason for getting me out of the shower*, he felt like saying as he walked to the phone, but instead answered simply, "Judge Boucher." He listened and his frown of annoyance became one of concern.

"Oh, no," he said. "When? . . . Of course. I'll be there within the hour."

He dressed and went downstairs to the kitchen, made himself a cup of instant coffee, and pondered the news he'd just received. District Judge Epson had suffered a heart attack. He was expected to recover, but as the new kid on the block, Jock Boucher was being asked to take over his docket in the interim. Had anyone given a thought to the fact that his own docket was already full? No matter. It had just gotten fuller. Boucher gulped down his coffee. He would have bolted from his house, but it was one of the most historic homes in the French Quarter, filled with period antique furniture he'd spent much of his adult life collecting. From such a majestic presence, one did not bolt.

The judge was granted admission to the underground parking lot of the Hale Boggs Federal Building without having to show his ID; he was recognized by security after only a short time on the bench. His vehicle had a lot to do with it. Of all the members of the federal judiciary of the Eastern District of Louisiana, Jock Boucher was the only one who drove a Ford F-150 pickup truck. No one knew he was also the only one who made weekly visits to neighborhoods decimated by Hurricane Katrina, where he would pick up and carry off refuse. After the oil spill, he had scoured beaches and wetlands to help with cleanup activities in any way he could, including the heartbreaking task of rescuing oil-soaked wildlife.

On this eventful morning he took the elevator up to his floor and walked the deserted hallway to his office. His administrative assistant was already at her desk, also having received an early call. She followed him into his chambers. About as good as government offices got, his private quarters were spacious but stark: thick gray wall-to-wall carpet, a large oak desk stained dark, a ponderous suite of sofa, chairs, and tables, and built-in bookshelves, so far largely empty.

"I've already spoken with Judge Epson's office," his assistant said. "He has a trial starting Wednesday, motion hearings today and tomorrow. Here's your copy of his calendar. You have docket call at nine, and it's a long one. I thought maybe we could just post a sign outside Judge Epson's court moving his cases here, unless you know how to be in two places at one time."

"Give me a minute to study his calendar." She started to leave, but he motioned her to stay. After a couple of minutes, he said, "We'll do this. Have Judge Epson's law clerk ask the lawyers appearing if anyone wants to reschedule. If both parties agree, have them prepare the orders for my signature. I'll move my docket call along as fast as I can, then I'll go to his courtroom and deal with whatever's remaining."

"Yes, sir."

He moved his own docket along at lightning speed and was ushered to Judge Epson's bench barely an hour late. The courtroom was empty.

"Where'd everybody go?" he asked.

Judge Epson's law clerk sat beside the idle court reporter. "Sir, everybody asked to reschedule. We've received dozens of calls from other attorneys asking the same thing. They prefer to wait and see when Judge Epson will be back."

"They got something against me?"

"It's not that, sir."

"Okay. Well, I guess I'll head back to my own territory." He rose from the bench to leave just as two federal marshals burst through the door next to the jury box, a prisoner held tightly between them, his hands manacled. They saw the judge and looked at each other curiously.

"Sorry, Your Honor. I thought we were in Judge Epson's court."

"You are. Judge Epson is in the hospital. I'm Judge Boucher. I've been assigned his cases till he returns."

"I think we'd better wait till Judge Epson gets back," the marshal said, and began to turn away.

"Stop right there," the judge ordered. "Bring that man here."

With obvious reluctance, the two federal marshals approached the bench, their prisoner shuffling between them. The man was as emaciated as a human being could be, with a thick gray beard hanging down his chest. He wore raggedy street clothes, not an inmate's jumpsuit.

"What's this man charged with?" the judge asked.

"Contempt, Your Honor. He was brought in this morning."

"Let me see the file."

Again the reluctance of the marshals was obvious, but one stepped forward and passed a couple of sheets of paper to the clerk, who handed them up to the judge.

"This warrant's twenty years old," Judge Boucher said. "Is it still good?"

"Well, Your Honor—"

"What I mean is, is the underlying judgment still valid? After this length of time, if it hasn't been revived, it's probably unenforceable. Is the contempt civil or criminal?"

The two marshals looked at each other.

"You don't have to answer that," Judge Boucher said, reading the file. "Most judges don't know the difference. I'm going to give this man the benefit of the doubt. Undo his handcuffs."

There was movement under the man's bushy gray beard. It was a smile. Rather than hold his hand out for the cuffs to be unlocked, the prisoner dropped his arms, and the cuffs fell and clanked to the floor.

The judge cracked a smile himself. "What's your name, sir?"

"Bob Palmetto, Your Honor."

"Have you eaten lately, Mr. Palmetto?"

"I had something yesterday, sir."

"Are you hungry?"

"I wouldn't mind a bite."

"Good. Tell you what I'm going to do. One of these two gentlemen is going to my office to get on the computer and check the records to see if there are any other warrants or outstanding enforceable judgments against you. The other marshal is going to stay here while you tell me about this contempt order Judge Epson entered against you all those years ago."

"I'd be happy to, Your Honor."

"Good. Sandwich and a Coke all right? I'll have someone bring them here."

"Could you make that a Diet Coke, Your Honor?"

Disposition of the matter took about as long as it took to eat the sandwich. Palmetto had been held in contempt for failure to appear and produce documents in a case that was later dismissed on plaintiff's motion about a year after the contempt was ordered. He stated that his business had been burned to the ground about that same time and any documents he might have had were long since destroyed, thus rendering moot any basis for contempt. The marshal returned and admitted that he could find no other judgments against him. The two marshals and court reporter were dismissed. Only the judge and the former fugitive were in the courtroom, the judge escorting the frail man to the exit.

"Off the record," Judge Boucher asked, "why didn't you appear in court that day?"

"I'd have been killed, just like my lawyer was," Palmetto said.

"Oh? And just who might have killed you?"

Bob Palmetto turned and pointed his bony finger toward the now empty bench where, for the last twenty-five years until this morning, District Judge Epson had presided.

CHAPTER 2

EARLY THAT EVENING, JOCK Boucher sat in the hallway outside Judge Epson's hospital room. There was a small army of people there, mostly lawyers. There were one or two people from city hall, and a man he recognized but couldn't name.

"Who is that?" he asked a man standing near him. "I've seen him somewhere."

"John Perry," the man said, "CEO of Rexcon Energy."

A doctor came off the elevator and saw the crowd. He shook his head.

"Folks, I'm sure Judge Epson appreciates you all being here, but he's recovering from a heart attack. I'm going to have to ask you all to leave."

He began herding the group toward the elevator. Jock approached him.

"Doctor, I'm Judge Boucher. I've taken over Judge Epson's responsibilities. I just wanted to assure him everything's—"

"Thank you, but you're the last person I want him talking to, at least now. I want him to forget he's a judge, if that's possible. Please, I don't mean to be rude."

"I understand," Boucher said.

"Now," the doctor said to the group, "I'm afraid you'll all have to leave."

As he got on the elevator, Boucher noticed John Perry speaking to the doctor. The CEO was allowed admission to the judge's hospital room.

A widower, Judge Jock Boucher lived alone, which meant that despite his judicial stature, he still had to take out the garbage. He was engaged in that task after returning from the hospital later that evening. Foot traffic was common on Chartres Street and he had not yet equated his new position with the need for enhanced security. He did not notice the man who approached him from behind in the dark until the man reached out and tapped him on the shoulder as he bent over the massive plastic refuse bin he had wrestled to the curb. Boucher spun around, fists clenched, ready to defend himself with his bare hands.

"It's me, Judge."

He could barely make out the figure in the dark, but the man was close enough for him to notice how skinny he was. "Palmetto?"

"I shaved my beard. Sorry, didn't mean to startle you."

"What do you want?"

"A favor."

"Let's go in the house."

"No, sir, I'd rather not. This will just take a minute. My lawyer was murdered twenty years ago and they never found who did it. He had prepared a report he was going to deliver to the FBI the next day, but he was shot. The report was about Judge Epson."

"What about Judge Epson?"

Palmetto looked around. "I don't want to go inside your house. Do you have someplace we could sit down outside?"

"I have a courtyard around back. Come on."

They walked up the drive to the back of the house. The courtyard of the old home was dense with foliage, some plants the offspring of two-hundred-year-old bushes and trees, part of what the earliest residents of the French Quarter had called, with disdain, "the jungle." Palmetto took a seat on a bench facing a stone statuette. He looked up at the star-filled sky and said, "Energy. It's all around us, everywhere in the universe. Someday . . ." He sighed. "But we're addicted to oil."

"Mr. Palmetto . . ."

"Have you ever heard of methane hydrate?" Palmetto asked.

"Methane is a gas, sometimes called natural gas. It's a relatively clean-burning fuel, but can be dangerous. It has caused explosions in coal mines and offshore wells. A hydrate is when a gas combines with water and freezes."

"I'm impressed, Judge. Methane hydrate is the gas trapped in ice under the seabed and formed under high pressure and low temperatures. It could be the largest source of energy on earth. There's at least twice as much of it as all the other fossil fuels combined. It could replace oil and make offshore drilling a relic of the past, and could meet all our energy needs for the next two hundred years, maybe more. But extraction is complicated." He looked to make sure his audience of one was listening. The judge wasn't missing a word. He continued. "It's volatile and a greenhouse gas. If it escapes in quantities, it could cause climate change beyond any scale yet imagined. I invented a way to exploit it safely. Then people got killed. They died trying to protect me and my discovery. I'm a geophysicist. I invented a way to get the gas up to the surface safely. You understand?"

"I'm not a scientist, I'm a jurist," Judge Boucher said.

"Well, you'll understand this next part. In a lawsuit the judge can force parties to produce testimony, documents; right?"

The judge looked at his watch. "It's getting late, Mr. Palmetto."

"Here's what happened. Rexcon Energy learned of my discovery. They brought a groundless lawsuit against me claiming what I discovered about methane hydrate extraction, I'd stolen from them. They got the court to make me produce evidence of my own discoveries, and the judge just turned it over to them. They stole it. They had the judge in their pocket. My lawyer—his name was Dexter Jessup—got tired of losing every time he went to court to fight their demands. He discovered the judge was being paid a lot of money. Dexter was going to go to the FBI. He was with me the day before the meeting. He left my office and was never seen alive again. No killer was ever found. The case was never solved."

"This happened twenty years ago," the judge said.

"Yes."

"Is Rexcon, or any energy company, extracting methane hydrate today? I don't believe I've ever heard of it as an energy source."

"I've been waiting twenty years for this and the time has finally come. The Mideast is a mess, we can't do a damn thing about it. We lose the Suez Canal and we've got to take our tankers around Africa—through pirate-infested waters. Our biggest Mideast supplier, Saudi Arabia, may not have as much oil as it wants us to believe. They refuse to publish estimates of their provable reserves, and their major field is now pumping out more salt water than oil. The demand for natural gas keeps rising. There are new industrial and commercial uses, but demand is going to explode when we start using it as a transportation fuel. There already are truck and bus fleets that run on natural gas, and the big automakers say they will have cars that will run on this fuel in the next few years. Then watch demand outstrip supply. Also, new methods of onshore drilling may present a threat to our most valuable—and most vulnerable—natural resource, fresh water. An abundant clean-burning fuel off our own shore starts to look pretty good—especially when it won't cause oil spills. Political instability of our foreign suppliers, ecological dangers of offshore oil drilling—it's the perfect storm. There's going to be a lot of attention paid to methane hydrate now, just you wait and see."

"You said it was a greenhouse gas."

"That's if too much of it escapes into the atmosphere. I also said I knew how to extract it safely. My process for the extraction of methane hydrate will be much more like mining than drilling, more ecologically friendly. No oil spills. Now it's economically viable. It's taken twenty years to get to this point."

"And you think Rexcon is going to use the information they stole from you with Judge Epson's help."

"I know they are. The problem is, they don't know everything. Remember, I didn't produce certain documents."

"Which you swore under oath were destroyed in a fire."

Palmetto said nothing. He leaned forward and tapped his temple with his index finger. "Nobody ever asked me to produce what was in my head. I stopped putting anything on paper a long time ago. I've also done a lot of work on this over the past twenty years."

Jock Boucher sighed and leaned back in his chair. "This has all been very interesting. But you asked me for a favor. What is it?"

"The FBI looked into Dexter's allegations of Judge Epson taking bribes. They wrote their findings in a report. Guess what they did with that report? They gave it to Judge Epson, that's what, and it never saw the light of day. Now that you're running his court, I thought maybe you could find out what he did with it."

"And just why do you think I should look for this report—if it exists?"

"Because a good man lost his life when he saw wrong and tried to right it. I want to believe that you have the same values."

Judge Boucher sat shaking his head.

"Okay." Palmetto stood. "Just do this one thing for me. Look at the background, the family of Dexter Jessup. That's all I ask. Will you do that for me?"

"I'm handling the dockets of two federal courts," Boucher said.

"Ask your law clerk to do it. It won't take half an hour. If you don't feel like going further after that, I won't bother you again."

"I'll think about it," the judge said. "Now you'd better be going. You take care of yourself, Mr. Palmetto." Boucher extended his hand.

"And you, Judge," Palmetto said, grasping Boucher's hand with both of his.

Then he was gone.

CHAPTER 3

THE NEXT MORNING ROLLED over Judge Boucher like thunder. He had a stack of motions from Judge Epson's court to review and sign, and an emergency hearing in his own court: a plaintiff seeking a temporary restraining order. He didn't have time to catch his breath till noon, and it was then he recalled his previous night's visitor. He called for his law clerk.

"Julie, see what you can find out about an attorney by the name of Dexter Jessup. He was murdered about twenty years ago. And see if you can find out anything about his family. I know you're busy, but I'd like to get this off my mind."

"Of course, Your Honor."

She returned in two hours.

"Dexter Jessup was shot in a roadside killing twenty years ago," she said. "He was a prominent and respected attorney, from a long line of lawyers. His father wrote *Jessup on Evidence*. It's still the leading textbook on the subject."

"*That's* why that name sounded so familiar to me," the judge said. "I used that book in law school."

"Dexter's grandfather was prominent as well. He was a member of the state supreme court back in the fifties. I couldn't find much about the man's murder. There was an investigation by the FBI, and his death did apparently lead to some kind of an inquiry of the district court, but I could not find any record of it. That's about all I could find. I could dig deeper."

"That's all right. Thanks for your help."

He jogged, he lifted weights, but the favorite exercise of Judge Jock Boucher at the end of a demanding day was the punching bag. He'd done some boxing in the army and had been a pretty fair pugilist, but he'd put all that behind him when he became a state judge more than a decade ago. Practice bouts sometimes left cuts and bruises and it just didn't do for a jurist to appear in court with a lacerated face. It distracted the jury. But the punching bag, that was a great outlet for frustration and aggression, and still one of the most complete workouts there was. A judge's day utilized one body part only. Even vocal cords were rarely used. The lawyers did the arguing, his response was limited to one or two words. At the end of a full day, the mind was numb. Many judges anesthetized the brain with the liquor bottle kept in their desks. That wasn't his way—not that he didn't enjoy a sip of bourbon or a glass of wine when the occasion merited. But to wind down from the pressures of work at day's end, his choice was a seedy gym in a black neighborhood where nobody knew or cared about position, because none there could claim one. Except for those working out in the ring, no one ever even bothered to look at anyone else, each in his own private world. He had a crummy old locker with a cheap combination lock. He stripped and changed into his gym shorts, T-shirt, and boxing shoes, put on his gloves, and for the next hour he whaled.

After this brutal session, the bag shown no mercy, he returned to his locker for his shower flip-flops and a towel. There was an envelope at the bottom. He picked it up and looked around. Intent on the bag, he hadn't seen anyone near his locker. He opened the envelope and took out the single page. The handwriting was illegible, but he knew the author. Like doctors, scientists had horrible handwriting, as if it were a part of their training. In this case it was a geophysicist. He read:

They want me dead. I have to go. Marcia Whitcomb was also killed, just a poor legal assistant. Ruth Kalin disappeared, lawyer in his office. The Jessups are a pretty impressive family, right? Where's the justice, Judge?
P.S. If I were you, I'd stay out of places like this.

B.P.

The old man had spunk. Boucher was sure that he'd gotten himself picked up yesterday after learning of Judge Epson's heart attack and had followed him home last night, and followed him to the gym this evening. Timid men didn't go around tailing federal judges. But Palmetto was scared enough now; scared enough to run. He put the letter in his pocket. Looking around the gym, Jock Boucher realized the scientist was right. If a stranger off the street could walk in and access his funky old locker with no one noticing—or caring—maybe this was no longer the best place for him. Anonymity minimized security concerns, but federal judges were not exactly anonymous. He emptied his locker for the last time.

Arriving home, he didn't even make it ten feet before the phone rang; Judge Epson was calling.

"Hello," Boucher said. "How are you feeling? I tried to stop by yesterday evening, but your doctor said you couldn't have any visitors. He said he especially didn't want you discussing any court business. . . . Well, I've got to get something to eat first. . . . Eight o'clock? You sure that's not too late? . . . Okay, see you then."

The hallway outside of Judge Epson's hospital room was deserted when Boucher arrived. He knocked on the closed door.

"Jock, that you?"

"It's me, Judge."

"Come on in."

The patient was sitting up in bed. He was clean-shaven and his gray hair was neatly combed. He looked like he could get up, put on street clothes, and walk right out. He motioned his visitor to take a seat in a recliner next to the window. "Thanks for coming," he said.

"You're looking really good, Judge," Boucher said, "but is this okay with your doctor? He sure didn't want me talking to you last night."

"He worries too much. How are things going?"

"Better than I expected, at least for me. I'm afraid you'll have a plateful when you get back. Just about every lawyer has rescheduled pending your return. At least the newly filed cases are being split evenly with the other judges."

"I heard you handled one of my bench warrants, an old contempt case."

"I did. The judgment was void. I dismissed it and let the fellow go."

Epson frowned and looked straight ahead. "Wish you hadn't done that. You know where this fellow is now?"

Boucher wondered if he'd made himself clear. He'd dismissed the matter. Epson's court no longer had jurisdiction over the man.

He studied the judge's face and answered simply, "No." He decided not to tell of his subsequent run-in with Palmetto. The interest in this single matter, with everything else the senior judge had going on, not the least of which was his heart attack, was unsettling. He didn't like the feeling. Judge Epson seemed to sense this and forced a smile.

"Well, it's water under the bridge," Epson said. "Probably best to get that ancient history off the books. How did the old guy look? I have a vague memory of him being an odd sort."

"He was skinny as a stick, with a beard halfway down his chest. Looked like he'd been living in a cave. After he shaved the beard, he looked almost normal."

"I expect to get out of here day after tomorrow," the judge said, changing the subject. "I'll convalesce at home. Get some work done from there. My situation shouldn't be too much of a burden on the rest of you."

"The important thing is for you to get well. Like I said, everything is under control. Maybe you should think about taking some time off."

"I might," Epson said.

Boucher knew the meeting was at an end. Epson was beginning to tire. He stood. "If there's anything you need, just call."

"Thanks, Jock. And thanks for coming by." A tepid handshake was offered, the judge staring into space. Maybe it was just fatigue.

In the hallway, waiting for the elevator, Jock Boucher slapped himself on the forehead. "I'm an idiot!" he muttered. He knew why Epson had suddenly had such a vacant look on his face. Palmetto's damned beard. He'd mentioned how he looked clean-shaven. He'd admitted seeing the man after the hearing—apparently not something Judge Epson wanted to hear.

Alone in his room, Epson made a call from his cell phone. When the party answered, he said, "We might have a problem." Then he hung up.

Jock Boucher slipped out of bed late that night. He went to his study and turned on his laptop. He went online and confirmed that Marcia Whitcomb, assistant of the assassinated lawyer Dexter Jessup, was deceased. Oddly enough, she had died within days of her employer. He could find nothing on the other lawyer Palmetto had mentioned, Ruth Kalin. She seemed to have vanished without a trace.

He turned off his computer and the desk lamp and sat there in the dark. Everything Palmetto had told him so far had checked out. He thought about the FBI report allegedly given to Judge Epson. Could it still be in his records? The question stayed with him as he returned to bed and, finally, to sleep.

CHAPTER 4

BOB PALMETTO LAY IN the dark on the lumpy mattress of the cheap motel, hands folded behind his head, skinny bare legs crossed at the ankles, reminiscing. How many dumps like this had there been? Twenty years times three hundred and sixty-five was over seven thousand, and at least a third of that number had been spent in one fleabag or another. Cheap hotels and motels preferred cash and didn't give a damn about driver's licenses or credit cards. Their accounting was as ghostlike as their patrons, and that suited him fine. In fact, it had kept him alive.

He had prepaid for the night and as usual was awake before the dawn. A metabolism like his didn't require a lot of sleep. There was no checkout in this kind of a joint; you grabbed your stuff and walked out. He would do some walking today, making about four miles per hour, maybe eight hours, maybe more. He would walk to a smaller town and if it took him a day to find one, it didn't matter. Small-town bus stops, like cheap motels, weren't too curious about a cash customer either. He wanted to put a good walk, then a good bus ride between him and the town where there were people who wished him harm.

For the last twenty years, Bob Palmetto had spent his nights in cheap dives, but he lived his days in public libraries and Internet cafés. There was a time when he traveled with a pack of diskettes, then disks, then flash drives. Now he carried nothing. He'd discovered cloud computing and his whole life's work was—at least at this moment—in the ether, waiting for him no matter where the long and winding road took him. And no documents, at least not in paper form. He was not the only one who lived in a paperless world. Some of the world's greatest scientists made their work available for their own use and others' via the Internet. Infinite galaxies of information were now available anywhere in the world. Now a cyber-discovery he had recently made determined his direction and his next destination.

Palmetto was impatient to get going, but knew it was best to wait till the sun was full in the sky. Not many men hiked the open road as in days past, and those who did might arouse the curiosity of a passing patrol car—especially in the dark. When he judged the time to be about eight o'clock both by the sun and the amount of traffic on the road he would travel today, he left the motel. He carried a backpack and wore hiking boots, aiming for a woodsy look that also helped to avoid unwanted attention from the local constabulary. If you looked like you were passing through, they tended to leave you alone, and a hiker by definition was on his way somewhere else. He crossed the highway in order to walk against the oncoming traffic. It was safer and he had an understandable aversion to things moving up on him from behind. He started getting hungry about ten, but kept pushing until the sun shone straight-up noon.

Palmetto realized that with the old contempt charge expunged, he wouldn't have the same worry as before about checking into places, but caution was still his companion. It was still best not to leave a trail for the wolf pack to follow. As he hiked the highway, he talked to himself. It was a habit he'd developed as his walks had gotten longer and longer. It was a comfort to him and made the loneliness a little more bearable. It was a one-way conversation. He'd promised that if he started answering himself, he'd stop.

Palmetto checked the position of the sun in the sky. He was heading northeast. He had a long way to go, but he'd be closer to his destination by the end of the day, and even the slightest progress gave him peace of mind. It was a paradox. He was excited, he was eager, but he was not hurried. A good day's walk, a good night's sleep, maybe tomorrow he'd continue his overland journey by bus, maybe even by rail. Watching the country pass during the next several days, he'd have time to think and to plan his strategy for his next objective. He knew what he needed and he knew where to find it. The challenge was to obtain it for his particular use, and in this he knew he must not fail.

There was a new spring in his step as he thought about his destination. He was going to a place where like-minded people shared his respect for earth's final frontier, the ocean. Bob Palmetto was headed to the Marblehead Oceanographic Institute, Marblehead, Massachusetts. He needed a submarine.

"Can't find him anywhere," the caller said. "A photo taken twenty years ago and the description of a skinny old man in dirty clothes is not a lot to go on. We know he did not take any public transportation out of New Orleans. We don't think he has a credit card or a driver's license. This guy's a needle in a haystack."

"Keep looking," John Perry said. He hung up, then called Judge Epson in his hospital room. "You up for a visitor?"

"You've been blacklisted," Epson said. "Nurse took my blood pressure just after you left last time. Your visiting privileges have been revoked. Can it wait till tomorrow? The doctor said he might release me if there are no more 'surprises.' It will be better at home anyway, more private."

"Fine. I wanted to tell you that the judge who's taken over your court was asking about me when he was at the hospital the other night."

"He hasn't taken over my court!" Epson said. "He was appointed to assist with my caseload because he's the new kid on the block. Just about every case is being continued till I get back."

"You know him well?" Perry asked.

"Nobody does."

"Let's talk about him next time we get together."

"We can if you want, but he's not getting close to my business."

"Good. We'll talk soon." Perry hung up.

Jock Boucher couldn't keep his mind on his work, not good for a federal judge. He'd done a little more research and learned that Marcia Whitcomb died of natural causes in her home. No autopsy. She was twenty-eight. What natural cause took a young woman in her prime? Ruth Kalin had graduated magna cum laude from Loyola University College of Law. She could have had her pick of top law firms in New Orleans, yet went to work for a sole practitioner, then just disappeared. Why'd she pick Dexter Jessup as her first employer—because he was a crusader? A crusader who ended up a martyr? Were those other lives sacrificed as well in whatever was going on then? He turned off his laptop, stood, and paced around his desk.

The lawsuit against Palmetto had been dismissed almost two

decades ago. Back then, paper files were kept in the building for ten years, then sent to federal archives. He didn't want to go that route if he could avoid it. He was pacing when there was a knock at the door.

"Come in," he said. It was Julie, his law clerk. She had papers in her hand.

"Anything wrong, Judge?" she asked.

"No. Why?"

"You seem distracted. This motion, you signed it in the wrong place." She showed him the misplaced signature.

He shook his head and sighed. "What was I thinking?"

"Obviously not about a request for extension of time."

He looked at her. She was bright and self-assured, mature enough to know the world was no bed of roses.

"Julie, did you know what you wanted to do when you finished law school?"

She looked at him. She'd worked for him a short time. He had not asked much about her. Her academic record spoke for itself.

"Your Honor, I have the next twenty years of my life mapped out."

Boucher was thinking about Ruth Kalin. She too must have planned her future. Working for Dexter Jessup was no fluke, and her disappearance was not an act of caprice.

While in law school and thinking about his own future, Boucher had briefly considered the FBI as a career path. He'd had two interviews with a young agent named Ted Neely. They'd even gotten together a couple of times to play handball during the courtship before Boucher decided neither was for him: neither the Bureau nor handball. But he'd run into Neely over the years and greetings were always cordial and on a first-name basis. None of which was sufficient reason for Boucher to be calling him late that afternoon with a question of a sensitive nature. Neely replied with a tone of bonhomie that they revive their old friendship, even suggesting they meet that same afternoon, why waste time. He'd not acknowledged his question, Boucher noted as he hung up, which in itself was some sort of answer. Neely had proposed they meet halfway between the district court and the FBI building. His choice of venue was odd, a Baskin-Robbins near 610 and Elysian Fields Avenue.

The FBI man was already there when Boucher arrived, their two cars the only ones in the parking lot. Not a lot of call for ice cream on a chilly, cloudy late afternoon. He bought a single scoop of Rocky Road and joined the agent at one of the small tables away from the window.

"What'd you get?" Boucher asked by way of greeting.

"Pralines and cream. Means I have to add a half hour to my run tomorrow."

"You picked the place."

The man did not offer a handshake as Boucher sat down—strange for one renewing a friendship—and he barely looked up. His hairline was receding, Boucher noticed as he engaged in the universal and irresistible assessment of one not seen in a while. Other than that, it seemed that here was another FBI agent with whom it was impossible to avoid clichés and stereotypes, from clothes and shoes (which he had seen coming in) to haircut. Neely was older than when he had last seen him of course, but these people didn't age, they hardened.

"You have something to ask me," Neely said. "Ask away before I'm tempted to go back for seconds."

"This is about something that happened twenty years ago. You had recently joined the Bureau, I think."

Neely dipped a taste from the tiny plastic spoon and studied his frozen confection as if he were reading tea leaves. A frown of concentration turned to a wry smile.

"I heard you'd taken over for Judge Epson after his heart attack. This is about that lawyer's murder, right?"

"Partly. The lawyer had a case before Judge Epson at the time he was killed. I heard there was some sort of inquiry into Judge Epson's conduct. Did you know anything about that?"

"I wasn't involved." Neely took another spoonful of pralines and cream. Boucher shrugged as if to say, *Well, that's that.* "But I heard things," Neely added. "Even the new kid hears things. The buzz was that Judge Epson had taken bribes. A report was written up, you know, justifying time spent and requesting further direction—asses are covered in these kinds of situations by asking higher-ups to call the shots—and word came back from D.C. to lay off. Let it go. Something like that could only have come from the director, but I'm just guessing. All of it was way above my station."

"But there was a report," Boucher said.

"To my knowledge, yes. There was a report. But D.C. buried it. I can't swear to this, but I think they told Epson what they'd found. He was told to clean up his act. Given a reprieve."

"Given a reprieve for accepting bribes?"

Neely bent forward. His voice was lowered. "At the time, Epson was presiding judge over a very important racketeering trial. Years of preparation. We couldn't afford to have him compromised in the middle of that. It would have done much more harm than good. The scales were weighed, the bribery business was buried. He was given a pass and told to mend his ways. I guess he did. That was the end of it." He sat back up and added a further reflection.

"Though he was long dead then, Hoover's shadow still loomed large over the Bureau. Maybe it always will. Anyway, Epson owed us. I'm pretty sure we used the occasion to remind him of that over the years. It's a bad position to be in, Jock. Don't ever let yourself get in hock to the Bureau."

Neely stood up and offered a handshake. "My advice to you is to forget about this. Don't make waves. It was good to see you. Take care."

Both hands were cold and clammy from the ice cream. Neely left. Boucher looked down at his cup. His Rocky Road had melted.

CHAPTER 5

JUDGE EPSON WAS RELEASED from the hospital with his doctor's admonitions: "No visitors, and *please* try to stay off the phone." John Perry was waiting for him at the house, the judge having called him from his cell saying he was on his way home. So much for the doctor's advice.

"You're looking good," Perry said.

"Bullshit. I look like one of those cartoons that's just seen a ghost. Maybe I did. Maybe it was me."

The two men sat in Epson's study. The room was modeled after a Victorian-era library, with bookshelves floor to ceiling on three walls. Behind the desk were French windows that opened onto a backyard with large shade trees. Designed for tranquillity and contemplation, it hit the mark, though tranquillity was not in the air this afternoon.

"We didn't find Palmetto," Perry said. "God only knows where he's gone."

"I just wonder where he's been for twenty years," Epson said.

"I'd sure like to know what he said to that judge."

"I can find out easily enough."

They were interrupted by a knock on the door. A maid stuck her head in. "Your office is on the line, Judge. Do you want me to take a message?"

"No, I'll take it." He picked up the phone. Perry watched as Epson's face turned from pale to a ghostly white.

"What's wrong?" Perry asked.

"The son of a bitch has gone to the FBI. He was asking about that inquiry twenty years ago."

Perry showed no reaction, not the faintest hint of emotion. This ability was his strength, had won him many a boardroom battle, and helped him to climb and remain at the top of the corporate ladder. He studied his manicured nails and asked, "Can we make Boucher a friend?"

"I doubt it," Epson said. "He just got appointed. He's probably full of himself and overflowing with ideals. Cynicism doesn't usually set in till after the first five years."

"I leave him to you. Take care of it." In this manner a federal judge received his orders as if he were a foot soldier. Perry got up to leave. "I hope you'll be back at work soon," he said. "Unpleasant things seem to happen when you're away."

"I'll be back within the week," Judge Epson said. "Count on it."

John Perry didn't need anyone to show him to the door; he'd been in this house before. He walked the flagstone path to the driveway and his car. In contrast to the slow pace of his footsteps, his mind raced. Despite what he'd just said, he would leave nothing to Judge Epson; there was too much at stake. He would take care of what had to be done. He got in his car, called his office, and was reminded he was expected at a charity function that evening and his wife wanted to know which of his tuxedos she should put out for him. He answered, hung up, and smiled at the range of thoughts that had just run through his brain in less than a minute. From the sublime to the mundane, it was all in a day's work for the man who would provide the greatest country on earth with enough energy to last the next two hundred years. Perry made a stop before going home, to arrange a matter that couldn't be discussed over the phone.

Matt Quillen hated the sight of blood, and had equal disdain for loud noises; ironic aversions for a professional killer. He'd been offered the assignment because he never failed, and accepted it without hesitation for the same reason he accepted them all. He needed the money. Being one of the best meant that his client list was short, and it could be a long time between jobs. Though he was well paid and his lifestyle was not extravagant, the money went only so far. The timing of this assignment was particularly welcome. He asked the obvious questions, and the not so obvious. One aspect stood out. He was tempted to smile but knew better. Never in front of a client. But when asked when he could do it, he said, "Tonight. There's no time to waste."

After Perry left, Quillen searched the medicine cabinet in his house. He found what he was looking for. There was a certain genius to his manner of operation. If a SWAT team had come busting through his door at that very moment, they would have found no weapons, only generic and nonlethal medications. Among his talents, he was a pretty damn good chemist. Nonlethal chemicals took on a new character under his direction. It was all in the mixing. In his home medicine cabinet he had all he needed to commit a murder. Timing. It was always about timing. If the client had come one day later, he would have had to devise a different strategy. But tonight he knew it would be as sure a thing as anyone in his business could want.

*   *   *

He began his assignment at four a.m., his favorite time, darkest before the dawn and all that. From experience—he hadn't always been an assassin; he'd spent his early adulthood in law enforcement—he knew that cops patrolling on the nighttime shift had lost their edge by that hour. The house's security apparatus he analyzed in no time. He wasn't even earning his pay tonight; this hit was a gift. He put on surgical gloves, wrapped his shoes in foot covers, and entered through the back door. God, night-lights, in the kitchen and up the staircase! Could this get any easier? He'd brought a penlight but wouldn't need it; he could walk through the house unaided. He found the stairs and slowly ascended. The art of his craft was the entry, then getting close to the victim without setting off alarms. If there was any challenge it was here, but in this house there was no problem. He found the master bedroom and opened the door slowly. Sounds of sleep. The deepest slumber occurred at this time of the morning. To ensure his safety and his success, he took from a shirt pocket one of the two tools he had brought with him. It was a narcosis-producing aerosol in the shape of a fountain pen. From generic components in his home he'd formulated his own concentration of fentanyl and butorphanol tartrate, synthetic opiates related to morphine, used both by doctors and veterinarians, which would metabolize in the liver and be expelled, impossible to trace. He reached around the door and sprayed, closing the door quickly. He looked at his watch. The knockout spray would send anyone in the room into a stupor—the only deeper sleep would be death itself—then it would dissipate. Quillen had learned early not to trust everything he'd been told about a victim's lifestyle. Wives, kids, nurses, lovers straight and gay—there could always be surprises behind closed bedroom doors. He waited, counting time in his head, opened the door again, and walked to the side of the bed where his target lay.

With the victim immobilized by the knockout spray, the easiest thing to do would have been to squeeze the nostrils while keeping the mouth closed. This method he'd employed successfully a number of times but didn't want to use on this job because there was the slightest chance the police might assume a pattern and investigate more thoroughly. Quillen preferred avoiding any inference of a crime even having been committed. Also, suffocation was boring. This situation offered the opportunity for a little creativity.

He looked down at the unconscious figure, then unbuttoned the top three buttons of his pajama top, folding it over. He pulled out his second and final tool, a hypodermic needle. He removed the protective cap, reached down to the man's armpit, and plunged the needle in. Underarm hair would hide any sign of skin puncture. He pressed the plunger and injected sodium nitroprusside—from his own prescription, from his own doctor, to treat his own hypertension. The concentrated mixture he'd formulated flowed into the body. In this case, combined with drugs Epson had doubtless been given after his heart attack, it would bring death—and controversy. Fingers would be pointed, but not in Quillen's direction. He replaced the cap on the used needle, put it back in his pocket, and returned the way he had come. Half an hour later, he was home and preparing for bed. There was only one drawback to the timing of this particular kill: it would not make the morning paper. Matt Quillen liked the image of bad news on the doorstep. Maybe next time.

CHAPTER 6

RADIO AND TV STATIONS interrupted their regular morning programming with the news.

"Federal District Judge Roy Epson died in his sleep this morning. He had just been released from the hospital yesterday. Questions are already being asked about whether his medical team erred in releasing him so soon after his heart attack."

The flag above the Federal Building was at half staff. Boucher ran into two other judges in their private elevator. One was well informed.

"He had an overdose of antihypertension drugs in his system. Drove his blood pressure down like a rock dropped from a cliff. I hope his cardiologist has a good malpractice carrier."

"Does he have family?" Boucher asked.

"No children. Four ex-wives. Five divorces. You figure the math on that one."

"He married and divorced the same one twice?"

"Bingo. I only met two of the ladies, but I bet each one is having a meeting with her attorney as we speak. Judge Epson's married life was an annuity for divorce lawyers. Seriously, Jock, Epson's death is going to mean a lot of work for you. We're all drowning."

"I know. I just hope I'm up to it."

"Hell," the other judge said, "just do what I do, which is just what my law clerk tells me to do. There's a reason we hire the top of the class. They know more than I can possibly remember."

If you had a complaint about a sitting judge, and if you had the nerve, you went with your complaint to the chief judge of the district. There complaints lived or died. At the end of the day, Boucher called on the chambers of Chief District Judge Arnold Wundt.

"Jock Boucher, this is a pleasant surprise." Judge Wundt walked across his office and greeted him. "Come right in. You know, I was planning to give you a call."

Arnold Wundt had been on the bench for thirty years and had decided to retire. For more than a year he'd taken on no new assignments. His office oversaw the administration of the district's judicial affairs. How much the senior judge was involved personally in these matters and how much he delegated was known only within the office that Jock Boucher now entered. He looked around. You only had to switch the photos and diplomas and it could have been the office of any judge on the bench, including his own. The men did little to personalize their working quarters. At least the women jurists had flowers brought in. The two men exchanged handshakes. It being after six and with all but one of Judge Wundt's staff having gone for the day, a drink was offered. It was against his routine but Boucher accepted. A glass on the judge's desk indicated His Honor was already a step or two along the path. If the cut-crystal decanter that the judge pulled from his desk was any indication of the quality of the liquor contained within, Boucher was being offered some high-class hooch straight up, no ice.

"Hope you drink bourbon. I understand you're a boy from the bayou."

"My grandpappy made the best moonshine whiskey in the parish, I've been told," Boucher said. He raised his glass.

Judge Wundt returned to his chair behind the desk, dropping his huge frame rather than lowering it. "It's a shame about Roy."

"Roy?"

"Judge Epson. It came as a shock and a surprise. Shit, if anyone around here should be dead of a heart attack, it's me."

That statement was hard to argue. Wundt was overweight and his face was mottled from alcohol. He took short, shallow breaths, maybe one in ten a deep one to compensate for inadequate oxygen intake. Boucher debated bringing up the subject he'd come to discuss. This man had one foot on the banana peel.

"Something on your mind," Wundt said. It wasn't a question.

Boucher studied the dark amber liquid in his glass, rolled it around, held it up to the light. "Not sure I should. I didn't know you and Epson were close."

"Who the hell said we were close? I knew his first name. We worked in the same building almost thirty years, doing more or less the same thing. We'd speak in the elevator and we'd see each other at functions. Oh, we'd help each other out with a case now and then, always with an eye out for the quid pro quo, if you know what I mean, but close? Judges don't get close, not with each other, not with anyone, if they're smart. You'll see soon enough. Anyway, you came here for a reason. Nobody comes to me without a reason. I'm listening." The judge put his elbow on the armrest of his chair and rested his jaw on his fist, staring at the man before him as he'd stared down lawyers and litigants for decades.

Boucher swallowed the remaining bourbon in his glass, letting it burn its way down his throat. "A long time ago, Roy Epson did something he shouldn't have," he said. "I was told about it. I met with an FBI agent I know who confirmed it."

"What'd he do?"

"He took a bribe."

"That's all?"

"He might have murdered someone."

"Any proof of that?"

"Not that I'm aware of."

"Then don't repeat it. You know better than that."

Wundt stood up, took the decanter, and poured one more shot each. He leaned against his desk and said:

"We all fuck up. Good intentions, bad intentions, it doesn't matter, sooner or later we all fuck up. Thing is"—now he swirled the liquor in his glass and looked down into it—"we can't afford to let the world know when we do. I'm not talking about judicial decisions, I'm talking about a judge stabbing somebody in a bar, driving drunk in drag, beating his wife and breaking almost every bone in her face. Someone has to do what we do, and sometimes behind decent legal minds lurks every personality disorder imaginable. It's like flagpole-sitting. We're perched up there, no real human contact, with everyone staring at us from below, wondering if we'll fall—or jump. Some of us snap."

"Are you saying Roy Epson *snapped*?" Boucher asked. "Seems to me he accepted bribes. Maybe worse. Why was there no follow-up?"

Wundt studied the carpet. "The FBI looked into it and gave their findings to Judge Epson. Why? Maybe they found no proof of any of the allegations. Maybe they wanted something to hold over him. Maybe they realized what a can of worms could be opened by charges of a jurist unfit for his job. Such a claim might have called into question the finality of every judgment he ever made and open a floodgate of motions to relitigate. Who knows? Anyway, he's dead. Soon he'll be buried. Let him rest in peace. Let it go, Jock."

Boucher stood up. "I'll try," he said.

Judge Wundt watched him leave, shaking his head.

CHAPTER 7

A TEPID, FLAT SOFT DRINK and half a stale tuna sandwich on his desk were unappetizing reminders that he was starving. Fatigue could no longer be ignored either. Boucher dismissed those who had soldiered on with him after normal working hours, and took the elevator to the basement and his pickup and headed home.

The local radio news station was still reporting on Judge Epson's death, but added little more to the elevator account he'd gotten that morning. The two shots of bourbon had made him sleepy. He was almost too tired to be driving and fought to keep from weaving into the next lane, raising his chin, stretching his jaw muscles with a mighty yawn. He drove just under the speed limit. Traffic was not heavy. He noticed, then focused on a pair of headlights in his rearview mirror. After ten minutes there was no doubt, he was being followed. Palmetto was back. Well, it would be interesting to hear what he thought of Judge Epson's death, and a caffeinated drink, hot or cold, was what he needed at this point. He pulled into a convenience store. Palmetto followed and pulled up right beside him. Only it wasn't Palmetto.

A woman in her mid- to late forties got out of her car. She

walked to the hood of her vehicle, standing between him and the entrance to the store.

"Judge Boucher, my name is Ruth Kalin. God, I haven't spoken that name in twenty years."

He approached her, holding out his hand. She took it with a firm grip.

"I'm very pleased to meet you," he said.

"You know me?"

"Bob Palmetto mentioned your name."

She looked around nervously, a habit ingrained over two decades. "Could we go someplace and talk?"

She was wearing a jogging suit and sneakers. It gave him an idea.

"I've just joined a new gym. No one knows me there." He gave her directions and they left in their separate vehicles.

Twenty minutes later he pulled into a strip mall. There were few cars out front. He nosed into a parking space and she pulled in next to him. They entered the gym and headed to a far corner and the juice bar.

The judge ordered a couple of Cokes. They sat down and two cold cans were set on the table, then they were left alone.

"Excuse me," Boucher said. He popped open his drink and took a big swallow. "It's been a long day."

He studied her, comparing the actual person to the image he had formed. He had pictured a young, idealistic woman in her twenties. Even allowing for the passage of two decades, the mental image he'd formed of her was more flattering than the reality. Not that there was anything wrong with the woman sitting across from him, not at all, but she looked older than he would have imagined. Then he realized. It was not aging, it was not the loss of youth. It was the theft of what was once a part of this person, something no cosmetic surgery could restore. Gone were her hopes and dreams. But aside from the dry skin and worry lines around the eyes and mouth, the woman looked healthy, even fit. Her complexion was Mediterranean, somewhere between Italian and Middle Eastern; her black hair, with patches of gray, was short and curly. She was slim, but any hint of a figure was disguised by her attire. She wore no jewelry, not even a watch.

"I have to assume you learned of Mr. Palmetto's appearance before me," Boucher said. "I understood you two hadn't spoken to each other in over twenty years."

"We didn't even speak back then," she said. "I never met the man; knew him only by name and description. Neither of us appeared for that court hearing after Dexter was murdered. When I heard Judge Epson had died, I called the district court and found out you had taken over his docket and that Palmetto had been brought to you on an old warrant. I haven't practiced law in twenty years, but I still know how to get information out of a court. I knew that Palmetto's appearance wasn't a fluke and figured he had turned himself in to you. If he thought he could trust you, maybe I can too. Did he mention me on the record?" she asked.

"No. We spoke briefly after I released him, then again . . . later."

"What did he say about me?"

"Like you said, that you were to meet him at court all those years ago. Dexter Jessup was shot and you disappeared. He was afraid you might have met the same fate as Dexter."

"I would have."

"I have a hard time believing that."

It was like sticking a pin in a balloon. She seemed to collapse right in front of him and her olive skin paled. He placed his hand on her arm.

"I didn't say I don't believe you," he said. "I'm hearing things lately that I'm having a hard time accepting."

"Maybe I should go," she said.

"Please don't."

Now she studied him. "Twenty years." She sighed, then stared into his eyes. "When I heard Judge Epson was dead, everything came rushing back like it was yesterday. The life I had was destroyed because of the crimes of arrogant, dangerous men. I'm trusting you," she said, "and I don't know why. Because Bob Palmetto did? Like I said, I never even met the man." His hand still rested on her left arm. She placed her right hand on his, continuing to stare into his eyes, unblinking.

"I'm putting my life in your hands. I think Judge Epson killed Dexter Jessup. I can't prove it, but Dexter was shot by someone he knew, somebody he let get close to him. Judge Epson knew Dexter was going to the FBI. They told him. You guys in that Federal Building are one big fucking cabal." She looked down and removed her hand from his. "Sorry, but it's true."

"Why would anyone want to kill you?"

"You know the answer to that. Dexter had evidence of crimes committed by a federal judge: that the judge accepted bribes from John Perry. Before he could present this evidence, he was killed. I worked for Dexter Jessup. Please, Judge Boucher; you're an intelligent man."

"This has nothing to do with intelligence. You're telling me a federal judge is a killer, you have no proof, and you waited twenty years till he was dead to speak up about it." Boucher pulled a five-dollar bill from his money clip to pay for their Cokes. "Come on, let's go." They exited and stood outside. People were walking past them.

"Get in my truck for a minute," Boucher said. When they were seated in his truck, he spoke with a husky whisper. "Judge Epson is dead. The matter is closed."

"How did he die?" Ruth asked. "Was there anything peculiar about his death?"

Boucher said nothing. He had thought something about Epson's death was odd. He had met the late judge's doctor. The doctor had denied him access out of concern for his patient. It didn't follow that the same doctor would be careless about releasing Epson from the hospital prematurely.

"They said Dexter's assistant, Marcia Whitcomb, died of natural causes," Ruth said. "She was twenty-eight and in perfect health. Something similar will be said about Judge Epson's death, just wait."

"He had a heart attack. He didn't fake that." But Boucher wasn't even convincing himself.

"Let me ask you something, Judge. If I knew you met with Palmetto, how many others know?"

"Judge Epson knew. It was his case. You found out because it's now a matter of public record."

Ruth's eyes bored into his. "Judge Epson was killed because what he did all those years ago has come back to haunt someone who still has a lot to lose—John Perry. If you can't see that, you're in the wrong profession. What's worse, you're in the wrong place at the wrong time. Judge Boucher, you're in danger. Believe me, twenty years ago I was right where you are now. You must protect yourself. You wouldn't be the first federal judge to be murdered. You wouldn't even be the first this week." She opened the passenger door.

"Wait," Boucher said. "I need to know more about this. Would you, uh, like a drink?"

"I don't drink," Ruth said, "but you can buy me dinner if you know a place where I can get in dressed like this."

"Do you like fried chicken?"

"I do."

He knew just the place. He led the way, Ruth following in her own car.

What had started as a lunch counter in the 1940s had become an institution over the decades, its specialty New Orleans–style fried chicken. Run by an octogenarian who kept her Cajun recipe a secret even from her own family, it had been discovered and praised by some of the country's greatest chefs. The place was crowded when they arrived, and soon they were lost in the anonymity of the hungry throng. Judge Boucher spoke as they waited for their table. He pointed to a wizened old woman scurrying about.

"That's the owner," he said. "This place was destroyed by Katrina and she was relocated to live with her family in Kansas. One day she just left without telling them, flew back to New Orleans. She was found sitting on the doorstep of her destroyed restaurant. The police thought she was just another homeless person. They found out she was a celebrity. Folks got together, raised money, rebuilt the restaurant. It's another example of the resiliency of the spirit of New Orleans."

He paused for a minute, then asked, "How did you survive all those years?"

"I lived with friends and family, and I became a personal trainer," Ruth said. "I went to my clients' homes and they paid me in cash. I learned how to become invisible."

"Not exactly the life you planned. Why did you go to work for Dexter Jessup in the first place? With your academic record, any of the top firms would have been glad to have you."

"We were engaged," Ruth said. It was not a direct response, but it answered all his questions.

The chicken didn't taste as savory as usual on this evening—no fault of the chef or her secret recipe. Boucher was caught staring as they ate.

"What's wrong?" Ruth asked.

"I can't help but regret that you were robbed of the life you chose, the life you deserved."

"As T. S. Eliot said, 'I have seen the moment of my greatness flicker, and I have seen the eternal Footman hold my coat, and snicker, and in short, I was afraid.'" Ruth shrugged. "So I went into hiding. I survived—so far."

"Do you still think you're in danger?"

"I'm sure they gave up on me, at least until Palmetto reappeared. Now I'm a question mark. Someone will want an answer."

"You took quite a leap of faith in coming to me."

"Yes, I did. Now I pray that you will do the right thing for the right reason. Judge, John Perry is dirty. I want to see he gets what he deserves. It's taken me years, but I found what is needed to put him away."

"Like what?"

"You'll know when the time is right," she said. "Now I have to go. Thanks for the dinner, it was delicious."

He stood and she kissed him on his cheek, whispering, "'I am Lazarus, come from the dead, come back to tell you all, I shall tell you all.'"

He watched her walk away, T. S. Eliot's words ringing in his ear. He rubbed his cheek where she had kissed him. It burned like he'd been branded.

Boucher headed back to his new gym to work the excesses of the day out of his system. After nearly an hour with the punching bag, he followed with twenty minutes in the sauna. He drank no less than four full glasses of water, and felt himself purged. He showered and dressed.

There were still two or three men working out when he left. A liquor store several doors down was doing a brisk business, but all other commercial activity in the strip mall was done for the day. He walked to his truck, unlocked the door, and climbed behind the wheel. He sat on it before he saw it and jumped, hitting his head on the roof of the cab. Someone had placed a package inside his vehicle. He pulled it out from under him and looked at it. A large envelope, papers inside. He checked his doors and windows for a break-in; everything was secure. But someone had gotten in. A car passed behind him, its lights briefly illuminating his cab before it went on its way. He glanced at the first sheet, the dim light of the parking lot just enough for him to read the title. He replaced it carefully in the envelope. This package deserved special care; Dexter Jessup had died for it. It was the report he never gave, the document that got him killed, which Ruth Kalin had guarded with her life for two decades. He would see her again, this he knew for sure. And when he did he would ask her where in the hell she learned how to break into a 2004 Ford F-150 FX4, his pride and joy.

CHAPTER 8

JUDGE BOUCHER'S TRUCK COULD barely squeeze into the narrow drive alongside his house, but he considered himself lucky to have as much space as he did. Built in the 1820s, his "raised center hall house with Doric columns and twin staircases," as guidebooks described it, was one of the landmarks of the French Quarter, and had originally included gardens on both sides, a rarity at the time, as landscaping was usually kept in back, out of sight from pedestrian traffic. In addition to the utilitarian driveway, the venerable property included a Spanish-style courtyard, and former slave quarters—the only part of the house he didn't like and consciously ignored. He had spared no expense furnishing the home with original period furniture and was a prized client for a number of antique dealers around the country. The house had been owned by many historical residents, including a Confederate general and a major twentieth-century author.

This literary feature was particularly appealing to the woman who came to the front door to greet him after hearing his truck pull into the drive. Seeing her, Jock bounded from his truck and up the stairs to the main entrance like the track star he once had been. They embraced between the Doric columns.

"I thought you weren't coming until tomorrow," he said. He took her hands and looked into her face, not sure of what he saw.

"I finished early and thought I'd surprise you. I hope I did the right thing."

That was it; there was doubt in her eyes. "Why on earth would you say something like that?"

"There was a woman," she said. "When the taxi pulled up, there was a woman. It looked like she was hanging around waiting for you. She looked frightened when she saw me, and took off. Jock, if you're seeing someone else . . ."

"Was she about your height, with short curly black hair, some gray?"

"It was dark. I don't know. Maybe."

"I know who it was, and no, I am not seeing anyone. I have to get something out of the truck. Go on in, I'll be with you in a second." He turned before descending the stairs. "Thanks for the surprise. Malika, I'm delighted you're here."

Malika Chopra was the first woman he had dated since losing his wife to breast cancer five years ago. They had been seeing each other for almost a year now, though their relationship was the long-distance kind. Jock couldn't travel because of his work, and Malika was always on her way to or from somewhere. But their reunions kept the magic going. Malika's beauty was breathtaking. Born in Mumbai, educated in England and the United States, she was carving out her own niche, creating a new position in the rapidly changing world of publishing. Quasi-agent, quasi-publisher, she represented authors, both novelists and screenwriters.

Later, after they had kissed and made up for lost time and sat in their robes before the salon's original brick fireplace, Malika tried to joke about the woman she'd seen on her arrival, but she quickly sensed it was a serious matter and didn't push.

"Actually," Jock said, "this is unusual. I can never talk about my work with you because I don't discuss pending cases. But this one is ancient history. The woman you saw worked for a lawyer who was murdered decades ago." He told her of Palmetto, Judge Epson's death, his meeting with Ruth Kalin—and the envelope sitting on the coffee table at their feet.

"I have no idea why she came here. We met earlier this evening. She could have spoken to me when I went back to the gym but instead she somehow got into my truck and left this. I don't know why she didn't talk to me there—unless someone scared her away. Then she came here and ran away a second time? I don't get it."

"I could tell something was on your mind other than me," Malika said.

She gave a sideward glance and a shake of her head toward the bedroom, through the open door of which could be seen an antique two-poster bed with recently rumpled sheets.

"Oh, no," he said.

"It wasn't a total disappointment," she said, running the nail of her index finger around the curve of his mouth to his chin, down his neck to his chest, then his stomach. "But you did seem distracted."

"Second chance?" he asked.

"Of course." Hand in hand, they returned to the bedroom, and as they had been on nights such as this for almost two hundred years, the lights in the house on Chartres Street were extinguished. He focused on his lovemaking, then both soon fell asleep.

Jock woke hours before dawn, giving himself enough time to explore the contents of the package Ruth Kalin had placed in his truck. He had even more questions than before. There was more than Dexter's report in the package. There was something else that looked like a research project she must have worked on for years.

There were graphs and charts. Jock had no idea what they meant. He put the package in his safe, the most secure he'd ever been able to find. The kitchen refrigerator was built on hidden extension slides; a stopper underneath was locked or released with a light kick, and the fridge could be pulled out with no effort. A wall safe was installed behind, with a combination unforgettable and easy to dial from an angle, 6-6-6, the number of the beast.

Jock put the package in the safe, then walked out his back door to the courtyard and its statue of Saint Jude, the patron saint of lost causes. He paused before the old stone piece and mused. Dexter Jessup had gathered enough evidence to implicate a sitting federal judge in a serious crime. He had been a lawyer, not a professional investigator. If he had been able to gather such evidence with his limited resources—and no doubt he had at least intimated to the FBI what he had found in order to be granted a meeting with them—then why had they not followed through, especially after his murder? Maybe, like Judge Wundt had suggested, they wanted something to hold over Judge Epson. That was a scary thought.

"But I really don't have the slightest idea," he said aloud.

The silent Saint Jude's hand was raised in benediction.

The first thing Jock did on reaching his office that Friday morning was call the Federal Records Center in Fort Worth, giving the case number and requesting the complete file on Palmetto's lawsuit. Being as old as it was, the case was not available in the district court's computerized Case Management/Electronic Case Files System or on PACER, the Internet Public Access to Court Electronic Records system. Only the original paper file was available. Boucher was told he would have a copy on Monday. Direct requests from jurists received priority.

The clerk had been working archives for ten years and he had never seen a similar instruction: the file contained a number he was to call if it was ever requested. This he did, giving the name of the party requesting the case files.

CHAPTER 9

BY THE END OF the day Friday, Judge Boucher was exhausted. He had put in fifteen-hour days. He had a weekend guest, and needed a break. He bade his stunned staff farewell at four p.m. that afternoon and headed home.

"Hello, house, His Honor is home."

Malika rested her head on the back of the sofa. Jock bent down and gave her an upside-down kiss.

"Any strange women hanging around today?" he asked.

"I wouldn't have noticed them if there were," she said. Next to her on the sofa were several advance reader copies of books scheduled for publication, called ARCs in the trade, and a laptop, BlackBerry, and an iPad. All were proof she'd had no problem keeping herself busy.

"You up for an evening out?" he asked.

"*Toujours, monsieur. Où voulez-vous aller?*"

"*Tu.* With a lover it's *tu*, not *vous*."

She rose from the sofa and walked into his arms. "Where do '*tu*' want to go, *mon amour?*"

He locked the fingers of both hands behind her back and began to sway. "I want to dance some zydeco, eat some crawfish, and drink cheap beer. I want to show you a Cajun good time. Tonight, we return to my roots." He released her after a quick kiss, walked into the kitchen, and returned with two beers.

"There's a funky place near Lake Pontchartrain. It's like nothing you've ever seen, I guarantee." He pronounced it *gar-on-TEE*. "This old icehouse fills up on Friday nights with some of the most unique people in all the United States, black Cajuns."

Malika had learned about Cajuns on her first date with Jock Boucher: descendants of French expelled from Acadia, which was now northeastern Canada, in the late eighteenth century. Many of them emigrated to Louisiana. She knew that black Cajuns were descendants of slaves from the twenty-two Cajun parishes around New Orleans, and many of them lived in small isolated communities deep in the bayous.

"Will they be speaking French?"

"Some of them speak French using idioms from the time of Voltaire."

"You're kidding."

"Nope. And the music. Zydeco, it's as unique as the people."

They toasted with their beer cans. "I like seeing you this way," Malika said.

"What way?"

"Exuberant. It suits you."

"You mean more than my judicial bearing?"

"I would like for you to leave your judicial bearing outside the door of this house, or better still, leave it in your courtroom."

"You got it, babe." He looked at his watch. "We need to get ready. It's a bit of a drive. Dancing doesn't start till later, but we've got to eat first."

"What do I wear to this, what did you call it, icehouse?"

Jock smiled. "The dress code is pretty eclectic. Some folks are elderly and—these are poor people, you understand—they come wearing their best-night-out clothes. Some of the older men wear zoot suits they've had since the fifties, padded shoulders, double-pleated trousers, wide-brimmed hats, pointy-toed balmorals and brogues that must have cost them a fortune back in the day." He shook his head with wonder. "Wow, those cats are cool. Tonight, *ma chérie*, we are going to *laissez les bons temps rouler*! And you just watch your man strut his . . . exuberance."

She excused herself to dress and returned minutes later completely transformed. She wore a scarlet silk tunic with extensive gold embroidery resembling a Coptic cross from the neck to her waist, with more embroidery at the hems of the flared sleeves. The tunic covered her hips and was worn over capri pants of the same-colored silk, which fit like a second skin. On her feet were golden slippers.

"It's a kurti," she said to her stunned admirer. "You like it?"

"They're going to love you on the bayou," Jock said.

As they drove from the city to Lake Pontchartrain, Malika listened to the story of Judge Boucher's family, none of whom had ever traveled more than one hundred miles from their small community of Toulouse.

"It had been named by some pioneer planter for the city in France, but none of the folks living there could read, and none had ever been anywhere. They were descendants of slaves. When someone from the capital showed up and asked them what the name of their little town was, they told him, and a sign was put up. The sign read TOO LOOSE, and nobody knew it till my grandfather got himself a sixth-grade education. I was sent to live with relatives in New Orleans when Mom died. Dad stayed there running his little store till he passed away. Nothing left of the village now."

"I bet your father was proud of you," Malika said.

"He was proud enough to burst, but he would tell me that my grandfather must be rolling over in his grave. Grandpappy favored the other side of the law."

They reached the bayou country and its two-lane causeways built on levees crossing one mangrove swamp, then another. Small towns formed where spits of raised dry land separated the marshes. Dusk had fallen, and before them a garish neon sign blinked next to a shack on the side of the road.

KISS MY ASS, SUCK MY HEAD, EAT ME, the sign read.

"Looks like just the place," Jock said, and pulled into a gravel-covered parking lot. He killed the engine and turned to his passenger. "Honey, you are about to learn the fine art of eating crawfish."

They were early to the crawfish boil, but not the first customers. A mom, dad, and three kids were digging into a small mountain of the shrimplike crustaceans. They looked up at the new arrivals, the children wide-eyed until the mother told them not to stare at people and to eat their dinner. They did as they were told.

"I'm surprised to see children here," Malika said, "with that crude sign out front. In fact, I'm surprised that kind of language is allowed on a public road." The waitress coming to seat them wore the same crude commands on her T-shirt.

"Hon," the waitress said, "that's one of the prettiest outfits I've ever seen. Where on earth did you get that?"

"It's made in India," Malika said, returning her smile. "Like me. But I bought this one on the Internet."

"Umm, umm. I had me one of those, my man would never let me out of the house. You folks hungry?"

"That's why we're here," Jock said.

She gave him an approving once-over as well. The judge was dressed in simple tan slacks, a blue oxford shirt, and Top-Siders. They were shown to a picnic table covered with newspaper. A young boy carried a large stainless steel pot and dumped its contents in the center of the table: a mountain of crawfish, ears of corn, potatoes, and whole onions. He flashed a dazzling smile for the benefit of the exotically dressed woman.

"We got beer, ice tea, and Pepsi," he said.

"Couple ice teas," Jock said; then, to Malika, "We've got a long evening ahead of us."

In addition to the crude language emblazoned on each worker's T-shirt, KISS MY ASS, SUCK MY HEAD, EAT ME was on half a dozen signs around the restaurant.

"Folks here don't find it offensive," Jock said. "It's how you eat these things. Now do as I do. Take one in both hands. Take the head in the fingers of your left hand, grab the tail in your right, and pinch. Good. Now twist. That's it. Okay, put the head down for now and bite down just to the tail. Chomp. Good, huh? The next part is optional but if you don't do it, you'll be treated like an alien. Take the head and suck out the juices." Malika watched him, then gamely followed suit.

"That's delicious," she said, "maybe the best part."

"Glad you like them. I thought you might."

"Just wait till I get you to Mumbai," she said with a coy grin.

Jock and Malika finished their mound of shellfish but declined the offer of another. Their principal destination lay ahead. "The zydeco place is not much farther," Jock said, "but I like to get there before the band and get the best seat."

They beat the band, but just. Two musicians followed them in the door and set up on a small raised stage. Jock picked a table nearly touching the dance area.

"Is that the band?" Malika asked.

On the small stage was a black drummer, skinny as a snake, with a single snare drum. His wrists were not much thicker than the drumsticks he held in bony fingers. Sitting next to him was a short stocky white man with a several-day-old beard as counterpoint to a head as bald as an egg. He pulled an accordion from a battered carrying case, and plugged in a mike to a portable amplifier. Both men looked hungover.

"Just the two of them? That's the band?" Malika asked.

"Usually guest musicians drop in and do a set for a beer, but the guys you're looking at right now are enough, believe me."

This was soon proven. Though the musicians sat with vacant stares for almost fifteen minutes, when folks started arriving and the tables closest to the dance floor were taken, the music began. The rhythm was largely a two-step beat on the snare. The accordion also played in staccato-like cadences. The lyrics were mostly single syllables, a few sounding remotely like French. But the audience was not here to critique. Nearly all in the room were on their feet with the first tune. When the song was finished, they stayed waiting for the next.

"We'd better get up there while there's still room," Jock said, and led Malika to the dance floor.

There was no routine, there were no steps to learn, and there was no way to imitate other dancers because no two in the room danced alike. Their moves were a combination of boogie, shuffle, bop, and polka. The only common element was pure enjoyment. When Malika's eyes met those of others, the looks she got were of welcome and approval. She was warmed by more than just the rising temperature created by so many bodies in such a small place. There were a number of elderly people on the floor, their movements restricted by age, but not their enjoyment. And they were dressed as Jock said, suits and frocks out of the fifties. Finally breathless, Malika begged for a break. They returned to their table.

The pulse of the room diminished as the band played a slow number. There was more affection shown between the oldest couples than those three and four decades younger. An old man made his way to their table as the accordion player announced they would take a break after the next song. The man was bent over with age, but he bent over farther out of respect as he spoke to Jock. Malika thought she recognized the words *petite amie*. Jock bent over to Malika and whispered in her ear.

"This gentleman served with our Fifth Army in World War Two and was wounded at the Battle of Monte Cassino. Soldiers from the Fourth Indian Infantry saved his life. He recognizes where you're from. He says it would be an honor to dance with you."

The old man looked at Malika with eyes that watered with age. She had no such excuse for the moisture rimming her own as she stood to accept. They were given plenty of room on the dance floor for the final song of the set, and warm applause when the dance was finished. She kissed the old man on the cheek, and he nodded and walked away.

"He must be ninety years old," she said, taking her seat.

"And he just danced with the prettiest girl in the place. That's a Cajun for you. Live till you die."

But fatigue soon hit. They still had to drive home. Two-lane blacktops built across swamps were challenging enough in the daylight.

"We'd better be going," Jock said. He paid the bill and put a fifty

in the musicians' tip jar. It was easy access to the exit with most people on the dance floor. They made it to the door.

"Just a minute, *mon ami*."

Jock turned around. A six-foot-five, three-hundred-pounder
was walking toward him, followed by two slightly smaller goons.

"I didn't get my dance," the big one said.

No mistaking the intent here. Jock pushed Malika ahead of him
through the door, handing her the keys to the pickup. "Get inside and
lock the door."

"Step outside," Jock said. "But I'll only dance with one of you at
a time."

"Guess I go first, then," the big one said, to no one's surprise.

The provocateur outweighed him by more than a hundred
pounds. His knuckles, nearly dragging on the floor, evidenced a significant advantage in reach, and those paws, now clenched, would be
decisive—if they landed. The bruiser stood with legs spread and long
arms held out from his sides, as if preparing for a gunfight rather
than a brawl. Jock stepped in close, holding his arms high like he was
ready to take a partner in his arms for a waltz.

"Well," he said, "let's dance."

"You stupid fu—" but the consonant never made it out.

Jock brought a knee to the man's groin, which merely brought
a muffled "*Umph*," not the reaction he was hoping for. He tucked
his chin into his neck, lowered his arms, then began his familiar
routine. The hulk had almost the exact dimensions as his punching
bag. Lightning-fast jabs struck the fellow's ribs, kidneys, and flabby
stomach. The thug had no room to swing, and most of his punches
hit Jock's upper back with little force. From a distance, with Jock's
punches landing almost too fast to see, it did resemble an awkward
dance. For several minutes he pounded nonstop, while his opponent

couldn't land a punch. And there were several more knees to the groin too. After one that he knew had hit the mark, Jock took a step back as the man bent over in pain, then leaned back, the windup, the pitch. His fist landed square in the big man's face, pulverizing a nose previously broken, sending blood spurting in all directions. Beaten, the man stepped back, screaming in pain, and fell to his knees. Because he was bending over at the waist, Boucher's right cross didn't have full force, but it had enough. He knocked the man out cold.

The second string of the goon squad now stepped forward, smiling.

"Ain't gonna happen. *Ça ne va pas arriver.*" From the shadows a frail figure approached: the old man Malika had favored with a dance. Though his gait was unsteady, his hand did not shake. In his gnarled fist he held a switchblade.

The two men laughed. "Get out of the way, old man. You think you can stop us?"

"Me? No. I'm just infantry. But I brought the artillery." With the sound of several pistols being cocked, four men lined up behind the old veteran, guns in hand.

Not another word was spoken. The attackers picked up their wounded member, retreated to their car, and peeled out of the parking lot, spewing gravel and dust behind them.

"They ain't from around here," one of the men said, clicking the safety back on his pistol. "Just wanted you to know that. The lady okay?"

"She's fine," Jock said. "Thank you. Thank all of you." They shared handshakes and backslaps, then Boucher returned to his truck. *"Au revoir,"* he said. The rescue party waved him good-bye, then went back inside to their dancing.

"Did he hurt you?" Malika asked as they pulled away.

"Never touched me."

"I'm sorry. I didn't mean to cause any trouble. I might have danced with them if they had asked me."

"Dancing was not what they had on their minds," Jock said. "They were looking for a fight. One of the other men said they weren't from around here. I didn't think so. They had New Orleans accents. Why would men come all the way out here from town just to start a fight? There are hundreds of bars closer. Unless . . ." He finished his sentence with an inner monologue: *Unless they were looking for me.*

Boucher drove through the bayous with care, and with an eye on his rearview mirror. Several times he thought he spotted a car tailing him, and with no place to turn off from the two-lane blacktop, there were some anxious moments. But there were no incidents and they reached the city's outskirts. The main event of the evening was waiting for them at home.

CHAPTER 10

TWO PATROL CARS WERE parked in front of Boucher's house, one blocking the driveway, both with lights flashing. There was a dark sedan parked in the drive. He parked bumper to bumper with the cop car denying him access to his driveway. People were ambling along the sidewalk in front of the house, but one of the officers kept them moving along.

"What's going on?" Boucher asked.

"Who are you?" a cop asked.

"I'm Federal District Judge Jock Boucher. This is my house. What is this, a break-in?"

"No," the cop said. "Who's in the truck?"

"A personal friend."

"Would you ask your personal friend to step out, please?"

Malika got out of the truck and walked to his side. The cop stared at her like he hadn't seen a woman in recent memory. "Where y'all been?" he asked.

Jock Boucher had had his fill of insolent men for one evening.

"I want to know what you're doing here at my house, and whose damn car is that in my driveway."

"You know, Judge, that's something we'd like to know too. Maybe you could step over here and help us out with that one. Better ask the lady to stay back, though."

The cocky officer walked to the sedan and stood next to the driver's door. The window was down. Boucher followed and looked inside.

"Oh, my God."

"You know her?"

"I know who she is."

"You have a name for us?"

"Her name is Ruth Kalin."

The entry wound was a black hole in her left temple. A dark line of blood seeped down the side of her face, a coagulated drop hanging from her ear like a pear-shaped ruby.

"She a personal friend too?"

Jock Boucher's fists were clenched so tight his nails dug into the flesh of his palms. At that moment a plainclothes officer arrived and approached the judge, bearing himself as if with a fatigue no amount of rest could cure.

"I'm Detective Fitch," he said. The two shook hands. "I know who you are, Judge," he said. "Why don't we go inside while they get the body and the car out of here?"

They entered the house. Fitch stood just inside the doorway. He took a look around. "You were out this evening?" he asked.

"We were. I arrived home to find the police out front and that car in my driveway."

Fitch looked at Malika and nodded his head. "Ma'am," he said, as a courtesy. He was waiting for Boucher to introduce her.

"Malika Chopra's a friend of mine from New York, visiting for the weekend," Boucher said.

Fitch asked her several brief questions, which she answered with crisp, short sentences. Apparently satisfied with her answers, he concluded with, "I'm sorry this had to spoil your weekend."

"I'm sorry for the poor person in that car," Malika said.

Even with the hangdog look on his face, you could almost see Fitch's mind at work as he stood there. He turned and looked out the window in the dining room. The patrol cars had left. The ambulance had removed the body, and the decedent's car was being loaded onto a flatbed. Boucher invited the detective to sit. The invitation was refused. All three stood like each was waiting for the other to make a move, but it was Fitch who was in control.

"You know, Judge Boucher, I should have my men do a search of your house, but under the circumstances . . ."

"Detective, if you want to search my house, go right ahead. In fact, my friend and I could check into a hotel and you could have the entire night if you need it."

Fitch reached around to the back of his head and scratched. "That's very understanding of you. Tell you what. Could you meet me at the Eighth District station on Royal Street Sunday morning? Won't be too many people around then. I'll do what I need to do here, then lock up after myself. I don't think we need to involve Ms. Chopra any further at this point."

"May we get a few personal items from the bathroom?" Jock asked.

"Of course."

He and Malika excused themselves and returned within minutes. Jock carried a small bag, which he opened for inspection. Fitch shook his head, not needing to look. Boucher led Malika to the doorway.

"We'll be back around nine in the morning. Will that be enough time?"

Fitch nodded. They left.

"Was that the woman I saw the night I arrived?" Malika asked as they got into his truck.

"Yes."

"My God, why? Why here?"

"I don't know. I really don't know." But he knew one thing. He had been foolish enough to be seen by hundreds of people with Ruth Kalin at the restaurant. Had he not been so careless, she might still be alive.

He drove the short distance to the Royal Orleans Hotel. It would have been easier to walk but Malika was upset. He asked her to sit in the lobby while he got a room. Aware of how it must have looked, checking in this time of night with no luggage and such a striking woman with him, he identified himself using his title, giving the excuse of a plumbing problem in his nearby home. He was given his key card and they went to their room. Malika walked in and sat rigid on the bed.

"How can you be so calm?" she asked. "That woman was murdered right in front of your house. And that fight earlier this evening; the two are connected, aren't they?"

He closed the door, double-locked it, and fastened the chain. He walked to the bed and sat beside her, taking her hands in his.

"It's too much of a coincidence for them not to be connected in some way. But I don't know how and I don't know why. If I seem calm, it's because of what I do. I've sat in judgment of people for the last ten years of my life. I've determined civil disputes and I've sentenced men to jail. I've seen evidence of murders more brutal than this. I've learned to be dispassionate about—"

"Dispassionate? Dispassionate about a woman's murder at your own home? I don't understand. I don't understand any of this."

He kissed her cheek, for an instant unsure if she would permit him. "I don't understand it either. But I will be working with the police and we will do everything possible to find the killer."

She wrapped her arms around him and buried her face in his neck, sobbing. "I don't want to read about you," she said.

He knew very well what she meant.

With the morning's first light he woke to see her eyes wide open, staring at him.

"Did you get any sleep?" he asked.

"A little. When do you have to meet with that police detective?"

"Tomorrow. I think that was very decent of him." He tried to read her face. It was a mask. "Would you like to do something today?"

"I know this sounds horrible," she whispered, "but could we do something today to keep from thinking about yesterday?"

He sat up in bed. "Yes. Let's get out of here. Are you ready to go back to my place?"

"I'm ready."

"I'm sorry," she said when they arrived at his house, "I didn't know the hotel was so close. We could have walked. It would have been easier."

"It's all right. How are you feeling?"

"Groggy and tired," she said. "Feels like a hangover."

"Coffee will help. Let's clean up and I'll make some. Service in the courtyard in half an hour."

She managed a wan smile but she stared at her feet as they walked up to the front porch, avoiding the chance of her eyes falling on any unpleasant surprises.

The morning was fresh, but not cold, the scent of blossoms heavy in the still and already humid air. With no breeze to stir them, the blooming plants in his courtyard created a mood of a very old funeral parlor. Jock sat in a wrought-iron garden chair. Malika joined him. She looked better, more in control of herself.

"I hope you like your coffee," he said. "I make mine with chicory. Did you know the use of chicory goes back to the time of Cleopatra?"

She took a sip, then smiled. "In India, particularly southern India, it is almost impossible to find coffee without chicory. It is a staple."

Her smile vanished. "You are involved in something very dangerous. You know that, don't you?"

"I thought we were not going to think about what happened yesterday."

"Is that easy for you?"

"No. It is on my mind right now. It will stay on my mind. But I've told you everything I know about the woman and there's nothing more to say. This is our—"

"Last day together," she said, finishing his sentence. "I'm sorry. We won't talk about it anymore. What shall we do today?"

"We'll start at the Court of Two Sisters. They've got a great jazz brunch on weekends. We'll do the Quarter like we've never done it before. That should keep our minds off unpleasant things."

Secret recipes, magic potions: the French Quarter's hospitality is a witch's spell baked in beignets, soaked in Sazerac. Surrender to its beguiling charm, and fears are banished, worries forgotten. This is the promise the tiny kingdom offers, and on the last day of Malika's visit, the promise was fulfilled. For the day, troubles were forgotten, or at least not mentioned again.

* * *

Next morning, Jock had wanted to see her off at the departure gate, but Malika had insisted otherwise and he dropped her off at the curbside check-in.

"See you soon," he said.

"Very soon," she said. This was their parting tradition. They were more into reunions.

From the airport he returned to the Quarter and his meeting with Detective Fitch. They'd not set a specific time, but Jock knew the detective would be waiting for him.

The Eighth District Police Station on Royal Street was another of the French Quarter's most historic buildings. Built in 1826, it had been the old Bank of New Orleans. Its elegant façade disguised the activities now conducted within its walls, ranging from the mundane to the morbid. Judge Boucher was expected and was shown to Detective Fitch's office, a mustard-yellow room with brown blotchy stains on the walls from bad plumbing. It was barely big enough for the three chairs and the desk behind which the detective sat. The judge stood in the doorway, his eyes drawn to the ashtray on Fitch's desk. Swiped from the Old Absinthe House, it held six or seven cigarettes, all crushed soon after lighting.

"Trying to quit," Fitch said.

"Good idea." Boucher still stood in the doorway. "You know, this is one of the ugliest offices I've ever seen. Color makes me want to puke."

"Makes me want to smoke," Fitch said. "I don't like it either and this is Sunday. Let's get this done so we both can get out of here." Boucher pulled a wooden chair away from the desk and sat down.

Detective Fitch's eyes were two black marbles buried beneath a protruding frontal orbit above and puffy purplish sacs below. It was like he was staring out of a cave. A permanent slouch gave him a world-weariness that his sagging face reinforced. This was a man going through the motions of life.

"Did you know the deceased?" Fitch asked.

"I recently met her." Fitch had asked this question the other night, but Boucher did not object. He described the circumstances, then added, "My girlfriend thought she saw her at my house Friday before I got home, but that's a guess. It was dark."

Fitch shook his head. "You only met her the one time?"

"Yes, once."

"Then she comes back to your place without being invited—"

"Was she shot at my place?"

Fitch drummed his fingers on his desk and looked at Boucher. He shrugged. "Maybe, maybe not. Someone wanted it to look like a suicide. Gun was in her left hand, but there was no gunshot residue."

Jock brought the picture back. Standing next to the car, driver's side, open window. Entry wound left temple. He brought another picture to mind. Meeting Ruth. First handshake. Firm handshake. Eating fried chicken, drumstick in her fingers.

"She was right-handed," he said.

"You sure about that?"

"I'm sure. I remember shaking hands and we went out to get something to eat the evening I met her. I can picture her eating. She was right-handed."

Fitch took out a pack of cigarettes from his shirt pocket. He tapped one out and was about to light it. Boucher glared at him. He put it back.

"That's a nice house you got," he said.

"Thanks."

"Not many judges can afford a place like that, even federal judges."

"Back before I was a state judge I was a trial lawyer. Got lucky with a couple toxic tort cases."

"So you're rich?"

"I'm comfortable."

"Then why the hell are you a federal judge? I know what you guys get paid. Work it out on an hourly basis with the overtime you put in, and you all make as much as a plumber."

"I believe in our judicial system—"

"Spare me." Fitch held up his hand. "I've worked with more judges than I can count, mostly city and state judges, but I've known some feds too. There's only one reason to be a judge—you like getting your ass kissed. And those who don't kiss your ass, you can kick theirs, to hell and back. That's my definition of power, kiss my ass 'cause I can surely kick yours."

"It sounds like you don't have a very high opinion of judges."

"I've been a cop for almost thirty years. I've known judges good and bad and crooked and straight. No, I don't have a particularly high regard for judges, but I don't despise them either. They serve a necessary function, like a traffic light. It's just the holier-than-thou shit that gets to me. I'm all for proper decorum in the courtroom and all that, but it builds egos that make a lot of them assholes. So I admit I grin a little when one of you gets caught with his dick in his hand."

"That's what you think about the murder of that poor woman? A judge caught with his dick in his hand?"

"That was my first thought," Fitch said, "body in the driveway of a judge's nice, expensive house. I'm sorry. It wasn't fair to you." He let out a long, slow sigh. "I had a nice house too, before Katrina."

"Where do you live?"

"Past tense. Lived in Chalmette. Don't live anywhere now. Got a place where I sleep, and I work here." He sighed a weary sigh. "You got an alibi for Friday night? She was killed about ten-thirty."

"Like I told you before, I went to hear some zydeco with my girlfriend at a roadhouse on Lake Pontchartrain."

"Witnesses?"

"Maybe two hundred. I got in a fight."

Fitch chuckled. "I don't see any bruises. You win?"

"I had help, infantry and artillery."

The detective didn't ask for an explanation, still chuckling. "Federal district judge brawling in a redneck bar. That's a good one, and I've heard judge stories you wouldn't believe."

"It was a Cajun bar, not redneck."

"Yeah, well, choice of venue doesn't change the cause and effect, from my perspective." He reached for his cigarettes again, but this time didn't pull the pack completely out of his shirt. "Listen, I gotta ask you more questions, but this shithole is getting to me too. You want to get out of here?"

"There's something I do on Sundays," Jock said. "You're welcome to come with me and we can talk while I do it." He explained his one-man salvage missions.

"One request," Fitch said. "St. Bernard Parish."

St. Bernard Parish was the only parish completely inundated by Katrina. Of nearly twenty-seven thousand homes, only half a dozen remained habitable after the storm. Six. In addition to the flooding, oil storage tanks burst, covering the area with a foot of black sludge.

"Found my wife's body a week after the storm," Fitch said. They were on the outskirts of Chalmette, the St. Bernard Parish seat, heading toward the town called Violet. "She was buried in oil. Don't know whether she drowned or suffocated, not that it makes much difference. I couldn't get out of the Quarter, with all that was going on. You ever been married?"

"My wife died of breast cancer," Jock said. "Five years ago. No kids. She was trying to get pregnant, before . . ."

"Sorry for your loss," Fitch said.

"Ditto. How about here?" Jock stopped the truck.

The few houses still standing were empty shells. Most lots were empty, nothing rising from the ground. Refuse lined both sides of the street. But for its cracked blacktop, the street might have been nothing more than a bulldozed path through a garbage dump. Stunted trees were the only signs of life. There was no sound other than a breeze teasing something hanging loose somewhere, banging it against a hard surface without rhythm or rhyme. There was no animal life, certainly no humanity: all washed away on fouled floodwaters.

They got out of the vehicle and began picking up objects closest to the road, mostly loose rotten wood and personal effects like the odd shoe, a coffee cup that remained inexplicably intact. The broken toys that spoke of monumental loss they left untouched. The fact that a black man and a seedy-looking white man could load the bed of a pickup without being harassed was further proof that this one-time neighborhood where friendly souls had once congregated was now a wasteland beyond concern or care.

"Federal judge and Eighth District detective picking up trash. Don't you just wish some wiseass would come by and try to give us some shit about looting?" Fitch said.

When the bed of the pickup was full, Fitch leaned against the side of the truck and reached into his shirt pocket. This time the cigarette was lit. After three puffs, he discarded it, crushed it under the sole of his shoe.

"Okay, Judge. Back to the inquiry. I gotta do my job. Why did the deceased come to you in the first place?"

As they drove back to the French Quarter, after properly disposing of the refuse, Judge Boucher repeated his narration of the chain of events, beginning with Judge Epson's initial heart attack. Not wanting it to become evidence and thereby losing control of it, he left out telling the detective about the report Ruth Kalin had given him the night before her death. His safe had not been found when the police had searched his house, and he'd been asked no questions that would require him to perjure himself. There were minutes of silence after he finished his account.

Fitch spoke. "I want to take a look at the case file on that lawyer that was shot twenty years ago. Cold cases have always intrigued me."

"That's a good place to start," Boucher said.

When they pulled in front of the police station, Detective Fitch offered a handshake before leaving and sealed the deal. "You're okay, Judge, sorry about what I said earlier, about judges, I mean."

"You're entitled to your opinion. Maybe I can change it."

CHAPTER 11

IT WAS MIDAFTERNOON MONDAY when Judge Boucher's assistant brought him the files requested from the Federal Records Center. He thanked her as if this had been a routine request, and she didn't act as if it were anything unusual, though after working for two federal judges and a magistrate over a period of more than fifteen years, this was a first for her. He asked her to close the door when she left, with instructions that he not be disturbed.

Discovery in law is a fact-finding process prior to trial. Its purpose is to allow parties in a lawsuit to properly prepare, and is based on the proposition that the free exchange of information will lead to the truth. The process is governed by state and federal rules to prevent abuse, and permissible discovery may include material such as written questions requiring sworn answers, oral depositions taken under oath, inspection of items or places that cannot be physically brought to court, and the presentation of documents. It was this final area where Judge Boucher found the elephant under the bed. Bob Palmetto was being forced to turn over trade secrets or go to jail. Never had Judge Boucher seen such obvious flaunting of the rules of discovery. Lawyer Dexter Jessup had put up a good fight, his objections valid and timely, but the files showed he was refused as a matter of course, and he was threatened with contempt of court more than once. The papers the judge held in his hand made a mockery of the justice system. His thoughts were interrupted by a knock at the door.

"Sorry to disturb you, Judge, but I'm going home now," his assistant said. "It's almost six. I'm going to lock the hall door."

"Fine. Good night." He didn't even look up, but continued turning the pages in front of him. In the silence of his chambers he knew he held proof of judicial wrongdoing in his hands.

"So what?" he said aloud. There was no one to answer, so he muttered his own response. "The judge was bent. The judge is dead. So what?"

He closed the files and locked them in his desk, rose, and left his office, puzzling over the killing of Ruth Kalin. He passed by his assistant's desk, on which lay a copy of that day's paper, which she must have bought from a stand in the lobby on her way home and brought back up to the office. The first report of Ruth Kalin's death had made the Saturday papers. There had been no calls to his unlisted number and he'd just said he could not comment on the matter to the few journalists hanging around his house—it wasn't like these were strange words coming from a federal judge. It was reported again on Sunday. The story had legs. By the Monday edition, it was number one with a bullet, front page, above the fold. His assistant had left the newspaper on her desk, folded so the leading headline was prominent: "Missing Lawyer Shot in Judge's Driveway." Right under this banner was the subheading, "Federal Judge Returns from Barroom Brawl to Find Body." Red lights blinked on the desk phone indicating incoming calls being answered by the recorder. *Good time to be somewhere else*, the judge thought as he took the paper and left.

*　*　*

Judge Boucher reconnoitered his own house. As he expected, the press was gathered and ready for a feeding frenzy out front. He drove away unseen. Where to go? He remembered Fitch's ashtray: the Old Absinthe House. Corner of Rue Bourbon—could there be a better address for a bar?—and Rue Bienville. It was a port in a storm, with a restaurant upstairs. At this hour there would be few diners. The owner of the restaurant greeted him, the consoling nod of his head saying that he had seen the day's papers. With Italians, discretion was an art form.

"Good evening, Tony. How about over there?" Boucher pointed to a corner table.

"You need a menu?"

Boucher shook his head. He knew this place well. "Caesar salad with oysters, and veal piccata. Glass of Montepulciano."

The proprietor returned and uncorked the wine. "On the house," he said, leaving the bottle.

Boucher finished his meal in solitude, then called for the owner. Tony came over. "Does Detective Fitch come here often?" the judge asked.

"He's downstairs in the bar now. If you need to go out the back . . ."

"No, no. He's on my side, I think. Is he by himself?" Tony nodded. "Would you ask him to come up?" Boucher asked.

Fitch was shown to the table moments later.

"I've already eaten," the judge said. "Sorry. Would you like some wine?" Fitch nodded. He raised his glass in a silent toast before sipping.

"You saw the papers, I guess," Fitch said.

"I did. Body in driveway, barroom brawl; none of this is going to do my judicial reputation much good."

"Yeah. It almost looks like the press has it out for you."

"The newspapers are just doing what newspapers do," Boucher said. "My alibi was printed. Who ever had a barroom brawl as a defense? At least I'm not a suspect, right?"

Fitch sipped. "This is good wine. No. As far as I'm concerned, you're not a suspect. It's likely the girl was shot someplace else and driven to your house in her own car. How was your dinner? Food good here? I never came upstairs before. This is nice." He looked around the room.

Boucher raised his hand again. "Tony, would you bring Detective Fitch a menu?"

"That's all right. Whatever the judge had is good enough for me." Fitch looked at Boucher, his elbows on the table, his fingers folded, forming a dome on which he rested his chin. "You know how to get a lifetime federal judicial appointee kicked off the bench?" he asked. "Catch him driving drunk dressed in drag. That's my favorite. But get him in a bar fight, then find a body at his house, that's not bad either. It looks like someone wants you to have one of the shortest judicial careers on record." He was brought his salad. "I love Caesar salad; never had it with oysters before.

"Judge Boucher," he said, "you got enemies. You've been on the bench less than a month and you got enemies. What the hell did you step in, son?"

"Twenty-year-old shit," Boucher said. "I can't believe the stink is still so strong. Sorry."

"Doesn't bother me. By the way, I looked into Dexter Jessup's case file."

"Anything interesting?"

"Maybe."

"Come on, Detective. What's your first name anyway? I buy a guy dinner, I should know his first name."

"It's Roscoe, but nobody calls me that, and that's fine with me. Never did like it much."

"So what should I call you?"

"Fitch. Just Fitch. How about you? I need to call you Judge?"

"If it's just the two of us, I'd prefer Jock. If we're in front of others—"

"It's Judge. I understand."

"So, what did you find?"

"It was a contact wound. Barrel of the gun was placed right to the back of his head. He had male pattern baldness. Back of his head looked like a bull's-eye."

Jock sat in silence. Fitch ate an oyster.

"He'd pulled off the road," Fitch said. "Motor was still running when the body was found, so it was discovered not long after the shooting. There were contusions on the right knee, so I'm thinking he got out of his car, saw the guy with the gun and tried to get away, slipped, and struck his knee on loose stones on the shoulder."

"Did he have a flat?"

"No, why?"

"Well, if the motor was running and he didn't have a flat tire, I wonder why he pulled off the road."

"Only answer I can come up with is that someone he knew flagged him down. He got out, saw the gun, and tried to run. Didn't make it. Anyway, it's all speculation. It was a half-assed investigation, partly because the crime scene was all fucked up."

"How?"

"Guy who found the body. He pulled right behind the deceased's vehicle, then flagged down others. Remember, not everybody had a cell phone in their pocket back then. Anyway, any chance of getting tire tracks from the perp's car was zero and any other clues were gone or compromised too. The scene had maybe half a dozen cars and people tramping around it before the first patrol car got there, so I'll cut the guys a little slack."

"So there was no evidence at the scene."

"What I'm telling you came from our cold case files. The files just have paperwork and photos. Anyway, physical evidence? Forget it. Our property room was underwater after Katrina. No way anything that old would still be there. Now, if you will let me continue . . ." Fitch took a sip of wine, licking his lips.

"Like I said. Contact wound. Barrel against the bald spot at the back of his head. It left soot. Almost like a tattoo."

Enjoying himself now, Fitch took a bite of romaine, then forked a thin sliver of Parmesan. Jock gritted his teeth.

"It was a .38 Special, gun was Smith and Wesson Model 10," Fitch said.

"Without a bullet, how can you know the gun and the caliber?"

"The caliber can be reasonably estimated from an entry wound. There's a measurable difference between a .22 and a .38. I know it's a Smith and Wesson Model 10 because of the tattoo. I put the barrel of one against the photo of the wound; perfect fit. Also, it was a Model 10 made between 1961 and the early 1990s."

"So we think the deceased knew the shooter, and we think the gun was a Model 10, one of which you just happened to have lying around. That's not much to go on."

"I'm not finished."

Fitch was served his entrée, took two bites, then continued.

"The S and W Model 10 Military and Police or M and P revolver was revised in 1961, adding a heavy barrel with a ramped front sight. The Model 10 was used in police departments all over the country, including New Orleans, until the early 1990s, when it was also phased out."

"Wait a minute," Boucher said. "A police car could have pulled him over. The weapon was a standard police-issue at the time. You know what you're implying? The shooter might have been a policeman. That could have been a reason why the investigation went nowhere."

"I'm going to finish this dinner before I say another word," Fitch said.

Jock had no choice but to let the man eat. Fitch chewed the last bite and wiped his mouth with his napkin. He took several gulps from his glass of water.

"I don't think it was a cop," Fitch said. "It's possible, but I don't think so. Cop shoots a guy he pulled over, it's because the guy presented an immediate danger, and the cop goes to some trouble to build a case of self-defense, justified response and all that. There was none of that here. Also, we've never had singles in patrol cars, they always partner up. Two cops in on a murder of a prominent lawyer? It's a possibility, I guess, but not a very realistic one."

"You say the gun and cartridge were used by law enforcement. That would include the FBI, wouldn't it?"

"Of course. There's even what they call an 'FBI load' to a .38 cartridge. Packs a bigger punch. There's something else. Using the same procedure—which I'm not saying would stand up in court—the gun that killed Ruth Kalin . . . ?"

"A Model 10 using a .38 Special cartridge," Jock said.

"Yeah," Fitch said. "But there's a lot of those guns and bullets around, and it wasn't the same gun in both murders, just the same model. The gun the woman had in her hand was a throw-down. Serial number was filed off. Cops use them when they shoot some-

one and need to claim self-defense. The bullet that killed her exited the right temple and went out through the open passenger-side
window. We didn't find it. We think she was shot somewhere else
and driven in her car to your place. Blood and tissue were on the
passenger seat, like she'd been pushed onto her right side. Shooter
bent her over, squeezed in, and practically sat on her. Also, the driver's seat was back as far as it could go. Her feet would have barely
reached the pedals."

"The gun being put in her left hand seems kind of amateurish to
me," Boucher said. "Especially with no gunshot residue on that hand."

"In the heat of the moment, criminals often overlook the obvious. She was shot in the left temple because that was the side that
was exposed. She had her windows down. Maybe she knew the killer,
maybe he was asking her directions. He was on her left side. That
was the side he got out of when he got to your place. It was easiest to
reach down, grab her left hand, and put the gun in it."

"It doesn't make sense to me that he'd put the gun in the left
hand of a right-handed person."

"He wouldn't necessarily have known she was right-handed.
How about this as another consideration? There's a common element in both murders. The victims, both of whom had plenty of
reason to be cautious, let the shooter get close, like they knew him.
From everything you've told me, there's one person they both knew:
their client, Bob Palmetto."

"Palmetto the killer? No way. If you saw him, you'd know. He
was dependent on Dexter Jessup. His lawyer was trying to save him
and his company. And from what he told me, he never even knew
Ruth Kalin."

"Well, you can't deny this: Lawyer Jessup gets shot. Palmetto
disappears. Lady lawyer disappears for twenty years, then she and

Palmetto surface at the same time. Lady lawyer gets shot, and now, where the hell is Palmetto? Maybe there was a crooked judge in the middle of all this—wouldn't be the first time—but you seem a little eager to fling mud at a judicial colleague, and a little overprotective of this guy Palmetto."

"And you've implied a police cover-up," Jock said. "That might say something about how you and I view our own professions. Anyway, I reject your theory about Palmetto." As he said this, he was wondering if his releasing the man had not been a mistake.

"If he were around, I'd sure have a bunch of questions for him," Fitch said.

"Such as?"

"Well, I'd want proof that he wasn't the one stealing ideas like that lawsuit claimed. And I'd sure want to check out his connection with Ruth Kalin."

The doubt in Boucher's mind flashed. The connection between her and Palmetto. There was something else—they had both sought him out in a short space of time, and they had both been to his house. Fitch was right. He and Fitch both had a lot to ask Palmetto—and Judge Jock Boucher had let him go.

"One more question," Fitch said.

"Yes?"

"What's for dessert?"

It didn't take long.

Next morning there was a note waiting for him on his desk: *See me now.* It was signed by Judge Wundt. Boucher could almost hear the words spoken, and thought, *Here I am, as close to the top of the ladder of life as one could hope to get, and I'm still taking orders.* It rankled, and his furor only festered more when he arrived at the chief judge's chambers and was made to wait for almost fifteen minutes. He was boiling over when finally admitted. Judge Wundt did not get up to greet him, did not offer a handshake.

"You know, Jock," Wundt said, "when we were together the other day, I wanted to say more. I wanted to tell you a little more about our brotherhood, about how we look out for each other; how we circle the wagons when it becomes necessary. I got the feeling you wouldn't have been receptive, so I held my counsel. I asked you to leave Judge Epson's past where it belongs. What did you do? Exactly the opposite. You requested the files from archives. Then there's a dead woman in your driveway."

"Judge, do you want a fucking letter from the detective in charge of the investigation saying that I'm not a murder suspect? I can have it for you in an hour. If that's not the purpose of this meeting, I have things to do. How the hell did you know I requested the case files from archives, anyway?"

"Since we're using the vernacular, I'll answer as follows. That's none of your fucking business. And the purpose of this meeting is not to ask you for a goddamned letter from some alcoholic has-been of a police detective. It's to ask you to take leave from the bench."

"What?"

"I think three months should be adequate. Maybe in that time you can give a little thought to the importance of unity between those of us who bear this responsibility."

"I came home and found a dead woman in my driveway. I had nothing to do with it and the cops know it. You're condemning me? You can't be serious."

A wry smile broke Wundt's stern countenance. He was enjoying this. "You're right, of course, and this would be a good time for all of us on the bench to come together and express a unity of belief in your innocence. Sadly, we can't do that. Your brawling in a redneck bar aggravates the situation. No, Judge Boucher, I've discussed the matter with my colleagues. It will be hard on us, of course—God, two vacancies on the bench—but we'll survive. You will take a three-month leave of absence."

"You can't—" Boucher said.

"You're right. I can't force you to take leave. You're appointed for life. But as chief judge it's my job to oversee the conduct of our judges. I can reprimand, or I can recommend further action. Take my advice. Take a leave. I think you will appreciate the value of coopera-tion when it's time to come back. Oh, and please, try to stay out of redneck bars in the meantime. That is all. Meeting adjourned."

Boucher stood, walked to the door, and turned. "The bar wasn't redneck. It was Cajun. Like me."

He left, the door slamming behind him.

CHAPTER 12

CONFLICTED: THE WORD SUMMED up Judge Boucher's feelings. He walked to the river that evening and stared out from the embankment down the Mississippi. The sun had set. A string of barges being towed looked like some prehistoric predator gliding through black waters, the lights of the tug's wheelhouse the yellow eyes of the beast. Was Fitch right? Had he jumped to conclusions regarding Judge Epson? Had he given Palmetto too much benefit of the doubt? Fitch had implied that the skinny old fart had played him like a drum, and the longer he thought about it, the madder he got. He had no idea where Palmetto had gone, but he had more questions for him—and he had a way to get him back, if luck served. Taking a leave from the bench might not be a bad idea, but he had an official act to perform before he left. First thing tomorrow. Standing looking over the brooding Mississippi, he took out his cell and speed-dialed Malika.

"Hi," he said. "How are you?"

"Fine. You?" Her voice sounded flat.

"I've been asked to take a leave from the bench till questions about that fight and the murder are resolved. I don't have to do it, but

I'm thinking it might be a good idea for a couple months. Maybe sort this stuff out in my head."

"What will you do?"

"Whatever I want, wherever I want. Other than a lot of time for contemplation, I haven't thought about specifics."

She asked about Ruth Kalin.

"I've met with the police. They don't have anything yet. These things take time."

"Where are you now? I hear something in the background."

"I'm not too far from the French Market; just staring at the river. You?"

"I'm in my apartment, getting ready to go to bed. I've been tired since I got back, and things have been hectic."

"Your voice sounds kind of funny."

"I'm tired, Jock. I haven't slept well. That incident, well, it upset me. I'm not as—what was your word?—as dispassionate as you."

He didn't know what to say, but at that moment she felt a lot farther away than New York.

"Jock?"

"I'm here. I just wanted to say hello. You go on and get some sleep. I'll call you soon."

"I'll try to be in a better frame of mind. Good night, Jock."

It was not one of their better conversations. He blamed Bob Palmetto for that too.

Boucher woke up next morning eager to face the day. He arrived at his chambers before his assistant and had the order drafted when she arrived. It was quickly typed, signed, and filed with the clerk's office. Before expiration of the ten-day period after which judgments became final, Judge Boucher rescinded his previous ruling and reinstated the contempt order against Robert Palmetto; a free man once again made a fugitive with the stroke of the pen. He would be totally unsuspecting. Sooner or later he'd be ensnared. This time it wouldn't take twenty years. Like adding a codicil to a will, Judge Boucher had added a unique instruction. He was to be personally notified whenever and wherever the man was apprehended. A one-of-a-kind kicker, he had given his home and cell phone numbers.

He wasn't the only one concerned with the whereabouts of Bob Palmetto.

Above it all. Figuratively and literally, that's how one felt in a private jet.

John Perry was economizing, using the Learjet 60 instead of one of the company's larger aircraft. Though it had a capacity of up to eight passengers, he'd had this one fitted for four, with two of the seats converting to a bed if he needed to rest or fancied one of the hostesses. Several politicians he transported were particularly partial to this unique aspect of in-flight service. His flight attendants were extremely well paid. They never said no; not that women ever said no to John Perry, whether compensated or not. He was in his mid-fifties, but his thick black hair had not yet begun to turn gray. His good looks had not faded; in fact, maturity added to his attraction. He had remained married to the same woman for almost thirty years. He'd seen careers ruined—and fortunes squandered—by extramarital affairs. When he got the urge, he'd hop on one of his jets and do it among the clouds with women whose only expectations were monetary.

On this occasion, though, sex was the furthest thing from his mind. Nor was he traveling alone. Two black leather seats faced each other with a table between them. Holes in the four corners held glasses, and a caddy fixed to the side of the table, not unlike the food trays used in old drive-in restaurants, held a bottle of scotch and bucket of ice. He and the man sitting across from him were engaged in serious conversation and did not want to be interrupted. The plane's flight plan would take them to the South Carolina coast, where the company's long-range helicopter, a Sikorsky S93, would transport them to a ship two hundred miles offshore. John Perry would see, before this day was out, some of the deepest core samples ever taken on planet Earth. And he would see his legacy: energy independence for what was once—and would be again, he thought—the greatest country on earth.

"What am I looking at, Bert?" Perry asked. The documents had been unrolled and were larger than the table's surface. Crystal glasses at the four corners weighed them down.

Bert Cantrell had been John Perry's closest confidant and master geologist for over thirty years. They were partners but didn't treat each other as such. To Cantrell, Perry would always be the boss. To Perry, Cantrell was his employee. It worked. In a business where the end justified the means, not only was one usually incapable of understanding the logic employed by the other, in many cases ignorance of the other's activities was bliss. But they had one thing in common. Both were ruthless to a fault when set on achieving a goal.

"These are substrata soundings we've taken of the Carolina Trough," Cantrell said. "They give the location and size of the methane hydrate fields and surrounding formations. Palmetto was working on geologic sequestration, among other things. His plan called for separating carbon dioxide from the methane and storing it underground. Carbon dioxide has been stored in geologic formations for aeons. But separating methane from CO_2 and storing it under the ocean floor is something new. We're just beginning to study the possibility and its effects."

"I can't believe it's taken us twenty years and we still can't find out what he did."

"What we think he did. The papers we got in that court case just reveal his theories. Sorry to hear about Judge Epson, by the way. We don't know if Palmetto actually produced results. Man, I wish we'd gotten him to come over to our side; if I could have just one hour with that guy . . ."

"I'd settle for one minute." Perry lifted his glass of scotch on the rocks with his left hand and took a sip. With his right hand he formed a pistol with thumb and index finger and fired an imaginary shot. "He and his damned lawyer nearly blew the whole deal."

"Yeah, well . . . we dodged that bullet."

Two hours later they were over South Carolina, descending to a small airstrip near the Atlantic coast. On the same strip, the Sikorsky S93 corporate helicopter was revving up for the final leg of the journey. Within minutes they were airborne again and heading out over the open ocean. Hours over the open sea, the research vessel was spotted, the red-ringed H on the aft deck guiding them to a soft touchdown. Perry had not spoken a word during this phase of the trip, and when asked why he'd been so silent he said, "I don't like helicopters." They were escorted belowdecks.

The lab aboard the ship was as complete as any geophysicist could have wanted. Half a dozen scientists were busy at computers. A larger screen displayed video transmitted from a remote camera on the ocean floor.

"Hey, guys, the boss is here," Cantrell said.

Only then did the scientists look up. Intrusions were not common and not welcome. The team leader introduced himself to the CEO and gave the names of his colleagues—each nodding and giving a wave and an expression that said, *I'm busy here.*

"Sorry for the interruption," Perry said. "Carry on."

The team leader, Ed Strake, explained the group's activities.

"What you see on this screen is the ocean floor photographed by our remote camera. It's fixed on the site where we're taking our core samples. Not much going on at the moment. The guys with their noses stuck to computer screens are analyzing data from our soundings. We're using Raman spectrometers, they're like lasers, to identify the boundaries of the field. We brought up methane hydrate; samples are in the freezer. Want to see them?"

"How did you find them?" Perry asked.

"We found these on the surface."

"You just pick them up?"

"Sometimes they're right there in the open, sometimes just below the ocean floor. Don't get the wrong idea, it's not like finding a rock—more like finding a diamond or a gold nugget. Sometimes where there are large deposits you do stumble across a surface sample, probably a piece broken off from a larger stratum. A hydrate is not as strong as rock, but it's twice as strong as ice. Also, if the pressure is constant, they remain frozen at temperatures above the melting point of ice. That's good news for extraction; makes it much more like mining than drilling."

He led them to a walk-in freezer. On a stainless steel table that resembled something from a hospital—or an abattoir—was a baseball-sized chunk of what looked like ice.

"Pick it up," Strake said.

Perry did. "Feels like Styrofoam," he said. He put it down.

"That's because a hydrate is a very poor conductor of heat. But it's ice. It melts. Watch this," Ed said. He flicked a lighter and held it to the chunk. The ice was immediately enveloped in waves of blue flame. The three men stared in silence. The ice was on fire. "Not much to look at, but this clump of ice comes from one of the biggest—and oldest—hydrocarbon deposits on earth."

"What's next?" Perry asked.

"That's up to you."

"What do you mean?"

"We need to clear the surface of the ocean bed. It's mostly sandy bottom but there is some sedimentary rock. There's a deep stratum of methane just below. You need to determine the manner in which we remove the top sedimentary level."

"We blast," Perry said.

Strake's eyebrows arched. "Underwater explosions deliver more energy than explosions aboveground. The heat from an explosion could melt the hydrate and release methane. The gas bubble expands because its pressure falls below the pressure of the surrounding water, until it collapses and forms a second bubble. Both create shock waves which can rise to the surface, creating a tsunami effect. Underwater blasting is very dangerous."

"Not if we limit the size of the blast. Tell him, Cantrell."

"We're just sweeping the surface of the seabed. We'll use low-velocity explosives, carefully placed. Heat rises, even in water, and with the temperature we have at that depth, there won't be a heat issue. By my calculations, the shock wave will be minimal and will in fact contribute to clearing the surface. There won't be any seismic effects. There are no reflecting surfaces or thermoclines on the seabed in the blast area, so the waves will just sweep over it and dissipate."

Perry smiled and put a hand on Strake's shoulder. "We'll blast. I'll tell you when."

Again silent in the refueled helicopter, Perry spoke only after they were heading back in the jet and the scotch was poured. He contemplated his glass.

"It's still risky," he said.

"Blasting?"

"Yeah. But we've got to get started. We've wasted too many years trying to get the federal regulators on board with this while everybody else is moving forward. Hell, New Zealand has announced it is going to be the first country to begin commercial extraction of methane hydrate. New Zealand, for Christ's sake—a country of eco-freaks, and they're beating us to this energy source. Well, screw the regulators. Do you know where we just were? We were two hundred miles offshore, the boundary of the U.S. exclusive economic zone. If we have to, we'll stay in international waters. Then they can't touch us." Perry sipped his scotch, then said, "We've got to find that fucker."

"Who?"

"Palmetto."

"John, it's been twenty years. He's old news. We're developing technologies he's never imagined. Why are you still worrying about that geezer?"

"Because he's a loose end. Because he could find himself another lawyer and claim we stole his extraction process and call attention to what we're doing. Because it could be twenty years ago all over again. I don't want him mouthing off now that we're so close. We've got to find him."

"He knows you bribed a judge. Nobody gave a damn then. Why do you think anyone would give a rat's ass now that the judge is dead? That makes no sense."

Perry leaned back in his seat. "Bob Palmetto should have been terminated twenty years ago. He needs to become a damned methane hydrate himself. Iced."

CHAPTER 13

PALMETTO LOVED HIS WINDBREAKER. It needed no folding and could be crammed into his backpack when he wasn't wearing it, which was seldom. Its synthetic fabric was impervious to wind and rain and it had a hood folded into the collar that could be unrolled to protect his neck and head. There was elastic at the wrists, a zipper up to the throat, and in low temperatures the drawstrings at the waist could be pulled tight, enabling him to use his own body heat as insulation like a diver's wet suit. *Forget Oscars, Pulitzers, and Nobel Prizes*, he thought. *The man who invented this jacket should have been honored, his name glorified.*

He stood on the dock at Marblehead. A brisk Atlantic breeze gave a mid-October hint of what the next few months would bring. A ferry bobbed idly on the water, the summer rush now over. Nearby streets where parking wars had raged for the past months were quiet, shops and restaurants extending a more civil invitation now that the tourist hordes were gone. The caliber of pedestrian was elevated. The man wearing the Sikh turban could be an oceanographic geologist; the Malay, an expert on zooplankton; the Aussie with his loud and unmistakable accent, a leading authority on coral reefs—and more than one of them could easily have been wearing Nobel prize medallions around their necks. These scientists were here as visitors to the Marblehead Oceanographic Institute, to learn from colleagues and to share knowledge they had gained. The man who invented the windbreaker would have fit right in, Palmetto thought. He zipped up his jacket and turned toward the town. Of course, two other things could also have brought these men of science to this charming New England seaside village: the vivid colors of autumn leaves, now in their final days, and clams—not to study the bivalve mollusks, but to eat them. Bob Palmetto gorged on clams. On his way back to the Institute, he bought a paper cone full of fried clams and ate them like popcorn as he walked.

He'd been coming to Marblehead for so long, everyone assumed he was part of the staff at the Institute. Though he'd seen security tightened over the years, he'd never even been asked his name. He was a routine visitor, and his routine never varied. Discarding the paper cone, now emptied of its fried contents, he entered the building that contained the oceanographic geology and geophysics department. He didn't get ten feet before a voice called out:

"Hey, Bob, when did you get back?"

A woman stepped forward and embraced him in the hall. Her auburn hair was cut short and she wore jeans, a beige Irish fisherman's sweater, and chukka boots. Admiring her utilitarian wardrobe, he held her hands in his with arms outstretched. He noticed her wedding ring.

"Mae, did you—"

"Me and Mark," she said. "I started helping him after his accident, and"—she patted her heart—"what can I say? It's crazy. We worked across the hall from each other for five years and never said a word to each other."

"What accident? How is he?"

"It was a freak thing. He was on one of our research vessels. A generator on deck got loose, slid, and pinned him against the ship's railing. His pelvis was crushed; a lot of nerve damage. The doctors say he might never walk again, but we have hope."

"I'm so sorry."

"No, no, no. No sorry stuff. Encouragement is what he needs. We treat it like a research problem. We work at physical therapy every day and we know we'll succeed." She put a finger alongside her cheek, and her expression changed. "You know something? You show up out of nowhere once a year and it always seems to be just after I've made a new discovery. I've just gotten results of a study you'll find interesting."

Mae grabbed his hand and led him into a room. On a stand was something that looked like a combination mini-submarine and Jet Ski. It was a remote-operated deep-sea exploration vehicle, and was the size of a compact car. Palmetto recognized it. The letters MBARI, for Monterey Bay Aquarium Research Institute, were printed large enough to be read from a distance and up to four thousand meters below the ocean's surface—as if literacy were one of many discoveries made at that depth.

"That's MBARI's Tiburon," he said. "What's it doing here?"

"On loan," Mae said. "We've been doing some experiments. We used it to help inject CO_2 hydrate slurry into subsea sediments more than three thousand meters deep."

"Geologic sequestration," Palmetto said. "What happened?"

"The purpose was to find the effect on single-cell foraminifera, organisms which play an integral role in the marine food chain. In a nutshell, some survived, some didn't."

"Conclusion?"

"We'd better be damned careful before we start exterminating life-forms."

Palmetto smoothed back the sparse strands of hair remaining on the top of his head. "There's a lot of interest in injection of CO_2 into the ocean floor. I don't think there's going to be much sympathy for a single-celled organism that never evolved from the seabed."

Mae sighed. "We do what we can. Why don't you go say hello to Mark? He's in the communication center. It's worked out well for him. He's happy there. If he can't go to sea, he can at least keep in touch with those who can. Go see him. And tell him you've been invited to dinner tonight. You look like you haven't eaten in a week."

"I get that a lot," Palmetto said.

He excused himself and walked to the communication center, where all research vessels of the Institute were monitored as they conducted their experiments around the world. A floor-to-ceiling map of the world showed the location of each of the research vessels. Via satellite, phone calls and faxes could be sent to and received by all ships at sea. Mark was sitting in his wheelchair with his back to the door, talking on the phone. Palmetto called his name. Mark leaned back in his chair as if he were going to fall, grabbed the wheels by their handrails, and literally turned on a dime.

"Bob Palmetto. How in the world are you?" he said.

Palmetto chuckled. "Man, you are hell on wheels. Good to see you, buddy. I've just come from Mae. She tells me you're in training for the Special Olympics."

"No, next year I'll be out of this thing and ready to run the Boston Marathon."

They shook hands, spent about fourteen seconds catching up, then got down to science. Mark was eager to show off their satellite communication equipment, and pointed to the location of each vessel of MOI's research fleet.

"The research vessel *Beagle* is in the Navy Yard at Norfolk. It transports *Lucy*, our mini-sub. We had some work done on the three-man mini-sub's manipulator arm. It's ready now and waiting for its next mission. The research vessel *Ahab* is in Tampa Bay," he said. "The smaller ships are here in port."

"Any research on methane hydrate?" Palmetto asked.

"We're not doing anything at the moment, but somebody out there is. Come over here." Mark wheeled himself over to the world map and with a laser pen pointed off the coast of South Carolina.

"There's a research vessel about two hundred miles off the coast of South Carolina. It's not ours, it's not Monterey's, and it's not from Scripps Institution of Oceanography. I've checked with all of them. But somebody out there is using a moored buoy tethered to some kind of transmitter on the seabed. Data is being sent from the seabed to the buoy to the vessel, then by satellite to somewhere on the Gulf Coast; could be New Orleans."

Palmetto felt hairs bristle on his arms and neck. "How are you getting it?"

"We're getting it because I'm probably the only guy in the world who's got nothing better to do than sit in here all day every day and I accidentally hit on their frequency. I've been snooping. Their encryption—if you can call it that—is transparent. It's almost the same as ours. I bet there's one or more of our guys out there. I just hope they're making more money than I am."

"What kind of data?"

"They've been marking off a field and taking core samples, as far as I can tell."

"Any idea how long they've been there?"

"I found them a week ago, so at least that long." Mark looked at his watch. "Mae did invite you to dinner, I hope." Palmetto nodded. "Then I guess we'd better close up shop and make our way home."

"I need to go to my motel room and freshen up."

"You do that. And check out. You're staying with us. No argument."

It couldn't be called running because both feet did not leave the ground during each stride, but on his way back to his motel room, Palmetto could have beat any runner hands down. He had wings on his feet, but when he got to his motel and tried several phone calls his feet were like lead as he paced his room, dragged down by frustration, fear . . . and failure. The day was here and he had failed to prepare for it. The phone numbers he had dialed, from scraps of paper yellowed with age, were no longer any good. He was a scientist, but he also had once been a businessman and he had lost one of the businessman's most important assets, his contacts. Palmetto, in his effort to survive all these years, had lost contact with those whose help he needed now. He had no one. Weighed down with frustration, he checked out of the motel.

Mark and Mae's home was a small Cape Cod, little more than a bungalow, with a hint of a front yard with a white picket fence and a large bay window, not far from the Institute. Mark answered the door when Palmetto knocked, took one look at his guest, and yelled over his shoulder, "You were right, Mae, a backpack, not a suitcase, and it's a small one." He laughed. "It wasn't even a bet. We knew you'd be traveling light. Come on in. Leave that in the hallway."

Palmetto followed his host into the living room, where a fire had been lit, more for atmosphere than heat. He sat on the sofa and heard a loud crash from the kitchen.

"Shit!" Mae yelled. She stepped into view. She was still wearing the jeans she'd worn earlier, but now they were splattered with what looked like blood. "I dropped a whole fucking bottle of red wine," she said as she collapsed on a dining chair. Mark wheeled to her side after a quick survey of the kitchen.

"Yeah, that's one dead soldier," he said; then, to her, "We'd better clean that up quickly or we'll never get the stains out."

He turned to Palmetto. "Bob, there's a ring of keys on a hook by the door. Would you mind taking the car and going to the supermarket? It's just about three miles straight up the road. You can't miss it. I've got handicapped plates, so you can park right in front. We'll have this cleaned up by the time you get back. If you need some money, my wallet's—"

"No, no. I'm an idiot for not bringing some wine with me. I've forgotten what manners I used to have. Not a problem. I'll be back in a few minutes."

The family car was a late-model Volkswagen. Palmetto couldn't remember the last time he'd driven a late-model anything, but keys still turned ignitions, automatic transmissions still shifted from p to r to d, and he was on his way. As cautiously as he drove, he could have walked faster. He should have.

He found the supermarket, pulled into a handicapped spot as advised, and hopped out of the car, anxious to complete his purchase and get back. This time he even ran. That was a mistake.

"Just a minute theah, mistuh."

He didn't even need to turn around. Whether it was the broad New England *a*'s or the drawn-out vowels of the Southern drawl, it didn't matter. A cop's command was the same regardless of accent or inflection.

"That your car?" the cop asked. He had been cruising the parking lot in his patrol car and seen a man jump from a vehicle parked in a reserved handicapped spot who showed no signs of a handicap at all, unless being on the slim side qualified—which it did not.

"No, sir," Palmetto said. "It's a friend's. He asked me to come get some wine. We're having dinner and his wife dropped—"

"Can I see your driver's license?"

Palmetto drew a deep breath, then with his exhale seemed to collapse in on himself. His shoulders sagged. His knees bent. For more than two decades he had avoided this moment, using more artistry and imagination in this singular endeavor than the most creative of men employed in a lifetime. He looked around him. A *supermarket*, for fuck's sake. Busted in a supermarket.

"No driver's license, Officer."

"Got some ID?"

"Not on me, Officer."

How he begged and pleaded. Geophysicist; guest of scientists working at Marblehead. Their house just three miles that way. No, he didn't know the address, but it wasn't far. Just minutes away.

"Well, the police station's just minutes away too."

Bob Palmetto rarely thought of food; it just wasn't that important to him. But that night, more than anything else on earth, he wished for the dinner that had been prepared in the home of his friends. He would have given anything to have been there for it.

CHAPTER 14

B Y THE TIME MARK and Mae had become worried enough to call the police and report their friend's failure to return from the supermarket, Bob Palmetto was gone from Marblehead, transferred to a federal holding facility in Boston. Though the phone literally shook in his hand as he did so, the custodial officer made a late-night call to the home of a federal district judge in New Orleans, obviously waking him.

"Keep him there," Judge Boucher barked. "I'll be there tomorrow on the first flight I can get."

Palmetto could not sleep. Seated right outside his cell were three guards who stared at him without blinking, believing they had in custody an international terrorist probably out to destroy the Western world. He'd tried to explain that the contempt order had been expunged and was answered with a sneer, "Tell it to the judge." He assumed he'd be arraigned, and could only hope it would happen soon. He turned over on his bunk with his back to the guards, feeling their eyes boring into him. Finally he fell asleep.

He woke with a spasm of terror. That which he had feared for decades had happened. He forced a sense of calm with slow, deep breaths, while trying to convince himself that this was all a mistake. He'd be hauled before a judge or magistrate, they'd check computer records just as Judge Boucher had done, and he'd be sent on his way with a sincere apology. The thought calmed him down, but didn't convince him. There was something unusual about his treatment—even though the guards who had sat with him through the night had left. There was no natural light in his cell and he had no idea what time of day it was. He was brought some food, mystery meat with watery rice, but he refused it, having no appetite and having discovered that the stainless steel toilet in his cell did not flush. After hours of being a model prisoner, anger began to take the place of fear. He was not a fugitive. This was a false arrest. He decided to stand up for his rights. Bob Palmetto hollered his demand . . . for a glass of water.

Boucher got the last seat on the early flight to Boston—coach class and at the rear of the plane. It felt like he was traveling incognito. The plane landed, and he rented a car, called the number he'd been given, and received directions to where Palmetto was being held. He was shown directly to the prisoner's cell when he arrived. Obviously Boucher had been checked out; there were plenty of electronic files on a federal judge.

Palmetto was wild-eyed when he saw him. "What are you doing here?" he asked, which was quickly followed with, "What am I doing here?"

Boucher had the guard unlock the cell. "Leave us for a few minutes. I'll be fine."

The guard left as ordered. The judge walked in, did not offer a handshake.

"What do you know about the murder of Ruth Kalin?" he asked.

Palmetto's mouth hung open. In this bizarre setting, it took seconds for the name to register. "Ruth Kalin?" he said. "The lawyer in Dexter Jessup's office?"

"Her body was found in her car . . . in my driveway." Boucher stared, looking for the slightest tell, any indication the man was lying.

Palmetto sat back down on his bunk. "I never even met her. I disappeared, she disappeared. I reappeared, she . . . God, they're going to kill me for sure." He began to shake. There was no doubt his terror was real.

Boucher put a hand on his shoulder. "I decided to try and find you before that happened," he said. "The detective working on Ruth Kalin's murder pointed out to me that you were the only link we had between the two murders and suggested that perhaps you had lied to me. I had to find out, so I reinstated the contempt charge, hoping you'd be picked up. It worked pretty damn well, I think." He looked around the cell. "How did they catch you?"

"I parked in a handicap spot."

"What?"

"Guilty as charged, Your Honor."

"Well, I'll be damned."

Boucher had Palmetto released into his custody with the stroke of a pen. He would rescind his most recent order when he returned to New Orleans. As they walked to his car he said, "Two months ago, I'm not sure I could have fixed a parking ticket. As a federal judge I can have a man thrown in jail across the country and get him out on my word alone. It amazes me."

"It scares the shit out of the rest of us," Palmetto said. "I owe some nice folks an apology. You can help. You owe me that."

It was about a twenty-mile drive north from Boston to Marble-head, and the business day was done when they arrived. Palmetto was able to find the home of his friends, recognizing the supermarket where he'd gotten busted, using it as a reference point. At least they'd picked up their car, he noted. They parked in front and walked up the drive to the house. They were seen through the large bay window. Both Mark and Mae opened the front door, saying, "What happened to you? We were really worried."

Palmetto looked sideways at Boucher and said, "You tell 'em."

It was all ad lib. The judge spun a tale about a mix-up in the files, and when he had learned of an innocent man's wrongful incarceration, he felt he had to set the matter straight. Personally. It was pure bullshit, but they bought it, in fact were given a heightened appreciation for the humanity and compassion of the federal judicial system.

As Palmetto retrieved his backpack, still in the hallway where he had left it the night before, he said, "Mark, I came here for a reason. I had hoped we might have discussed it over dinner"—he glared at Boucher—"but I, uh, got waylaid. Could I pass by the Institute in the morning? It's important."

"Of course, Bob. Anytime."

They shook hands and departed. As they walked to the car, Palmetto said, "Judge, I might need your help tomorrow."

"Mine? How can I help you?"

"I'm going to make a request to use a piece of their equipment. I need you to support me."

"I don't know that I—"

"Damn it, you're a federal judge. You can help and I'll tell you how."

They got in the car, Boucher driving. Palmetto explained what he needed and why.

"This could be important," Boucher said.

"I told you. Fasten your seat belt, Judge. I'd rather not have another run-in with the law."

They found a quiet seafood restaurant and talked till closing time, then checked into a motel and continued their discussion late into the night. Boucher told Palmetto everything that had happened since last seeing him: his meeting with Ruth Kalin before her death; his conversations with Detective Fitch. Palmetto was puzzled.

"Dexter Jessup was shot because he was going to go to the Feds and rat on a crooked judge. But why Ruth Kalin, and why was she killed after the crooked judge was dead? If it was her hanging around your house that night, I think she was going to ask you to close the book on the whole Judge Epson matter so she could get her life back. Somebody saw her and drew a different conclusion."

"Like what?"

"That she was working with me."

"Working with you on what? Something to do with why you're here?"

"Nobody knew I was coming here. I didn't even know myself when I left New Orleans. Maybe someone was afraid I might try to sue them. Maybe they were afraid you'd be sympathetic."

"No, I don't think it was about you, not directly. She believed Judge Epson might have killed her fiancé, but—"

"Her fiancé?"

"She and Dexter Jessup were engaged."

Palmetto was stunned. Boucher gave him a moment's silence. "He never told me."

"She also believed the assistant in the office was murdered. That's why she went into hiding. Ruth Kalin was terrified. But she was also a determined woman. She was out to get John Perry one way or another. The night before she was killed, she gave me a file. There was the report Dexter was going to deliver to the FBI and something else. I'm not sure exactly what it is, but it has something to do with Perry and Rexcon Energy. That might have been what got her killed. I haven't even told the police about it. Yet."

Palmetto couldn't stifle a yawn. He could barely sit up.

"You need to sleep," the judge said. "I doubt you got much last night."

"Very little." He stood and walked to the door. "I think the answer is at the bottom of the ocean," he said. Boucher attributed this confusing remark to the man's exhaustion.

Mark was at his computer next morning when they arrived.

"That research vessel is gone," he said.

"Good," Palmetto said. He sat down next to Mark and his computer screen. "That will make it easier."

"Make what easier?" Mark asked.

"Mark, we need to take the *Beagle* out. I need *Lucy*," Palmetto said.

"*Lucy*? Why?"

"I think that the vessel whose communications you intercepted was conducting an illegal offshore geophysical exploration," Palmetto said.

Boucher stepped forward and offered his first words in this conversation. "If the vessel you refer to did not have a permit for geological or geophysical exploration granted by the Bureau of Ocean Energy Management, Regulation and Enforcement of the U.S. Department of the Interior, then it was operating in contravention of

Volume 30, Code of Federal Regulations, Section 251.5." Both men looked at him with raised eyebrows. He stepped back and gave Palmetto a just-trying-to-help look.

"He's a federal judge," Palmetto said as explanation. "His knowledge of the law is encyclopedic. Seriously, Mark, I think I know who's out there. If I'm right we've got to stop them. They could be about to do something on the seabed that could have cataclysmic consequences."

"*Voilà*," Boucher said.

"He's Cajun," Palmetto added for the New Englander's benefit. "They like to show off their French." He turned to Boucher. "That's why Perry is still interested in me after all these years. He's afraid I could open the can of worms that Judge Epson kept a lid on. They've discovered a methane hydrate field and want to keep their discovery a secret."

"Bob, there are no offshore leases being let off the Atlantic Coast," Mark said. "After the drilling disaster in the Gulf, everything's on ice. And that research vessel was two hundred miles offshore. That's the limit of the EEZ, the exclusive economic zone. Beyond that, whoever is out there is outside U.S. jurisdiction and in international waters. They wouldn't need to worry about offshore leases—or regulatory oversight, for that matter."

"Who assigns the missions for the *Beagle?*" Palmetto asked.

"Well, theoretically I could," Mark answered. "But we don't send research vessels out on a whim. These are priceless scientific tools. We have budget restraints. I need scientific justification. It costs real money to send a ship out."

"Mark, these guys are rogues. If they're going beyond U.S. jurisdiction, we've got to expose them. I don't need to tell you the damage they could do out there. If that doesn't fall within the Institute's purview, I don't know what does."

"I don't know. . . ."

"You want more?"

"I need the strongest scientific justification you can get."

"Well," Palmetto said, "once upon a time, there were just three words that were enough to ensure funding for the entire space program. They should be enough to justify a single mission off our own Atlantic coast."

"What three words?"

"Beat the Russians," Palmetto said.

He typed search words on one of the computer's keyboards and motioned the others to read the screen when his findings appeared. The report told of a Russian mini-sub successfully bringing up a sample of methane hydrate from the bottom of Lake Baikal in Siberia, the largest freshwater lake in the world. It was the world's first extraction accomplished in this manner.

"Well, I'll be damned," Mark said. "I didn't know about that."

Judge Boucher read the screen. "I'd order your vessel to conduct this mission for national security reasons, if this were my jurisdiction."

"Okay, okay," Mark said. "The *Beagle* goes out. Just bring me back something good. Beat the Russians."

CHAPTER 15

THE CREW OF THE *Beagle* were notified. They needed a day to make ready, take on fuel and supplies. That left the evening free. Palmetto was keen to accept his friends' invitation for the dinner he'd been denied the night before. The judge politely declined. He would meet them in Norfolk.

Between Massachusetts and Virginia was New York City and an opportunity to see Malika. He called and asked her to meet him at the Plaza Hotel.

"Why don't I meet you there for dinner?" she said. "I have a presentation to prepare for a client, and I'm really behind. How about seven?"

He had taken it for granted she would spend the night with him, but something in her voice said this was not a given. He waited for her in the lobby that evening. She seemed pleased to see him, but carried no overnight bag, not even a large purse.

First it was cocktails in the refurbished Oak Bar, where a hundred years' worth of tobacco smoke had been cleaned off the Everett Shinn paintings of Central Park in winter. Their conversation was light, almost banter, with no questions, no mention of barroom brawls or bodies in driveways. After drinks they moved to dinner in the Oak Room, where the original wood-paneled walls and barrel-vaulted ceiling created the century-old ambience of an elegant retreat for robber barons.

"I don't know this city very well," Jock said after dessert, "but I feel that all I really need to know about New York is the Plaza."

"That's like saying there's nothing else in the French Quarter except the Royal Orleans," Malika said. "I wish you could stay longer than one night. I mean, how often do you come to New York? I'd like to show you my place. I'd like for you to be able to picture me when we're talking on the phone—since that seems to comprise such a large part of our relationship."

"Ouch," Boucher said. "Can you show me your apartment in the morning? I'd love to see it."

She smiled, nodding her head.

It was a pleasant enough evening. After dinner, Malika took a taxi home.

He checked out of the Plaza next morning and took a cab to Beekman Place. Malika's building had a doorman and a view of the Hudson from some apartments, but not her own. Hers was an alcove studio: a living room with a smaller area adjoining that served various purposes.

"Do you sleep on that?" He pointed to a Chinese opium bed in the alcove with decorative silk pillows.

"I do sometimes. But the sofa is also a convertible. Have a seat."

"It's nice," he said, looking around the apartment. "And you're right. Now I can picture you here."

"Actually," she said, "I wanted to say something and I thought this might be a better place than a restaurant. Jock, I want us to keep seeing each other and with all the traveling I plan to be doing, that shouldn't be difficult. I wanted you to see this little apartment so you would know how mobile I really am. I've got no strings. I think that's going to define our relationship for a while. No strings. Do you understand what I'm saying?"

"You want to see other people?"

"That's not what I'm saying, and no, I don't want to see other people. But I'm focusing on my work. If that involves a dinner out with someone, I'm not going to feel guilty about it. I don't want you to either."

"I don't know what kind of relationship that's going to be."

"It's going to be just about what it is now. How we feel about each other is going to be obvious within the first two minutes after we meet."

"So each reunion will be a surprise. I don't like surprises."

"For me, that's the way it is now." She took his hand and kissed his fingers. "I have career plans. I have hopes for us. But . . ."

"What do they call this, 'friendship with benefits'?"

She dropped his hand. "Don't be callous, and don't assume. If someone new comes along in either of our lives, c'est la vie. I hope, and honestly I believe, that the next time I see you, Jock, my heart will skip a beat as it always has. Till then, it's not good-bye, but au revoir. Till the next time our eyes meet. Then perhaps we'll know."

"When this matter is finished," he said, "I could come back here for a visit and you could show me your New York, you could come to the Quarter, or we can go wherever you like for as long as you like. Then we can—"

She put her finger to his lips. "We will talk then. Now you've got a flight to catch. Thanks for coming here. It was important to me."

They embraced and he departed. The doorman hailed him a cab and he rushed to the airport. Her plan worked. All through the flight to Norfolk he couldn't get the image of Malika sitting in her apartment by the telephone out of his mind.

Boucher arrived by taxi at the main gate of the Norfolk Navy Yard, showed his ID, and asked directions to where the R/V *Beagle* was docked. He looked around him as his clearance was checked. There were few people in sight at this scene of massive power in shades of gray. The light gray of the concrete wharfs and docks led to berths where the slate-gray vessels were moored, sitting in relief against the dark gray clouds that promised rain. The silhouettes of the naval ships above their decks were like skylines of futuristic cities. The only departures from the dominant gray color were the blue-black submarines, which were like ominous balloons floating on the surface: design simple, purpose lethal.

He was given a pass to get him through the rest of the checkpoints and directions to the dock of the *Beagle*. The vessel was easy to spot. Much smaller than the Navy's ships, it had a marine-blue hull and all above deck was white. On the stern was a large crane shaped like an A for lowering and retrieving the deep submergence manned vehicle *Lucy*. Boucher reached the gangplank and looked around for a familiar face. The one he saw was not one he expected. The woman he'd lied to trying to explain why Palmetto had been hauled off to jail waved to him from the ship. Mae, Mark's wife, was on this voyage.

"Come aboard," she yelled.

Boucher crossed the gangplank.

"Welcome," Mae said. "We're about to get under way. Bob is in the lab and asked that you meet him there."

A young crew member took the travel bag containing jeans and sweaters that he had purchased on his way from the airport, and led him belowdecks. Palmetto stood as Boucher entered the ship's oceanography laboratory.

"Welcome aboard," he said, pumping the judge's hand. "Do you have any idea how much time it takes to schedule a mission like this? Months. We did it in twenty-four hours, thanks to the Russians. They are still the greatest spur to our competitive spirit on the planet. We're going to take our sub down on an exploration mission. We bring samples back, we'll make news, give the Russkies a run for their money, and we'll ruin John Perry's day big-time. We'll also have an unimpeachable witness to our discovery, a United States district court judge. I'm going to let you figure out how we stop Perry if he's planning on operating in international waters."

"I'm not going down in any submarine."

"Think of it, Judge," Palmetto said, ignoring him, "it's the chance of a lifetime. You will see things few have ever seen. You might even see something *no one* has ever seen. It happens all the time."

As Boucher stood there trying to visualize the ocean depths, the ship began to move.

"We're under way," Palmetto said. "Let me show you your quarters and give you a tour of the ship."

"I want to see that damned sub," Boucher said.

They went back up to the main deck. Leaving port, they were passing the largest armada in the history of mankind, the U.S. Navy's Atlantic Fleet. It was midmorning, late for such a departure. The wind was brisk and from the east, the clouds low and dark gray. They would see rain within the next hour or two, was Palmetto's observation, but there were no storms forecast for the area. They were soon in open sea, still in sight of the coast. The change in heading from due east to south-southeast was obvious. Boucher stopped at the railing amidships and gazed at the Virginia shore receding from sight. He breathed deeply of the bracing Atlantic air, comparing it to the muskiness of the Gulf Coast, preferring the latter. The deep submergence vehicle was moored in its hangar in the middle of the deck toward the stern. They went inside.

Lucy looked somewhat like a snub-nosed guppy that had swallowed a marble. In fact, the sub was little more than a bathysphere—the optimal physical design for withstanding the enormous pressures at the ocean floor—encased in an outer shell. It had mechanical arms for picking up samples from the sea bottom that folded up like arms of a praying mantis under the "face" through which the pilot and two other scientists observed. The sub was secured to a carrier on tracks that permitted movement to the stern, and the A crane, which lowered and raised the sub to and from the ocean. Stairs and a platform permitted access and a peek into the spherical passenger compartment. They climbed up and Palmetto lifted the hatch.

"Come on, take a peek," Palmetto said.

Boucher bent over and looked in. "It's a good thing you watch your weight." The diameter of the hatch as well as the closeness of the quarters required that all who journeyed to the depths in this transport be on the slim side.

"Is it safe?" the judge asked.

"It's state-of-the-art," Palmetto answered. "It has the most up-to-date equipment, and its maintenance is impeccable."

"Is it safe?" he repeated.

"It's as safe as possible at forty-five hundred meters below the sea. That's almost three miles. Let's go see your quarters."

They walked back toward the bridge. Mae was standing at the rail gazing over the open sea.

"Mae, what are you doing?" Palmetto asked. She turned and faced him with a frown.

"I was thinking about my experiments. I'm allowed time for that, aren't I?"

He turned to Boucher and said, "Don't let anyone catch you mooning over the ocean. That's not done here."

"An oceanographer can't look at the ocean?" Boucher asked.

"Depends how and why," Mae said. "It all started on this ship after dinner one night. We got into an argument—no, a discussion—of Robert Frost's poem 'Neither Out Far Nor In Deep.' We feel our mission is to avoid the mediocrity that the poem criticizes. We look both far and deep in our research and try to avoid the seduction of the shallow glance. It's tempting to stand here and get lost in the sea's mystique. It hypnotizes, and that's a luxury we can't afford."

"I should read that poem again," Boucher said.

"There's a copy in your quarters and about a dozen other places aboard," Mae said. "It's a constant reminder to us." She looked at the sky. "We're going to get some rain and I've got work to do. I think we should all get below."

CHAPTER 16

BOUCHER SHARED A SMALL cabin with Palmetto and two other scientists, both at work somewhere else on the vessel. The early arrivals had chosen the upper bunks, denoting territorial rights by dumping their duffels on the beds.

"I'm going back to the lab," Palmetto said. "Are you going to be okay here?"

Boucher stowed his bag under the bed. "I'll be fine," he said. "When do we get where we're going?"

"About twenty-four hours from the time we left port; midmorning tomorrow, we'll be over the Carolina Trough. There are preparations and checklists for the sub. We'll start those about five in the morning. Life at sea begins early. But you have the rest of today to relax. Take advantage of it. I advise you to eat and drink sparingly. There's no crapper in the sub, and we piss in bottles. The less you have to expel, the more popular you'll be with your crewmates. Our descent will take us about four hours; we'll have a couple hours on the ocean floor, and the same time to ascend. We're talking about ten hours in close quarters. Sounds like a lot, but it goes fast. Believe me, it will be the most fascinating day of your life."

"I didn't say I was going."

Palmetto nodded and left.

Boucher lay down on his bunk, his hands folded under his head. He stared at the lattice of springs that supported the mattress above him and wondered what the hell he was doing here. He didn't ponder the question too long, realizing that lying prone was not the best position to be in at this stage of a landlubber's first ocean voyage. He felt the advent of seasickness and decided to go back up to the main deck. The rain had stopped. For two hours he stared at the horizon; maybe not out far nor in deep, but at least not over the side. When he got his sea legs, he was all over the ship like a spider crab. He asked questions, was given answers, and found his enthusiasm growing. Conscious that his were the only idle hands on board, he didn't spend too much time with or ask too many questions of any one person, and by late afternoon, he'd met the entire crew and research contingent. The *Beagle* carried a crew of thirty-six and a scientific team of twenty-four. The ship had been in port for repairs to the submarine's mechanical arm, and the personnel had not dispersed. Still, Boucher was amazed that they were able to prepare for this mission with as little notice as they'd been given.

A pleasant surprise that no one had told him about was the ship's small but adequate gym. There was no one around, his boxers and T-shirt looked enough like gym clothes, so he stripped and gave the rowing machine a workout. Closing his eyes, feeling the rhythm of the vessel as it cut through the sea, he imagined himself as a member of an Olympic scull crew. Had there been a way to harness the energy he expended rowing, he was sure he could have contributed to the progress of the ship. It was late afternoon when he returned to his cabin, timing perfect. He was first to shower and dress and was lying on his bunk in exactly the same position Palmetto had left him when he returned.

"Have you been there all day?" Palmetto asked.

"What else did you expect me to do?"

Dinner was served at six sharp: steak and potatoes. He ate half and pushed his plate away.

"You don't like it?" Palmetto asked.

"It's delicious," Boucher said, "but I can't eat a lot tonight. Busy day tomorrow."

Palmetto smiled. "What made you decide?"

"The Robert Frost poem. I read it in the cabin. I've got a chance to look far and deep. Chances like that don't come often."

Evening for the crew of scientists was not that much different from a night at home. Some read, there were several board games and DVD movies, and of course there was conversation. Though the passenger list frequently included guests from all walks of life, a federal jurist was a first and Boucher was the focal point of conversation. All were interested in the same question he had asked himself earlier—what was he doing here?

"I had to bust Mr. Palmetto out of jail. Next thing I know, here I am," Boucher said. It got a laugh.

"Judge, it's time to wake up."

Palmetto had given him a gentle nudge. Boucher opened his eyes. "What time is it?"

"Just after six. We made good time. We'll be coming up on our diving site in about an hour."

"What about the sub?"

"It's ready. See you on deck. I'm going to give Mark a call at the Institute and let him know we're here."

* * *

Rexcon's communication buoy bobbed on the choppy Atlantic surface. It was linked by cable to a monitor on the ocean floor where their surreptitious discovery had been made and charted. Sensors placed on the sea bottom were still retrieving and transmitting data to the buoy, which sent it by satellite to the corporate communication center in New Orleans. The buoy could also receive transmissions sent by any ship within a fifty-mile radius, and warn home base of any suspected poachers. It was in this manner that the call made by Bob Palmetto was captured and beamed up.

Bert Cantrell was copied on all communications from the ocean communication buoy. He saw the name Palmetto in the message and about fell out of his executive office chair. When he regained his composure he rushed into Perry's office.

"I just found Palmetto," he said.

"You're shitting me," was the response from Rexcon's CEO.

"He's on the research vessel *Beagle*. Take a guess where it's going."

"I don't have time for guessing games."

"It's headed for the Carolina Trough, the site of our methane hydrate field."

Perry stood up from his desk. "What did I tell you? I knew he was going to start poking around. What do you think he's doing?"

"They've got a submarine on that ship. Knowing that Palmetto is aboard, I think they plan to take the sub to the floor. He's probably going to look for samples. He does that and gets the word out, we've got complications."

"We have to see that doesn't happen," Perry said. "Take care of it as you see fit."

"You know what you're saying."

"I said do it."

Cantrell returned to his office. He had his own orders to give.

* * *

The sub was out of its hangar and had been moved on its tracks toward the stern and the crane. Boucher was hustled into it, his two deep-sea companions waiting. Mae sat in the pilot's seat.

"You didn't tell me you were in charge of this," Boucher said to her.

"You may call me Captain," she said. "Sit there," she commanded. "That's your monitor. You see what we all see. That's your porthole. You have to get your forehead right against that pad to see out. That's it."

As she spoke, the hatch above them was lowered and sealed. She continued. "We breathe our own air, over and over. This"—she pointed to a stainless steel tube just over a foot long—"is our CO_2 scrubber. It takes the carbon dioxide out of our exhaled breath, and traps it with the CO_2 absorber. We've got oxygen tanks here." She patted them. "They're essential to supplement our own air. Here's our air quality monitor. Too much CO_2, I open the tank and add oxygen. Toilet procedures have already been explained to you. Here's your bottle. I won't peek, promise. Here we go."

They were lifted, then swung away from the stern and lowered into the water. Still attached, they floated for an instant. With the radio phone, Palmetto announced they were ready. Boucher watched through his porthole. It was about the size of a snorkeling mask and, with his head pressed against it, felt like one. He saw the bubbles as the sub submerged. They sank into water that seemed bluer below than it had on the surface, but that began to change. It was like a sunset on a cloudy day. The water became darker and darker till it was black.

"I'm testing the lights," Mae said. Shafts of illumination cut through the void for only an instant. Test successful, the lights were extinguished to conserve energy. The black void was total, then suddenly Boucher saw what looked like a heaven filled with stars: pinpoints of light flashing on and off.

"Phosphorus," Mae said. "We're about a thousand meters down."

"That was fast."

"We told you. Time passes quickly on the way down, especially on your first trip. It's the return that can seem slow. You can keep looking, but there won't be much to see till we're on the bottom. Relax. If you want some music, there's a CD player, a headset, and a collection of disks. It's a diverse collection, a little bit of almost everything."

The head of Rexcon's research team received the approval he'd prepared for. With great care and expertise—for which he congratulated himself—he had planted detonators in the subsea soil to prepare the essential element of the process they were employing, the blasting of the surface of the ocean floor. His orders were relayed by phone. He recognized the voice of Bert Cantrell. His orders: "Detonation approved. Proceed."

CHAPTER 17

WE'RE APPROACHING THE SEABED," Mae said. "Depth sixteen hundred meters. I'm switching on the outside lights."

All eyes were on the three separate monitors as the ocean floor seemed to rise up to meet them. There was no visible sign of life. What the shafts of light revealed could have been barren desert, but for what looked like bubbles floating a few feet above the surface. Then the bubbles began to change shape. Mae maneuvered a light at one and it vanished, then reappeared in a different color, a translucent pink. Boucher watched as two of the bubbles made contact and became one; whether one popped or the two merged, he couldn't say. He turned to his porthole and as he did a transparent squidlike creature over three feet long fluttered in and out of his field of vision, inches away from the shell that protected them from the crushing pressure at this depth.

"We are on the side of the Carolina Trough," Mae said for Boucher's benefit. "It's pretty flat right here, but there's a steep drop off our starboard side. Ready for a little prospecting, Bob?"

"You bet." As fascinating as the marine life was, the prospect of finding the energy source that had absorbed him for much of his adult life meant more.

"Do you think we'll find any at this depth?" Boucher asked.

"Lake Baikal is sixteen hundred meters at its deepest point. If the Russians found hydrate at that depth, we should too," Palmetto said.

But after an hour, they'd found nothing—except of course some of the most extraordinary life-forms on the planet, including flatworms the size of a man, one of which crawled all over them, blocking portholes and covering them with a slime that distorted vision till it peeled off and floated away like a sheet of cellophane.

"I'm going to descend, climb down into the trough a ways," Mae said. "What do you think, Bob, another thousand meters?"

"Might not take that much. I never really expected to be able to just pick methane hydrate up like shells on the beach, but now that we know it can be done, maybe we'll get lucky."

It took them almost another hour, and the discovery was credited to Mae.

"Bob. Over there. Lower right-hand corner of your monitor, maybe twenty yards away. Do you see those mussels and tube worms on that mound?"

"Yes. They use methane like a food source. The tube worms may be connected to the hydrate too."

"Okay, I'm heading over there. It's right on the edge of that ledge, but there's enough space to set down. We're going to park on the ridge," Mae explained for Boucher's benefit. "It's easier to use the arms when we're at rest, and easier to get the sample into the vacuum chamber invented by none other than your illustrious submariner, Bob Palmetto."

Boucher looked up from his monitor at the man sitting so close to him.

"I did manage to do something beneficial with those twenty years," he said.

"He's being modest," Mae said. "He's got thirteen patents on deep-sea mining equipment and he's donated royalties on all of them to the Institute. Okay, we're on the bottom. Extending arms."

The controls were levers and handles below the principal monitor at her station. The elbow joints of both arms were flexed and the titanium appendages reached straight out as if offering an embrace. Then the "hands" dropped, fingers pointing down. They were lowered to the ocean floor. The fingertips raked the bottom to feel the surface. It was rocky sand, not too hard-packed, near-perfect consistency for collecting samples. The arms were lifted, turned, and placed over the grayish lump that lay on the surface. It looked to be about the size of a volleyball. The fingers were manipulated to form a claw and lowered over the object. The claw was tightened, fingertips digging into subsea soil.

"Are you sure that's methane hydrate and not just a rock?" Boucher asked.

"It's too soft to be a rock. See how the claws scraped it? Definitely methane hydrate. It's a piece that broke off the mound where the tube worms are feeding. Grab it," Palmetto said.

The fingers closed. The hands were raised. The clump was bigger than a volleyball. It was almost two feet in diameter.

"Hot damn," Palmetto said. "We beat the Russians with that one. Their sample was just over ten pounds. This one is twenty if it's an ounce."

"Worth the trip?" Mae asked.

"Mae, a new industry is beginning with this sample. The world has a new source of energy that will last us for centuries."

"If you've known it was here, Bob, why have you waited till now?"

"You want to help with that one, Judge?" he asked Boucher. "Go ahead. She has a right to know."

Boucher spoke, his low monotone almost hypnotic in their tiny egg resting on the deep-sea floor.

"Mr. Palmetto invented a process for the extraction of methane hydrate twenty years ago. His discovery was stolen from him, and several people involved were murdered. He's been keeping a low profile until recently, out of concern for his life."

"That's just a part of the answer, Mae," Palmetto said. "We can't afford to be dependent on imported crude oil any longer. The whole damned Middle East could go up in flames tomorrow and the world crisis would be devastating. We must develop this energy source that's right at our doorstep. It can't wait. I found out those who stole from me are planning to utilize my process and they don't appreciate the dangers. I've made substantial improvements in the last two decades. They do something stupid and it could set this viable source of energy back another twenty years. I must make it known what's here and how we can safely exploit it."

No one spoke. Keeping the devil from this deep blue sea would demand restraints that had not always been imposed, at least not uniformly, in this field of human endeavor.

For the next several minutes, the arms were manipulated with almost surgical precision, placing the sample in the container designed for this purpose. Actually, the sample was too large and pieces broke off as it was stowed, but finally it was in and the vacuum container was closed. Uniform pressure would be maintained as the sub rose to the surface.

Mae was in the process of returning the mechanical arms to their locked position when the sub was blasted off the subsea surface. Its front end rose up as if it were trying to stand, then it fell over backward. The three inside were thrown back and landed in a heap on top of each other. Whether their concussions were from hitting their heads or from the sound waves, which sped through water faster than through air, the three were knocked unconscious. They tumbled over and over, down and deeper into the Carolina Trough, reaching the limits of pressure their tiny cocoon could withstand, before the sub stopped.

Boucher regained consciousness, of a sort. He thought he had opened his eyes but was unsure. He could see nothing, not a single indicator light from a single piece of equipment. He thought he was moving his fingertips, but was unsure of that too. He could feel nothing. Of one thing he was sure: he was thinking, therefore, if Descartes could be believed, he was still alive. But for how long? How long had he been unconscious? He tried to breathe but could take only short, shallow breaths. The oxygen was running out, carbon dioxide building up.

His left arm was pinned under something. He extended his right, feeling along his side. Palmetto was underneath him. He knew it was Palmetto below because Mae was on top of him. That was a certainty. She was lying facedown right on top of him, her cheek nestled against his neck. Also, she had worn corduroy slacks and he could feel the ribbing of the material. He rubbed his hand along the textured cloth. It brought back a memory. As a young boy he'd inherited a hand-me-down pair of corduroy pants, his first pair of long trousers. He had hated them because they were too hot to wear on the bayou and too big for him. But as summer changed to fall he grew into them and discovered their inestimable benefit—they were indestructible. Sliding in the dirt, climbing trees; they saved him from skinned knees, and saved his butt from beatings because they didn't tear. He heard a soft whisper.

"Jock, would you please stop rubbing my ass?"

"Mae! Are you all right?"

"Well, you're making me horny, so I guess I am. How's Bob?"

"I don't know. I think he's underneath me."

"There's nowhere else he could be. I'm going to try to move."

He felt her weight lifted off him. He heard her as she groped her way in the dark. There was the sound of switches and buttons being pushed, but nothing happened. Finally, there was the soft whirr of a small motor, maybe a computer's cooling fan. A red light came on. It was like a homing beacon. Mae found another switch, and another indicator light came on. With this limited illumination, she was able to find the magnetized penlight she kept at her workstation. She started checking gauges, starting with air. "Jesus," she whispered. Boucher heard the whoosh of oxygen escaping from the tanks.

"Another two minutes and we would have been asphyxiated," Mae said, "or frozen. Damn, it's cold in here."

It took another entire minute before Boucher could draw a full breath. He lifted himself up.

"Shine the light on him," he said.

Mae directed the beam. He lifted Palmetto's head and felt blood on his hand. He pressed the neck for a pulse, feeling nothing at first, then just the slightest hint. "He's alive, but he's hurt."

"Sorry. I can't help. We've got to get out of here. We fell over two thousand meters. We're at our maximum depth. We fall any farther and . . ." There was no need to finish the sentence.

Mae turned off the oxygen and engaged the backup batteries. It took several minutes, but finally there was light. From the position of the equipment it was apparent that the sub was on its side. She contorted her way to the pilot's porthole and took a look out. "My God," she said.

Boucher pulled his sweater off, made a pillow, and placed it under Palmetto's head. Mae was still staring out, so he went to the other porthole.

"I can't make out anything," he said.

"You're looking straight down. We're on another ledge, I guess. I can't see what's holding us up." She reached for the radiophone.

"*Beagle*, this is *Lucy*. Over." She heard her transmission echo. Three seconds later came the response.

"*Lucy*, this is *Beagle*. What happened down there and how are you? Over."

"My God," Boucher said. "It sounds like they're in here with us."

"Yeah, our communications are great," Mae said. "We've spoken to the International Space Station from three miles deep.

"*Beagle*. We don't know what happened. It might have been an earthquake. We have fallen into the Carolina Trough and are now at our maximum depth. We're lying on our side against the trough. Running low on oxygen and battery power, and air quality is poor. The CO_2 scrubber isn't working properly. I don't know whether I can jettison ballast to begin ascent from this position. Over."

There was a long minute of silence.

"*Lucy*, you have no choice. You must begin ascent. Over."

"Will try. Over and out." She replaced the phone.

"What do you have to jettison?" Boucher asked.

"The sub has expendable steel plates. That's what makes us sink, and when we're done, we just unhook them to rise to the surface."

"It's that simple?"

"It's that simple."

They heard a moan and both dropped to Palmetto's side. He was trying to sit up but couldn't. Boucher caught him behind the neck as he fell back down.

"You bumped your head," Mae said.

"Tell me something I don't know," he answered. "Where are we?"

She told him their position, and their predicament.

"Well, we sure as hell can't stay here," he said. Again he tried to sit up, and did better on the second try. "This your sweater?" He handed it to Boucher. "Put it back on. You'll freeze to death." He looked at them. "What are we waiting for? Jettison those damned plates."

"Easier said than done," Mae said. "We're on our side. That means we're lying on half of them. The others are on top of us."

Palmetto gathered his knees to his chest, wrapped his long arms around them, and lowered his head in thought.

"Unhook them, or whatever you do," Boucher said.

Mae bent over the lopsided control board and flicked several switches. Nothing happened. "We don't have gravity working with us."

"But we have something else," Boucher said. He grabbed one of the CDs from the crew's collection. The silver disk mirrored the colored indicator lights in its grooves and illuminated the label. "When you said this collection was diverse, you weren't kidding. This is perfect."

He inserted the CD and unplugged the headset so the sound could be heard by all. The rhythm began: drums beating in 2/4 time, a single accordion. Boucher couldn't stand, he slumped. He motioned Palmetto to move aside, though there was no room for him to go anywhere. Nonetheless, he stepped toward Mae and said, "Would you care to dance, madam? It's zydeco. Think of it like a polka, but stomp your feet."

She stepped into his arms. In the deep-submergence vehicle, they moved to a Cajun beat. The sub swayed. It tilted. The shift in weight caused the vehicle to pitch and keel over, again tossing them, but not with the same violence as before. They listened as the sub scraped and grated against the rocky surface of the trough. They felt themselves fall off the ledge, deeper, deeper.

Mae screamed, "The plates aren't dropping!"

She jumped for the control panel and slammed her fist against the release lever. They continued to sink . . . then, slowly, the sub righted itself. Its descent ceased and they hung suspended, then began to rise. The music kept playing, the lyrics touting the talents of a "hootchie-kootchie man." A considerable amount of carbon dioxide was exhaled in their collective sighs of relief.

They all sat in whatever positions they found most comfortable. The ascent was a simple process, rising like an air bubble to the surface. Mae kept an eye on the depth gauge. After a lengthy period of silence she said, "We're back at the level where we got our sample."

Palmetto went to his porthole and looked out. "Mae, shine the light out there."

"We don't have much power left, Bob."

"Please. It's important."

Mae directed a beam across the seabed. "Look at that," she said. Palmetto was looking.

"That's a stratum of methane hydrate out there," he said. The surface looked like a field of dirty snow. "That was no seismic event that pitched us into the trough. That was a detonation. Somebody blasted away the surface and uncovered it. I bet the bastards knew we were down here." He turned to face Boucher, who was seated at his own porthole. "Judge," he said, "we almost joined the Rexcon victims list."

There was silence as all eyes were focused on the seabed.

"I can see the future," Palmetto said softly. "I can see hundreds of remote-operated backhoes collecting hydrate and depositing their loads into carbon fiber pods, bathyspheres that will separate CO_2

and serve as depressurization chambers; one linked to another like a giant string of pearls leading from the mining area on the ocean floor, perhaps rising to the surface where a liquefied natural gas tanker will be waiting; maybe the string of pearls will stretch all the way to the shore for processing and distribution. Not only do we end our dependency on foreign oil, think of the thousands of jobs that will be created. Can you see it?"

"We see it, Bob," his crewmates answered.

The sub continued its ascent without another word being spoken until Mae again broke the silence.

"We have about an hour and a half till we surface."

"You told me this would be the most boring part of the trip," Boucher said.

"Not this time. We've used up all the oxygen in our emergency tanks. We fell deeper than our planned depth, and we don't know how much time we were unconscious on that ledge. We're recycling our own breath, but the CO_2 level is too high. There won't be enough air to get us to the surface."

"Call upstairs and ask them how long we've been down," Palmetto said.

Mae got *Beagle* on the phone and asked.

"We didn't know just how to tell you. Longer than you should have."

"Do we have enough air to get to the surface?"

"That's a negative," was the answer. The tone of voice was flat, no emotion was expressed, but they all knew better.

She hung up the phone and looked at her mates. "We will meditate," she whispered. "It lowers your metabolism and you will need less air. Think of two syllables and repeat them over and over in your mind. Now close your eyes."

They did as ordered, though Boucher added an extra syllable. He repeated *Malika* over and over until his meditation became a hypnotic trance, though he knew it was really the lack of air. The three drifted in and out of consciousness, then surrendered to the dark void.

The divers from the *Beagle* were ready. The ascent of the sub had been monitored. The tower, or "sail," broke surface and they were immediately climbing onto it. The hatch was flung open and one diver jumped in, carrying a tank of pure oxygen. There was no priority among the passengers. He placed a mask over the first face he could reach and kept it there till he saw a response. Palmetto coughed and gasped for the air now filling the compartment. Mae was next to receive air. The diver lifted the barely conscious woman up to the hatch. She was grabbed under the shoulders, pulled free, and placed in an inflatable dinghy, where a mask connected to a regular diver's tank of compressed air was administered to her. The men were given the same treatment, then they were raced to the ship while some of the divers remained behind and began to ready the sub for its retrieval by the research vessel. Within minutes the three were receiving medical attention and the word had raced through the ship. They were safe.

CHAPTER 18

BOUCHER WOKE UP. PALMETTO was standing over him, his head swathed in bandages.

"How are you feeling, Judge?"

He looked around. Had they already made it to shore? The room he was in looked like a small ER. An IV had been inserted into his left wrist and its tube was attached to a bag hanging from a portable rack. He looked at it, puzzled.

"Just to rehydrate you," Palmetto said, then repeated, "How are you feeling?"

He shrugged. "I feel fine."

"I want to show you something," Palmetto said. "You feel up to a walk?"

Boucher looked at the IV stuck in his wrist. "Get me unplugged."

"Will do. Be right back."

Palmetto returned in a minute with the ship's doctor, as excited as when he had left. The doctor took Boucher's blood pressure, then unhooked the IV.

"Don't go jogging on deck just yet," the doctor said. "You all have had shocks to your systems. One more thing: Can you calm this guy down?"

Palmetto was practically jumping in place. "Come on, come on," he said.

Boucher dressed, then followed the amiable maniac to the lab. The vacuum storage container had been retrieved from the sub and placed in a refrigerated storage unit. Several scientists in white coats were waiting for them. Mae stepped forward and hugged him. She whispered in his ear.

"I woke up with you rubbing my ass. I passed out thinking of you rubbing my ass. Passing out meant we used less oxygen. You saved my ass."

They shared a chuckle as Palmetto glared at them. "Are we going to do this or not?" he said. Mae apologized, winking at Boucher as she pulled away.

Palmetto opened the vacuum container, reached in, and pulled out the clump of methane hydrate they had recovered. It had safely survived the adventure of the deep. He broke off a chunk and returned the rest for further study, then faced his audience. He pulled a cigarette lighter from his pocket and lit the chunk. The white ice was enveloped in waves of blue flame. It was like staring at a star.

"Ladies and gentlemen," Palmetto said, "you are looking at the next major energy source on earth."

As they gazed at the ice on fire, a voice in the group muttered low: "What hath God wrought?"

At that moment, no one knew.

The captain set a course due east for Charleston, scheduled arrival the following afternoon.

Conversation at dinner that evening was predictable. Everyone wanted to hear about the near disaster, not out of a sense of morbid curiosity, but from a scientific interest in how to better protect against such events in the future. Palmetto had little to offer, keeping his own counsel. Boucher understood his silence. He asked Palmetto to join him on deck after dinner.

They stood at the railing, staring into the darkness. Clouds covered the moon. Though it was a pitch-black night, none of the senses were deprived. It was a rolling sea and the ship climbed and dropped as it crested moderate swells, sometimes throwing a light mist into their faces. Diesel fumes from the engine mixed with the scent of salty air, and the sound of waves slapping against the side mingled with the churning wake created by the ship's prop. The black sea offered the sight of green luminescent phosphorus. They could even taste the sea by exposing their tongues. It settled lightly but unmistakably. The two men spoke.

"I have a feeling you're thinking about revenge," Boucher said.

"Actually," Palmetto said, "I've been asking myself who set those charges. To blow a layer off the bottom of the sea as neatly as slicing off a pad of butter, that was not risky, that was plain stupid and irresponsible. Those fools have proven my worst fears about them. Perry—I want to kill the son of a bitch."

"I'm going to have to try and stop you." Even in the dark, Boucher knew that Palmetto was staring at him.

"What are you going to find me in contempt of this time? Contempt of ship? Contempt of ocean? He tried to kill you too, remember? He's killed others and he'll kill again. Your fucking legal system is not going to stop him. I've been that route. It's a dead end, and that's not a figure of speech."

"Calm down," Boucher said. It was an order, and he knew how to give orders. Palmetto shut up.

"How do you end the life of a powerful man?" the judge asked.

"Is this a trick question? A bullet through the head would be my answer. A powerful man's skull is no thicker than anyone else's."

"No. You take away his power. Without it, he merely exists."

"You're talking nonsense."

"Am I? You know John Perry. You know what motivates him. What if it were all taken away? What if he were to lose his corporation, his wealth, everything?"

"I think he'd rather die. He thinks he *is* his company. If you're talking about a messianic complex, he's your textbook example."

"So if he were to lose his company, lose his money, if he were ruined financially beyond any hope of recovery, and, of course, if he were to lose his freedom . . ."

"I'd love to see that day," Palmetto said, "but you're talking about the head of a large and politically powerful energy company. There's no way the two of us could make that happen."

"Detective Fitch in New Orleans might help us."

"Oh, boy. Now we are three."

"But you have friends too."

"Me? I've been living underground for the last twenty years, remember? I don't have any friends. I don't even have any family left."

"I think you're wrong. I think you have more friends than you realize. There are quite a few people who are concerned about your welfare, and concerned about this new form of energy you have helped develop. I think they'd be inclined to help too, especially if it meant that Mr. John Perry and his company would be kept from causing damage to their precious ocean."

"You mean the Institute?"

"Exactly. Listen to me. I have an idea."

CHAPTER 19

THE *BEAGLE* DOCKED IN Charleston, finding berth in a decommissioned navy yard. Boucher and Palmetto bade the crew and scientists good-bye and took a taxi to the airport. They purchased tickets, cleared security, and stood in the departure area.

"Just be where I can contact you," Boucher said.

"I'll call you. I'm going to get myself a cell phone," Palmetto said with a smile. "I've wanted one for years."

"Don't forget what else I told you."

"I won't."

The mention of a cell phone was a reminder. Boucher called Malika as he walked to his own departure gate. She answered after the first ring, identifying his number.

"Where are you? What have you been doing?" she asked.

"Deep-sea diving," he said.

"I wish you'd be serious for once. I've been worried about you."

A near-death experience is best not related to a loved one via cell phone in an air terminal. Boucher gave her the light version of his adventure. It was thrilling enough. He arrived at his gate, saw his flight was delayed twenty minutes, took a seat, and they conversed casually.

He was amazed how colorless he made his thrill of a lifetime sound and promised to tell a better tale when they were together again. They said good-bye and he immediately placed another call. Fitch also recognized his number.

"I was beginning to wonder when I'd hear from you," he said. "I thought maybe you went off the deep end."

"How did you know?"

"How did I know what?"

"Never mind. If you're free for dinner tonight, I'm buying. I've got a few things to discuss with you."

"I'm not known for turning down a free meal. When and where?"

"How about K-Paul's at eight?"

"You know," Fitch said, "if people recognize us as regular dinner companions, they might start to talk."

"You're right. Try not to dress like a cop."

"I wouldn't know where to start."

It was good to be on terra firma, and to be home. There was just enough time for a hot shower and a change of clothes before dinner. He turned to look at his house from the sidewalk. He felt he was jilting the grand old lady. She deserved more of him than she was getting lately.

K-Paul's was crowded as usual, but Fitch had already arrived and secured a table. He waved as the judge walked in. Boucher smiled. Fitch was dressed for golf, probably the only civilian attire in his wardrobe that he wouldn't wear to the police station.

"So, where've you been?" the detective asked.

Fitch did not get the sanitized version and about fell out of his chair as Boucher told him. As impressed as he was with the story, the menu brought by the waiter was enough to change the topic of conversation. Fitch asked what kind of food was served aboard ship and seemed disappointed that steak and potatoes were the fare in such exotic surroundings.

"You must be hungry, then," Fitch said, studying his menu. "I'll have the blackened catfish," he said to the waiter. "So, why am I here?" he said once the waiter had left with both of their orders.

"I've got to get him. Before he gets me."

"Who, Perry?"

"Of course Perry. He's killed at least two people already. He won't stop there."

"That reminds me," Fitch said. "Since you've been away, that doctor who treated Judge Epson has been pitching a fit. He claims there's no way the medication he prescribed could have caused the judge's death. He was about to demand the body be exhumed and another autopsy be done before he found out that His Honor had been cremated. The doc didn't say Epson was murdered, but he came damn close. I also ordered another search of the judge's house: nothing. Perry had been there earlier, but nowhere near time of death. If someone killed Epson, it wasn't Perry. It was a pro. He slipped in at night, did what he did, and left without a trace."

Their plates were brought. "Do you know of any professional killers working here?" Boucher asked.

"If I could prove it, they'd be in jail. We've got the garden variety of violent criminals. This guy, though, if he exists, he's different and he's an expert. He didn't want it to look like a crime. No message was being sent here. And I think he knew he'd get fingers pointing the wrong way with an injection, assuming that's how he did it. Hell, the whole town knew Epson had a heart attack and was just out of the hospital. I mean, he could have just suffocated him. Do you mind if I eat?"

"Sorry. *Bon appétit.* So you think Perry's got a hit man working for him?"

Fitch nodded, his mouth full, his expression pleading, *Please let me eat.* Boucher let him finish.

"Ah, man," Fitch said, "I love burnt fish." Then he frowned. "So now you've got two things to worry about: a shot in the dark"—he made a pistol with thumb and forefinger—"and a shot in the dark"—with thumb and two fingers he mimed a syringe.

"Like I said, we've got to get Perry—and his cohorts."

"You going home tonight?" Fitch asked.

"That is where I live."

Fitch shook his head. "You barely escaped an attempt on your life, yet you sleep in a house without security. Anybody could walk in off the street. The locks on your doors are practically useless. I checked. You're not safe there."

"I know. I've been thinking and I've got a plan. I want to run it by you."

"Shoot."

"Don't say that," Boucher said, forcing a smile. He lowered his voice. "I've been thinking about going to Perry."

"*What?*" Fitch lowered his voice. "What?"

"Look. Perry knows I've been asked to take leave from the bench. He probably had a hand in it. I go to him and say I'm a disgruntled judge. I want to make some money. I'm going to tell him Palmetto died in the submarine accident, and that I have access to his research. I'll sell the information to him and use that as a way to get on the inside of his organization."

"Just what do you think you'll accomplish?"

"I think I'll find what I need to hang him."

The waiter returned offering dessert, but both declined. Boucher asked for the check, but when it came, Fitch grabbed it.

"This one's on me. Don't ask me why, you won't like the answer."

"Oh, come on, Fitch. This is not my last supper."

But the detective refused. He paid the bill, stood, and said, "To-night, I've got your back. Your place will be watched. But after to-night, I can't promise you."

"I appreciate that," Boucher said. "I'll be in touch."

"I hope so."

Fitch left the restaurant and Boucher walked home, dawdling like a tourist in front of the various businesses he passed that catered to the night trade, but not venturing inside any of them. For a full five minutes he stood on a sidewalk leaning against a streetlamp, hands thrust deep in his pockets, listening to a jazz combo. He knew Fitch would cover him. When he thought he'd given the detective enough time to set up his surveillance, he headed for home.

CHAPTER 20

REXCON'S OFFICE WAS NOT far from the Federal Building, and the irony was not lost on Boucher next morning. His routine had been that of a regular judge with regular judicial responsibilities. But the final turn, into the underground garage of the office tower, would lead him to a far different destination. From the garage to the lobby to the elevator bank that led to the floor where the executive offices were located, he proceeded with a confidence bordering on arrogance. He wore his navy blue suit, white shirt, and red tie, a power color combination, but inside his chest his heart beat like a hummingbird.

He approached the first secretarial line of defense and asked for John Perry. The receptionist asked his name and he used his title. That got him to the second tier. A second woman came out from a closed burled-mahogany door that must have been fifteen feet tall and asked him the nature of his business and if he had an appointment.

"Mr. Perry will know the nature of my business. I do not have an appointment."

"I'm sorry, Judge Boucher, but Mr. Perry is not available at this moment."

"I'll wait."

The lobby area on the executive level was massive, but there was only one small settee against the wall for visitors. There were no carpets. The decorator did not want to cover the expensive marble floor. Boucher's heels clicked on the flooring and he fought the temptation to tap-dance across the grand entry to the sparse seating. He sat, crossed his legs, and clasped interlocked fingers around his knee, striking a pose of pure contempt. *Just try and make me leave*, his expression said. Minutes later, a third contingent of the protective phalanx came out, a matched pair of women this time, dressed in different versions of executive administrative business wear.

"Judge Boucher," the first one said, "I'm sorry to keep you waiting, but I've looked through Mr. Perry's calendar and I can't find an appointment with you scheduled for today."

"As I said previously, I don't have one," Boucher said, without changing position. "Federal district court judges don't make appointments."

"Of course not," she said. "May I know the nature of your business?"

I could tell you, but then I'd have to kill you, Boucher thought and was tempted to say. He couldn't suppress his smile and wondered if the adrenaline rush was making him giddy. "It's a personal matter," he said.

The two women whispered to each other, and one left, returning the way she had come. The remaining assistant assumed a sort of at-attention posture, linking curved fingers of both hands in front of her midriff with her feet close together. "If you will wait just a moment longer, sir," she said.

"I'll wait all day if I have to," he replied.

A minute passed, then several more. The woman stood over him as still and as mute as a statue. He got the feeling that if he made any sudden move she would have sprung to life and leapt at him like a cat. Even the receptionist protected behind the bulwark of her desk was frozen in stiff silence. Boucher shifted position to break the tension, and just to show he could. Finally the other assistant reappeared. She stood by the mammoth doors and said, "Will you come this way, Your Honor?"

He stood and strode across the marble floor, the sound of his footsteps echoing. Down a short and thankfully carpeted hallway, the woman walked, then stopped before another massive door made of some rare exotic wood. She pushed it open with ease and motioned him to enter with a wave of her arm. He stepped into the inner sanctum.

The chief executive sat behind an oversized desk far from the doorway. He waited, watching as his uninvited visitor took several steps, before he stood and came out from his power position to greet this stranger in his world, this Daniel entering the lion's den.

"Judge Boucher, I don't believe we've met." Perry approached, and with an almost invisible glance motioned his assistant to leave and close the door behind her.

The two men met in the middle and shook hands, grips firm and testing as each stared into the eyes of the other as if this wasn't a greeting but rather a game of chicken to see who blinked first. Perry's office continued the theme of the reception area: open space, little furniture. Big difference—the office had carpeting ankle-deep.

Finally Perry blinked, disengaging his grip. "What can I do for you, Judge?"

Boucher looked around the office. There was an Oriental cabinet with collectible pottery, Southwestern or Mexican, against the wall to his right, a built-in bar to his left with fine crystalware on display, a sofa and coffee table behind him next to the door, and two leather chairs in front of Perry's desk. Toward these he nodded.

"Let's talk," he said, then walked to the chairs and took a seat. Perry followed him, seeking a way to regain the initiative in this, his own office.

"I knew your colleague, Judge Epson," Perry said.

Boucher dismissed this comment with a wave. "I'm not here to talk about him."

"I'm curious to know just why you are here."

Boucher drummed the fingertips of both his hands together: one-two-three-four-five, one-two-three-four-five. It was an annoying gesture. Perry masked his irritation, but just barely.

"I've learned something about methane hydrate recently," Boucher said. "It appears to be a very promising energy source. Those involved should make fortunes, wouldn't you say?"

"It has possibilities. It's going to be expensive, even dangerous. We could be years away from commercial production."

"I understand the Russians recently recovered samples from a lake bed, using a submarine."

"How did you know that?"

"I know more. Japan, China, India—all three have located massive fields, and are beginning extraction of methane hydrate. Think of those three economic powerhouses with their own energy sources. Might change the world's balance of power, don't you think? Of course, you are right. It is dangerous to produce. Undersea landslides causing tsunamis, greenhouse gases, separation and storage of carbon dioxide. What method do you favor, geologic sequestration?"

"What do you want, Judge?"

"Let me tell you what I don't want. I don't want to be making a hundred and seventy-four thousand a year for the rest of my life."

"You want a *job?*"

"I'd prefer to call it a pension. What did Judge Epson call it? I'm sure he didn't call it a bribe."

"I don't know what you're talking about." He'd been on the edge of his seat, but now Perry sat back, assuming a more comfortable posture. This conversation was taking an unexpectedly favorable turn.

Boucher smiled. He pulled out a three-by-five card from his shirt pocket and handed it to Perry. On it were written the last seven words the CEO had spoken: *I don't know what you're talking about.*

"I hardly know you, yet I know you. Mr. Perry, you're very predictable. I wouldn't have expected you to say anything else because it wouldn't look good on tape, would it? Where is the camera and the mike, in that curio cabinet? In the bar? I bet it's . . ."

He stood up and walked to Perry's desk and picked up a small bronze statue of an old horse head oil pump. He examined it from all angles, then smiled, holding it up.

"Right with my first choice, wasn't I?" He set it back down and returned to his chair. "In all honesty, I'm here because you are so predictable. With all the people you've had killed, I think it's pretty predictable that you'll come after me next. I'd kind of like to see that doesn't happen. I'm sure you understand."

Boucher folded his arms across his chest and stared into the eyes of the man across from him. His cards were on the table. Perry had to show his or fold. Seconds ticked on a clock somewhere in the office. Perry displayed a bad habit. He flicked the nail of his right thumb against his front teeth. It was a sign he was about to give in.

"Where's Palmetto?" he asked.

Boucher breathed an unnoticed sigh of relief. He knew he was in. He pulled a second card from his shirt pocket, shaking his head. This card he handed over, saying, "Again, predictable. I knew that would be your first question. I just didn't expect you to take this long to get to it. Where's Palmetto, you ask? The answer's in your hand. It's one of my favorite movie lines."

Perry studied the card. It read, *He sleeps with the fishes.*

"What does this mean?"

"I think you know. There was a 'seismic event' off the coast of South Carolina a few days ago. Unfortunately, a mini-sub from the Marblehead Oceanographic Institute was conducting research on the sea floor at the time. One of the submariners was killed. His name was withheld pending notification of next of kin. It was Bob Palmetto."

"How do you know this?"

"I was on the research vessel *Beagle.* Your next question will be what was I doing there, and my answer is that I had taken Palmetto into custody in connection with the murder of a woman named Ruth Kalin. He was found in Marblehead, where he was a guest of one of the scientists with the Institute. You can check that out. It's a matter of record. Palmetto had asked me to let him conduct one last research mission. I agreed. He was right. It was his last mission. Now it's time for you to talk. Not here; not with the surveillance you have in this office. Let's go somewhere else."

"Where?"

Boucher looked at his watch. It was not quite ten in the morning. "You like beignets?"

They left the offices of Rexcon separately and met at the Café du Monde, the oldest tenant in the famous outdoor French Market. For over two hundred years, beginning with Native Americans and followed by African-Americans, Spanish, French, Italians, Germans, even Moors from the Holy Land, traders from the world over had engaged in commerce on this spot at the mighty river's edge. The tradition of trading was continued by the two men who sat by themselves in a far corner with their café au lait and powdered-sugar-coated pastries.

"I don't need a judge," Perry said. "I'm not involved in litigation and I don't expect to be. Besides, I have friends there already."

"I know what you need," Boucher said. "You need what Palmetto entrusted to me. Besides, I don't plan on being a judge much longer. I've been asked to take a leave from the bench—as I'm sure you know—and I don't think I want to go back."

"What did Palmetto entrust to you?"

"I have his work product, all of it. Extraction of methane hydrate, separation of CO_2, a system of transporting the methane. Everything he had twenty years ago and everything he's done since. The man was a genius."

"What do you want for it?"

Boucher held up his right hand with five fingers spread. Then he raised his left hand—with five fingers spread.

"Ten million?" Perry wheezed.

Boucher nodded and bit into his beignet. He was quick with his napkin to wipe the powdered-sugar ring around his mouth.

"You'll be making billions," he said.

"Not for ten years, if then."

"You know that's not true. There's going to be a headlong rush into this energy source. It's a perfect storm: tension in the Middle East threatening our major oil supply; our four greatest economic rivals—China, Russia, India, and Japan—moving toward the use of methane hydrate; and the unpopularity of offshore drilling after the Gulf oil spill. Palmetto explained to me how methane hydrate extraction could be accomplished with little or no ecological damage. If the United States is not the first off the mark with extraction and production, there'll be no expense spared playing catch-up. It will be like the space race all over again."

Perry wrinkled his nose. "This smells like extortion," he said.

"Bullshit," Boucher said. "Palmetto's dead, the goose that laid the golden egg. I inherited and I'm trying to sell a valuable product at a fair price. You're not interested? I've always wanted to go to India. I bet they'd be glad to see me. I look at how you've handled this matter to this point and I have to say I'm glad I'm not one of your shareholders. I think you're too dumb to run your own company."

He finished his beignet while Perry fumed.

"I've got to see some proof," Perry said.

"Of course you do. Give me an office, a nice one on the executive floor. I'll bring in daily reports till you have everything I have. You'll be making deposits to my nominated account. With the final report, I leave. We won't be the best of friends, but we'll trust each other because it would be mad not to. I don't mean the emotion, I mean *m-a-d:* mutually assured destruction. We'll have enough on each other that one could put the other away for life. That's my life insurance policy."

"I need to think about it."

"Of course you do." Boucher stood. "It's not the perfect plan, but we'll come to terms. I know we will. You're predictable."

After a last dab at the corners of his mouth, Boucher turned and left the table. He did not look back.

CHAPTER 21

BOUCHER LEFT THE FRENCH Market. When he turned the first corner and was out of sight of Perry, his legs went weak. He hugged the first lamppost he came to as if he were staggering drunk. Drawing on his wits and pure adrenaline, he had gone toe-to-toe with the killer on his own turf, the man who had almost succeeded in ending his life thousands of leagues under the sea. He let go of the lamp, stood up straight, and took a deep breath. As if to celebrate his accomplishment, two street musicians, one playing a slide trombone, the other a euphonium, started blowing a mean version of "Do You Know What It Means to Miss New Orleans." The judge slipped a twenty into the hat on the sidewalk. The music made him realize it was good to be alive. He turned the corner at the next block and an arm reached out and grabbed him, pulling him into a doorway. It was Fitch.

"You ain't dead yet, I see," the detective said.

Boucher wanted to hug him, still elated over his achievement, and grateful in the knowledge that the night before, this man had stood guard over him.

"I wangled a spot inside his company," he said. "He said he'd think about it, but I'm in, I know it." He poked his head out of the doorway and looked around. "You want to join me Sunday for my cleanup run? I'll tell you all about it then."

"Pick me up at ten," Fitch said. "Now go work it off. You're too damned excited."

Boucher walked home, changed into his exercise clothes, and got in his truck. He drove to his gym and parked outside. He couldn't help but think of Ruth Kalin, her brutal murder and the last time he saw her alive. He parked and went inside. Thoughts of the woman's death stayed with him and anger replaced the nervous elation he had felt earlier, both emotions rooted in the same source—John Perry. He blasted the punching bag for the next hour with such ferocity that the proprietor watching him almost came over to tell him to take it easy, out of concern for both his customer and his equipment.

Sunday morning broke with a sultry, musky dampness. Boucher sat in his courtyard in shorts and a T-shirt, sipping his coffee. This house was not made for a man to live alone, he thought as he picked up his phone and called Malika. They spoke for half an hour. She was in L.A. One of her clients had been offered a movie deal for his novel. It meant big money for both her and the client. This was a first for her and she was excited. Today was a day off. She would be playing tourist. Doing things they should be doing together. He hung up not liking the way his life was going. A sultry breeze blew in his ear and whispered, *So change it.*

He picked up Fitch at ten in front of the run-down apartment complex where he lived. For a time both were silent. Fitch spoke first.

"I know why I'm in a bad mood," he said. "What's your problem?"

"Malika's in L.A. doing the town and I'm stuck here with you. You don't look so cheerful yourself."

"My doctor says I need to cut down on my drinking."

"You'll feel better if you do."

"I'm also pissed because I'm getting nowhere with the homicides piling up around you. I spoke with an ex-FBI friend who says they wouldn't help with any of this, even if I asked them. They'd pass on bribing a federal judge because the case is cold and they wouldn't want a turf war with the DA's office. He says they've got a short list of hot issues and if you're not the flavor of the month they won't look at you."

"That's not why they won't help." Boucher recounted what he had learned about Epson and the FBI.

Fitch sighed. "Don't know why I'm surprised. Cronyism ain't unheard of around here. Anyway, what do you plan to do in his offices?"

"I don't know. Part of this is that old adage about keeping your friends close and your enemies closer. Part is just a feeling that I'm going to find something that will put him away."

"You—the guy he'd whack in a heartbeat—you think he's just going to leave incriminating evidence around for you to trip over? You're dreaming." He took a cigarette out, then put it back.

"I'm going to be giving him information that's worth a fortune," Boucher said. "He's going to like having me around."

"I think you're crazy." Fitch took out the cigarette again and placed it in his mouth, just sucking on it, not lighting up, then asked, "Where we going?"

"Nowhere. I'm just going to drive along the coast."

No cleanup today; it was a journey of reflection. Katrina, the oil spill, coastal erosion. Natural and man-made disasters had wreaked havoc on these wetlands and beaches but, as always, there were signs of the resilience of the land and its people. Fishermen still plied their trade on calm waters and couples could be seen walking hand in hand on sandy beaches. Ibis stood like marble statuary in the shallows and brown pelicans glided effortlessly on gentle air currents. In a single vista were signs of hope, and signs of dire warning. Neither was lost on the two men as they drove.

"Let's go by my office," Fitch said. "I want to give you something."

"The other evening you raised a good point," Boucher said. "I'm not sure it's such a good idea for us to be seen together—especially at your office."

"It's Sunday afternoon, for Christ's sake. Anybody who's not blind, deaf, and dumb is in front of a TV watching the Saints. For just a few precious hours on an autumn weekend everyone can forget about natural and man-made disasters. Martians could land in New Orleans on a Sunday afternoon during football season and nobody would know it. Besides, if Perry or his mob say anything about us being together, tell them you're still a person of interest in a murder that showed up in your driveway and I'm bugging the shit out of you about it. I agree to question you out of the office, out of respect for who you are and all that. Believe me, they'll buy that sooner than they're going to buy your line about being Perry's new Best Friend Forever or whatever the fuck it is."

They drove to the Eighth District station.

"Come on," Fitch said, "it's in my office."

"Well, I'll be damned," Boucher said when they entered. "You painted the place."

The sickly yellow walls were now a fresh eggshell white.

"Yeah, and what else?" Fitch asked. Boucher looked around.

"There's no ashtray on your desk."

"Now you know why I'm not Little Mary Sunshine. I'm cutting down on my drinking *and* my smoking. Thank God for great restaurants, 'cause that's going to be the only joy I've got left."

He sat down at his desk and unlocked the top drawer. "Here," he said, handing Boucher what looked like a quarter.

"What's this?"

"Tape it under the insert of your shoe."

"What's it for?"

"It's a GPS locator. It's for finding your body."

"That's a morbid thought," Boucher said, studying the small thin disk.

"That's police work," Fitch said. "Anyway, you want to get Perry, you know it might cost you your life. I don't want you to die in vain. If I know where your corpse is, I might be able to pin it on him. I said 'might.'"

Boucher chuckled.

"What's so funny?" Fitch said.

"You as Little Mary Sunshine."

Fitch declined the offer of a ride back to his apartment. He was going to find a bar with the biggest plasma TV, free pretzels and popcorn, and the cheapest beer. During a Saints game, temperance could take a hike.

Judge Jock Boucher went home and watched the game alone. He got a call at halftime.

"You're on," Perry said. "Start tomorrow."

Boucher called the Massachusetts number Palmetto had given him and uttered two words into the recorder.

"I'm in."

CHAPTER 22

THE WIND SHIFTED DURING the night and the temperature dropped twenty degrees. With the humidity still high, there was a definite chill in the air when Boucher woke the next morning. This was good. He was ready to go to work. The chill gave him an edge.

Like so many others beginning the normal workday routine, he was on autopilot as he drove to the city center and pulled into the federal courthouse out of habit, albeit a habit of only a few short weeks. The security guard allowed him access without question. He left his truck in the federal building parking lot. Parking privileges had not been taken from him, and it was a short walk of a couple of blocks to the office tower and Perry's corporate headquarters. This morning, when he got off the elevator at the executive offices floor, the greeting he received was much different than what he'd experienced during his first visit. He was welcomed. The receptionist in the large lobby offered a smile, as did Perry's two administrative assistants. All three women, he noted, were quite attractive, an observation that had escaped him earlier, when focus—and fear—was concentrated on a mission whose result could have been much different.

"Good morning, Judge Boucher." The speaker was the woman who had asked his business before. "We were told to expect you. Mr. Perry asked that you be shown right into his office. He's in a meeting elsewhere but will be with you shortly."

"I don't mind waiting here in the lobby."

"I'm sure you'll find it more comfortable in his office." She held the door open for him and showed him into the CEO's office. Boucher chose a chair next to Perry's desk and sat down.

"Judge Boucher." Perry's voice came from a hidden speaker. The judge turned around, looking for the source.

"I'm on the intercom," Perry said. "I'm down the hall with my chief geologist, Bert Cantrell. I'd like you to meet him. We'll be there in two minutes. Did Dawn offer you coffee?"

She came through the door that instant carrying a silver tray and coffee service. "I have it here, Mr. Perry."

"Thank you, Dawn," Perry's disembodied voice said. "See that Judge Boucher has everything he needs."

"I will, sir."

She wore a tan skirt, white silk blouse with the top button undone, and beige high heels. Her jewelry was a single strand of pearls and gold scalloped earrings. She wore a stainless steel lady's Rolex. Her hair was too dark for blond and too light for brown. Golden highlights caught the morning sun. Little makeup, white even teeth. All this Boucher noticed in less than a second. Summation: beautiful.

"This is a French roast," she said, pouring from a sterling silver pot into a fine china cup. "If you have a preference, please let me know."

"French roast is fine. Next time I'd like a little chicory." Boucher was testing. Accommodation to small details was a good sign.

"I like chicory too," she said. "We don't have any right now, but I'll be sure to get some." She handed him his cup, bending over and offering a view of her breasts supported by a push-up Wonderbra. She stood up slowly.

"Mr. Perry has assigned me to help you. Please let me know if there's anything you need."

Boucher nodded. "Thank you," he said, "for the coffee." He sipped. "It's delicious."

Dawn turned and left him—reluctantly, it seemed, or maybe the reluctance was his. He wasn't alone for long. Perry and another man entered just seconds later, as if exits and entrances were all choreographed in this organization. Perry had said he was bringing his geologist, but the person with him could not have looked less like a man of science. He was in his fifties, wore a buzz cut, had a thick neck that grew out of a barrel chest. If there was a stereotype for a former Marine—there are no ex-Marines, the corps proudly claims—this guy was it.

"Judge Boucher," Perry said, striding toward him, "I'd like you to meet Bert Cantrell, my right-hand man, and in the whole damn country he's the best geologist and geophysicist—which means he studies rocks and reports, dirt *and* data. He and I built this company."

Boucher stood and offered his right hand, anticipating and preparing for the bone-crushing handshake he knew was coming. He was not disappointed, but gave as good as he got. This man would challenge him. His grip spoke volumes.

"Bert and I have been discussing your offer," Perry said. "I couldn't make such a decision without him. We have decided to give you a trial run. If we feel what you have is of sufficient value to us, then the arrangement you and I discussed is on. If not, you go your own way and we go ours. Deal?"

Boucher looked at both men, studying their faces before answering. "I'm going to be parsimonious with my information until our arrangement is—"

"Parsimonious?" Perry interrupted. "Come on, Judge. This isn't a courtroom."

"It means you're not going to get an information dump right off the bat. I'm going to dole it out carefully. It won't take that long for you to decide to accept my proposal."

"That's fair enough." He turned to Cantrell. "Parsimonious; I thought he was talking about the damned fruit."

"That's persimmon," Boucher said.

"Whatever," Perry said. "You agree to a trial period. You'll turn your information over to Bert; he and I decide whether it's worth anything. We've set you up an office down the hall, and Dawn will be your assistant. She'll help you with anything you need." He paused. "Well, then, I guess we're in business. Welcome aboard, Judge."

"I'd prefer not to be called Judge," Boucher said. "My first name's Jock."

"Jock it is, then," Perry said. "Bert will show you to your office."

"Let's do that, then I'll excuse myself for the rest of the day. I will organize the material I'll present tomorrow." He turned to Bert. "And I'll have it ready by noon. I'm assuming that typing is among Dawn's attributes, in addition to the obvious."

"Don't underestimate Dawn," Perry said. "I don't pay her a six-figure salary because of her looks. She's got an MBA from Wharton and speaks three languages. There's no deadwood around here, Jock. The receptionist in the lobby is also a registered nurse. I hire based on merit. If it comes in a pretty package"—he smiled—"I try not to hold that against them."

*   *   *

Boucher saw his assigned office, had a few words with Bert, then excused himself. He retrieved his pickup and drove home. There he waited. Palmetto had promised him that a package would be delivered today and that he'd better be home to receive it. The midday sun had softened the early morning chill and he could not sit still. He went out back and walked his garden, alternately looking at the plants, his cell phone, and his watch. It was after nine in L.A. He dialed. Malika's phone was turned off or she was out of range. He couldn't remember a time when he'd been unable to reach her on her cell. He put his phone back in his pocket and went inside. He waited, wasting hours staring at the inside of his historic home, feeling disconnected from the things around him that he had loved perhaps not for themselves but maybe as markers, symbols of his success. He didn't feel too successful right now. He called Malika again. This time she answered. She was laughing, out of breath. He could hear a male voice in the background, then a muffled sound that told him she had her hand over the phone and was trying to get someone to be quiet.

"Hi, Jock," she said.

"I tried to call you earlier."

"Yeah, I saw. I'm sorry. I had to sleep late this morning. We went to a cast party last night and—"

"Who's we?"

"Jerry and I. Jerry's my client. We had the chance to meet a director who might do the movie of his book. He'd just finished a picture, and this cast party, well, it was outrageous. Guess what? He wants me in the movie too."

"Who, your client?"

"No, the director. His name is—"

"I don't care what his name is." There was silence. "How much longer will you be in L.A.?" he asked.

"I'm not sure." Malika's voice was flat. "There are things I need to do here."

"Well, call me when you get back to New York," Boucher said. "I won't interrupt you again while you're so busy."

"All right. Good-bye, Jock." She hung up.

He stared at the phone in his hand as if it would offer some explanation for the terse conversation just concluded. What did this woman want? She had said she wanted to be with him. Now she's out West doing God knows what. Was this jealousy he was feeling—or anger over his own uncertainty about their relationship? He shunted Malika and their unresolved issues to the back of his mind.

For the next three hours he sat reading in his living room, trying to ignore his century-old Seth Thomas mantel clock, each tick of the timepiece like a small mallet beating inside his skull. The sun was going down when he heard a truck pull up and stop in front of his house.

"Finally," he said aloud to hear his own voice. Breathing a sigh of relief, he went to his front door and opened it as the courier mounted the steps to his porch.

"This the, uh, Boucher residence?" He pronounced it *butcher*.

"I'm Jock Boucher."

"Package for you."

He signed for the package, then took it back inside. It was about twelve by eighteen inches, three inches thick, weighed maybe ten pounds, and was very securely wrapped. He took it to the kitchen and set it on the table, pulled a knife from the block of his chef's knives, and carefully cut the tape, slit open the package, then pulled out the contents—a notebook computer, a cell phone, and a small box with bits and pieces of plastic. There was a four-page letter from Palmetto in small-font, single-spaced geek-speak, giving instructions on the care and use of the equipment he'd just been sent. He read the letter, then read it again. It was too much to comprehend in one sitting. He returned to the section dealing with the notebook computer, its adaptations, and its intended use. After several readings, Boucher did manage to ascertain that Palmetto was trying to teach him about cloud computing. Apparently, the information he would be turning over to Perry was somewhere in this cloud.

What he gathered was that the cloud was like some kind of a remote database that you could access from any computer but you didn't keep the data on the hard drive. That meant you didn't have to worry about your computer being stolen, only about the cloud being hacked. But that seemed like a good thing in his position. Boucher was about to access the cloud when the new cell phone rang.

"Hello?"

"This is Bob," the caller said. "I see you got the package. I've been tracking it on the Internet. How are you doing?"

"I was about to go online."

"You can do that in a minute. I wanted to tell you about your phone. We've installed a few apps."

"A few what?"

"Applications. Programs. Listen to me carefully. First, any call to or from this phone is secure. You don't need to worry about that. But don't call any of Perry's or Rexcon's numbers with it, and don't make any calls with it from inside their offices. They'll know it's enhanced. Now, it has what I'll call a combination camera, laser measuring device, and CAD software program. To start the program you press the icon that looks like an eye and put the phone in your shirt pocket. You need to take off your jacket for it to see. It sticks up just above the seam of your shirt pocket. The camera is at the top. There are a couple floors I want you to walk—"

"Wait a minute. What does it do?"

"It makes floor plans."

"You're kidding."

"Do I sound like I'm kidding?"

"Why do you want floor plans of executive offices?"

"First, to know where you are in case there's a problem."

"That's taken care of," Boucher said. The disk Fitch gave him was at that moment taped under the insert in his shoe.

"Yeah, right. You've got a GPS locator in your shoe. I knew that when you answered the phone. That's so James Bond. With this system we know not only precisely where you are but everything that's around you: desks, cabinets . . . we even see hardware in the walls. But that's not all. When you walk their laboratories—"

"What laboratories? It's an executive office building."

"They're going to take you to their laboratories. When they see what I send you, they will take you to their hearts, clasp you to their bosoms, and—"

"You're coming unglued." He could hear Palmetto laughing. "And you're off the reservation," Boucher said. "I'm looking for evidence of criminal activity, not trade secrets. And where did you get this spyphone?"

"It was augmented by a guy here at the Institute. We call him Squeeze because of what he can compress into a cellular phone."

"What is an oceanographic institute doing making cellular surveillance equipment?"

"You of all people know how important communications are to every one of the Institute's missions. This is just an adaption of applications they use every day. You take care of this phone. It just might save your life. Okay, it's time to get you into the cloud. Open your laptop. Let's get you started."

CHAPTER 23

BOUCHER ARRIVED AT REXCON'S offices early next morning, parking in a public lot two blocks from the office tower. At eight-thirty when he arrived things were already under way. Dawn had his coffee ready and he had documents for her. He asked that they be transmitted to Bert Cantrell. Sitting alone at an obviously expensive desk, he took his phone from his pocket, held it below desk level, and stared at it, half expecting Palmetto to appear on the screen and say howdy. That didn't happen and he sat there with nothing whatsoever to do, feeling somewhat foolish. Dawn came in, refreshed his coffee, and said that Mr. Cantrell would be in to see him as soon as he'd finished reviewing the documents. Midmorning, Cantrell burst into the office.

"Brilliant," he exclaimed, papers clutched in his hand. "Have you read this stuff?"

"I have," Boucher said. "It looked to me like a simple and inexpensive solution to a complex problem." Palmetto had coached him to say that.

Cantrell sat on the edge of a chair across from the desk and leaned forward. "The separation and storage of CO_2—it's incredible. This process also makes for a safer transmission of methane. If his cost projections are accurate, this process can compete with onshore natural gas production. Outstanding." He stopped, remembering that although on his own turf, he wasn't necessarily talking to a member of his own team. He stood up. "It's a good start, but there are gaps."

"There'll be more tomorrow," Boucher said. "But with the next installment, my audition is over. Our deal goes firm."

"Let's see what you bring us next," Cantrell said, "then we'll decide." He started to leave.

"I have a question," Boucher said.

"Yes?"

"Where's the executive washroom?"

"I'll show you the layout of the floor," Cantrell said, "so you know your way around."

"Thanks," Boucher said. He took off his sport coat and draped its shoulders over the back of his chair.

He was given the tour. They even stuck their heads into Perry's office. He wasn't there. Jock returned to his own office and was putting his sport coat back on when Dawn entered.

"Can I get you anything?" she asked.

"I'm done for the day. You know, I don't think I'm going to be keeping you very busy. I hope you have other things to do."

"There's always something," she said, collecting the cup and saucer from his desk. "Till tomorrow, then?"

"Till tomorrow."

The moment he got in his truck, the phone in his shirt pocket rang and vibrated, tickling his chest.

"Works great," Palmetto said. "I'm looking at a copy of the floor plans right now."

"I can't imagine why," Boucher said. "There's nothing of interest on that floor."

"You don't know that. Your phone's sensors tell me that Perry has a very large safe built into the wall of his office. It's behind the bar; quite a piece of work. I don't think he had it built to keep his gold watch in. Cantrell keeps a lockbox in his desk. It's not made of tin. There's something I want you to do tomorrow. Your desk is too close to the window. Ask that it be moved closer to the door."

"Why?"

"There's a jamming system built into the exterior walls and windows of the building to protect against eavesdropping. It's interfering with your phone. If you're sitting closer to the center of the building, I think we can get it working better. It has a range of fifty feet, so get within that distance of your target and we'll do the rest."

"Could you please tell me what you are talking about?"

"Everybody there has a cell phone," Palmetto said. "The men keep theirs in their shirt or jacket pocket and the women keep them in their purses. We can use your phone to turn every cell phone on that floor into a microphone, without its owner knowing. We can adjust their phones' settings to silent ring and automatic answer, then just call them and we've got a remote listening device. Just stay away from the walls and windows. Now go on home, and, by the way, take the battery out of your old phone when you get there. They can do to you what we're about to do to them."

"So I can't use my personal cell phone? I have a friend; that's the way she contacts me."

"You can't use it till this is over. It won't be too long. Now move. You're in a public parking lot and you look suspicious just sitting there in your truck."

"You know where I am now?"

"I do and I know it's going to cost you fifteen dollars to get out of that lot if you don't move in the next three minutes. Get on home. I just saved you five bucks."

"One more question."

"Yeah?"

"What's my blood pressure?"

"One-twenty over seventy. Pulse seventy-five. You're good."

"I'll be damned," Boucher said. "I was only kidding."

"Like I told you, we've got apps for everything."

He wouldn't be calling Malika, and now she couldn't call him—at least not on his own cell phone. But she knew his home number. She could call him there. He went home and spent the afternoon conversing with Palmetto on their super cells. It wasn't so much a conversation as it was a science class. The information he would be handing over tomorrow was pretty much Palmetto's pride and joy, his raison d'être in life. He had developed a system for recovery, collection, storage, and transportation of methane hydrate using materials never employed in the energy industry. He took pains preparing his protégé.

"They're the same principles we've been using for the last hundred years," Palmetto said. "There's almost always gas associated with oil. GOSPs—gas/oil separating plants—are used in the production of oil to remove contaminants and to capture the associated gas for commercial use. That's what I did, I just did it underwater; very deep underwater. And I'm separating gases from gases, not from petroleum. Otherwise, it's much the same. Oil at the wellhead is under pressure; methane hydrate at the bottom of the ocean is under pressure. You already know that the bathysphere is the best design for deep-sea pressure, but obviously we can't use titanium for every aspect of underwater production, it's far too expensive. What I've been working on for the past twenty years are components that can withstand those extreme pressures. You with me?" he asked.

"So far," Boucher said.

"I started experimenting with carbon fiber. You know what that is?"

"They use it to make race cars."

"Racing, aerospace—it's used in many industries. It's strong under high pressure, it's light, which is an advantage transporting it over the open ocean, and it's even useful in filtration of certain gases. I have developed carbon fiber with various polymers to be used at different depths and for different purposes: pipes for transmission, bathysphere-shaped chambers for depressurization and processing. I can build an entire underwater plant from carbon fiber and polymers. When we're finished with a site, we can pack up and move on without leaving so much as a footprint on the ocean floor. In a nutshell, Jock, the variety of carbon-fiber-based components is the essence of my process."

"Is that what they were trying to get from you in that lawsuit?"

"Twenty years ago I was just getting started. I've done a lot of work since then. But yes; that's what got Dexter Jessup killed."

"Now you're just going to give it to them?"

"I'm going to give them just enough to whet their appetite. Anyway, you are going to put them out of business before they can use it."

"I thank you for your vote of confidence but you know this is no sure thing."

"I don't want to hear you say that again," Palmetto said. "Think positive and we'll make it happen. Always remember, you are not alone."

"I'm never alone with that damn phone in my pocket." He hung up and looked at his watch. Evening was nigh. He'd spent the whole afternoon at home and his landline had not rung. Not once.

As much as they love the Quarter, residents of New Orleans sometimes prefer to relax in more subtle surroundings, and when they do, the Garden District is the locale of choice. It was an old plantation till the 1830s. Wealthy Anglos bought homes there because they didn't want to live with the French and the Creoles in the Quarter. Originally there were two homes per block, each with large gardens, hence the name. It still has one of the largest collections of antebellum southern mansions in the entire country. At the end of the nineteenth century, many of the lots were subdivided, and Victorian homes were built between the older residences.

Boucher needed to get away from home and the phone that did not ring and wanted a different ambience. He drove up St. Charles Avenue to the Columns Hotel, where the bar catered to those seeking sedate sophistication—and could claim one of the best bartenders anywhere. It was officially called the Victorian Lounge. One entered the room through twelve-foot, three-hundred-pound mahogany doors. The former dining room of the original owners of the mansion, it offered a mahogany bar, and fifteen-foot ceilings from which hung the original German stained-glass chandelier. Queen Anne–inspired wood panels adorned the ceiling and an ancient-Greek-inspired frescoed frieze covered the wall. This was no ordinary bar.

Though not a regular, he was recognized by the bartender and greeted as he took a seat.

"Haven't seen you in a while, Judge," the bartender said. "How's it goin'?"

"Can't complain, Mike. How are things with you?"

"I don't owe my bookie; figure I'm ahead of the game. What can I get you?"

"How about a bourbon with a splash of bitters?"

"Brand?"

"Maker's Mark will be fine, thanks."

The best bartenders have two things in common: one, a good pour, and two, knowing when a customer wants to talk and when he doesn't. Judge Boucher wanted to chat and Mike was just about to oblige but then stepped back and moved to the far end of the bar. Boucher noticed this and, as he sipped his drink, sensed someone standing next to the bar stool on his right. He did not look.

"Good evening, Judge." The woman's voice addressing him was familiar. "I don't believe I've ever seen you in here."

He turned to face her. "Dawn. It's nice . . ." Not another word came out. She was standing close to him and it was like being poked with a cattle prod. The way she looked, from twenty feet away she would have had the same effect. Dressed for evening, she was stunning, wearing the simplest of black cocktail dresses, a diamond necklace and pavé diamond earrings, no watch, and a platinum ring with a huge pearl set in diamonds. Her hair looked softer in the subdued lighting, a strand falling down her forehead, just begging to be put in place. He refrained, the temptation almost too much.

"Yes," she said. "This is a nice place. It's my favorite, though I don't hang around in bars all that much. Do I, Mike?" she asked the bartender.

Mike saw an invitation being extended and approached them. "You don't come by often enough for me, Miss Fallon. You know Judge Boucher?"

"We've recently met," she said, "though not in social circumstances. He doesn't seem to recognize me out of uniform, so I guess I'd better order my own drink."

Boucher snapped to her none too subtle hint. "No, please. What would you like? Would you care to sit down?"

"I'm sorry," she said, "but I've never mastered the art of mounting and dismounting bar stools in form-fitting evening wear. How about a table?"

The lounge was not crowded and there were several tables available. Dawn ordered a champagne cocktail and they moved from the bar. He pulled out a chair for her, then seated himself. The bartender brought their glasses.

"I went to a gallery opening of an artist I like," she said as if answering a question—or addressing a speculation—"and was on my way home. I live nearby. I am not spying on you. I'm not supposed to begin that assignment until tomorrow. What brings you to my neighborhood?"

"You live nearby?" Boucher asked, flustered and unable to string more than five words together.

"I live in a mausoleum my family has owned since 1895. It's a few blocks from here." She sipped her champagne. "You?"

"I have a place in the Quarter. My home is old too." He sipped his bourbon for courage. "But I love it. I love places with history."

"Well, mine certainly has that. It was a bordello before my family bought it; the fanciest house in the Garden District. I've gotten rather obsessed with it, I'm afraid. Other than the kitchen, bathrooms, and essential electricity, I've kept everything faithful to the period. All the furniture is authentic. I've restored it as a stately home, not a turn-of-the-century cathouse."

Boucher chuckled and took a hard hit from his glass to settle himself. "How long have you worked for Rexcon?" It was a question he didn't want to ask, but trying to avoid it made it all-consuming.

"Next month will be my tenth anniversary. I started with them after graduating from Wharton, and I went to business school right out of college. Before you try to guess my age I have to tell you I received advance placement and finished Tulane in two years."

He did the math in his head.

"I'm thirty-four," she said before he had concluded his calculations. "Never married, not even close; I'm an old maid. And you? Are your bones starting to creak yet?"

"So far everything seems to be in working order. I know I'm getting old, though, because I only know the names of a few current movie stars and none of the new recording artists."

That led to a discussion of favorite music, and the next time he glanced at his watch, an hour had passed. "Have you had dinner?" he asked.

"No, and I'm famished."

"Do you have a favorite restaurant?"

"Commander's Palace," she said without hesitation.

Another talent of top bartenders: they know when their clients are ready for their check. Mike was walking toward them with the bill before Boucher even turned around to call him. He paid and they made their exit, Dawn slipping her arm in his as if out of habit. Walking along St. Charles Avenue, Dawn pointed out architectural details that gave the old homes their character.

"I've always loved Victorian architecture," she said. "Places like this."

They stood before a massive blue and white gingerbread structure with gables, a corner turret, and matching awnings: a Victorian masterpiece, Commander's Palace.

"I'm sure you've eaten here before," Dawn said.

"It's been a while. I remember celebrating here when I received the news that I'd passed the bar exam."

"So it's a special place for you too. Good."

Dawn was greeted by the maître d' like visiting royalty, and it wasn't all affectation, old families in New Orleans being revered. They were seated and Boucher excused himself to go to the men's room. He was drying his hands when he heard the voice coming from inside his sport coat.

"You picked a bad time to get up. She's making a call from her cell right now and you're out of range."

"Palmetto? The phone didn't ring and I sure as hell didn't answer it."

"It's always on. You're monitored constantly. Don't complain about it. It's your security guard."

"I thought I might enjoy an evening out."

"Yeah, and of all the gin joints in all the towns in all the world she walks into yours. Surely you're not that naïve."

At that moment a man came in to use the restroom. Palmetto went silent. But when it was again just the two of them he was back on.

"I don't mind you enjoying the evening, but for God's sake ask her something more on point. Get off the damned antiques, okay?"

Boucher said, "I don't like this."

"Maybe you don't, but at the end of the day it's what's going to keep you on the green side of the grass. Now get back in there and get her talking. And by the way, I think she likes you."

"That's none of your goddamned business," he muttered, but Palmetto seemed to have signed off.

Returning to his seat, he noticed Dawn was closing her purse, probably putting her cell phone away. He'd been out of range in the men's room, otherwise Palmetto would have known who she'd called and what she'd said. He had to admit the obvious: they had not met by chance this evening, despite what she had told him.

"I just called my boss," she said as he sat down. "I told him we were together and he told me to get as much information out of you as I could. I said I'd try, but I lied. Like I said, I wasn't supposed to start spying on you till tomorrow. Do you mind if we just enjoy the evening?"

"That suits me just fine." *Screw Palmetto*, he thought.

They ordered, and while waiting for their dinner he asked about her background, and if she had any family.

"I'm the end of the Fallon line in New Orleans," she said. "I had an older brother, but he was killed in Iraq. The house and I are all that's left. Your turn."

"I'm it too. I grew up in a small black Cajun town on the bayou. I was an only child; lost my mother when I was young and my father a few years ago. At least he lived long enough to see me become a judge. It meant a lot to him."

"I'm sure it did. But you're not a judge now, are you? I mean, working for Rexcon, obviously that's not a part of your judicial duties."

"I'm taking a break," he said, making it clear he didn't want to say anything more on the subject. She dropped it.

"What do you do at Rexcon, when you're not minding stray visitors like me?" he asked.

"Mostly SEC compliance stuff. A lot of forms. Very dull. Ah, just in the nick of time, before I bored you to death."

The waiter arrived with their dinner and the conversation turned to food, particularly that in front of them. Commander's Palace was world-renowned for its Creole cuisine, and for the fact that the majority of its ingredients were local; "one hundred miles from dirt to plate" was their credo.

"Your ancestors must be turning over in their graves, your being here with me," Boucher said, picturing them looking down on the mixed-race couple.

"You're so right. If I was caught out in public in their neighborhood with a Cajun, it would have caused a scandal. And a black Cajun? They'd have banished me. But I'm color-blind and those days are gone, thank goodness."

She made the remark in such an unaffected way. It made him smile.

After their dinner he walked her home, and like a young suitor he stood on the front porch as she unlocked the door with its beveled glass inserts, wondering if there would be a kiss, and if so on the cheek or the lips.

"Would you care to come in for a nightcap?" she asked.

"Thank you, no. Perhaps another time. I've got a lot to prepare for tomorrow. It's kind of a make-or-break day for me and your organization. If they don't like what I give them, it's au revoir."

"I think you'll be with us for a while longer. I've put in a good word for you, and I have influence there." She smiled, leaned forward, and kissed him on the mouth, light but lingering, then drew away. "We'll have our chance to get to know each other better."

"I look forward to that."

At the bottom of her porch he turned. She blew him a kiss before entering and locked the door behind her. It was a short walk to the hotel where he had parked, and where he had begun this delightful evening. He started the ignition on his vehicle and was reaching for the radio to find some jazz.

"Told you she liked you," Palmetto said. "Where'd she kiss you?"

"On the front porch, you Peeping Tom. I could have you thrown back in jail, you know."

"You and I are beyond all that now. By the way, I'm sure you realize SEC compliance can be anything but boring."

"That occurred to me too."

"So this lady might be an important piece of the puzzle."

"You were warning me away from her earlier this evening."

"I just said her meeting you was a pretty strange coincidence. But she seems sincere. I don't think she's lying, not that she's said much yet. Ask her some hard questions. The phone also has a polygraph app."

"You're joking."

"Nope. That one's going to make its inventor rich, I can tell you. Ask some hard questions."

"Okay," Boucher said. Speaking of hard questions, he had one or two of his own and called Malika. He didn't give a damn if Palmetto was listening, and if that lie-detector thing really worked, well . . .

Her phone rang and rang. He was just about to hang up. Once again her answer was breathless.

"Hello?"

"Have I caught you at a bad time?" he asked.

"Well, I mean no, not really. The phone was in the car and I had to run to catch it."

"Where are you?"

"Napa Valley. We're scouting locations. We'd just pulled in to this charming place to do a wine tasting."

"So you can't talk."

He heard her sigh. "What is it, Jock?"

"It's nothing," he said. "I shouldn't have called."

"It's just that I'm busy now. I told you that. Can't this wait till I'm back in New York?"

"Malika, I—"

"Jock, it will have to wait."

That's what he missed, he realized. These damned cell phones; clicking them shut was nowhere near as satisfying as slamming down a receiver. Those old phones could really take a beating and were practically indestructible, but these new devices were abysmal failures when it came to relieving one's anger. He called her right back and planned his speech as he listened to the *chirrrp, chirrrp* of his call ringing through. *It's over,* he would say, *we're through. C'est fini.* But the call went unanswered. Jock clicked off his phone, drove home, and took his anger and unresolved issues to bed with him for the night.

CHAPTER 24

JOHN PERRY SPENT MOST evenings in his office, not at home. He got along well enough with his wife—they could spend hours not speaking and thus not annoying each other—but his son drove him nuts. Twenty-two years old, still living at home, and unable to hold a job. Just the sight of him sprawled in front of the TV, unshaven and lethargic, made him want to grab the sloth by the neck and throw him out the back door for good. But Mama defended her boy and berated the father for his insensitivity. "I'm not insensitive, I just can't stand him," Perry had told her more than once.

Bert Cantrell had no such domestic problems because he had set a bachelor's course early in life and had never strayed from his chosen path. He'd spent many a late evening with his business colleague over the years. Many useful ideas, some quite profitable, had come from these sessions. Perry was a big-picture guy, while Bert was all about details. Bert had just explained the gist of the information they'd received from Palmetto.

"So it's worthwhile?" Perry asked.

"It's worth a fortune," Bert responded.

"How long do we keep him around?" Perry asked.

"It depends on what we get next. He's holding back, that's obvious; but what he doesn't know is that I can fill in the gaps. I haven't exactly been sitting on my hands all these years."

"I don't want him around any longer than necessary," Perry said.

"I don't like the idea of doing in another judge."

"They have accidents just like everybody else. Besides, Judge Wundt told me this guy would not be missed."

"He said that?"

"In so many words," Perry said. He rose from his desk, taking his empty glass to the bar. He mixed himself a scotch and soda, loosened his tie, and sat on the settee. "Lifetime appointments don't necessarily guarantee a long life."

At that moment, Perry's desk phone rang. He stood up. Walked to his desk and answered his private line. "Hello. . . . You are? . . . That's great. Good work. Get to know him. Find out whatever you can about him. We'll discuss it tomorrow. . . . No, my cell phone is in my desk drawer and turned off. I don't want my wife calling me. Thanks. You too. 'Bye.

"That was Dawn. She's having dinner with Judge Boucher. That could be useful."

Perry stood at his desk. It looked like he was staring at a spot on the far wall. "It's time to fish or cut bait," he said.

"Meaning?"

"Meaning I've made up my mind. I've spent millions over the years bribing regulators and politicians. Just when I've got everything set, we get an oil spill, they reacted in their typical knee-jerk fashion and put a moratorium on offshore exploration. Now they're limiting new leases while they continue to study the cause and effect of the oil spill. That could take years, especially on the East Coast. And now we've got this windfall from Palmetto. Well, damn it, I'm not going to wait any longer. We're going ahead—over the two-hundred-mile limit, in international waters. I don't want to make a lot of noise about this. We just do it. I don't want some damn judge hanging around here and talking about 'international protocols' or some shit no one could enforce anyway. We get what he's got, then he's gone."

Bert went to the bar, mixed a drink, and they raised their glasses in a toast. "I've been waiting for this for more than twenty years," he said. "We are about to advance the science of energy exploration more than any company that has ever existed, and we're going to do it on our own terms."

Perry raised his glass. Theirs were two egos on a collision course with reality.

Boucher woke early, did a half hour's worth of calisthenics, fixed himself a pot of coffee, and flipped between CNN and Fox to get their widely varied interpretations of the day's events. He printed out the latest from Palmetto, showered, dressed, and headed for the office. Dawn was waiting for him. Her smile seemed a little brighter, her welcome a little warmer.

"I enjoyed the evening," she said.

"Me too." He walked into his office and remembered what Palmetto had asked him to do. "Dawn, could we get someone in here to move this desk closer to the door? It gets a little too much sun for me where it is now."

He gave her the file he had brought and she took it down the hall to Cantrell's office. She was there for some time, and in the interim two men came and moved his desk to his requested spot. He was now a few feet from the door, less than twenty feet from Dawn's desk, and closer to both Cantrell's and Perry's offices. He sat down and his cell phone vibrated almost immediately. He took it from his pocket, reluctant to answer it. He had a text message. Palmetto approved the new desk location.

Dawn was seated across from Perry's desk. Bert stood behind him. If they were expecting any scintillating revelations, she thought, they would be disappointed.

"We had drinks, then we went to dinner at Commander's Palace. He walked me home and that was it. We talked about antiques and stately homes. His house is in the National Registry just like mine."

"Wasn't he suspicious that you just bumped into each other?" Bert asked.

"I'm sure he was, at least at first. But I wasn't lying to him about where I had been, because that's what happened. He was in my neighborhood, I was on my way home and stopped into a local bar for a drink. There really was a gallery opening, if he cared to check. It was all perfectly natural."

"Do you think he'll go out with you again?"

"I think he will," she said.

"Good," Perry said. "I want to know what his real agenda is here. Find out." She was excused.

"Well?" Perry said when she had gone. "What have we got from him this morning?"

"Good stuff. Palmetto's been busy all these years," Cantrell said. "He's filled in some holes in our research, that's for sure. But I'm thinking with what he's given us and what we already have, we're ready. If we're going to start extraction in international waters, you're right. We don't want that judge hanging around our offices."

Perry said, "Then it's time to plan the endgame."

"Let's get him to the lab," Cantrell said. "Invite him to observe our testing. A lot of things can happen in a laboratory."

"That's an excellent suggestion."

"I'll need a little time to get things ready."

Perry looked at his desk calendar. "How about Friday?"

"Fine. Let me go and talk with him," Cantrell said. "He's waiting for me."

Bert Cantrell bounded into Boucher's office. He reached his long arm over the desk, offering a handshake.

"We have a deal," he said, grabbing Boucher's hand. "Perry has approved your payment and the first installment will be wired today. We're ready to begin. I'm going to organize some lab tests; test some of the data we've received from you. Why don't you join us? I'm sure you'll find it interesting."

"I'm sure I would," Boucher said. "I'm not finding enough to occupy myself with here, other than moving furniture around."

"You don't really have to hang around here, you know. Why don't you take Miss Fallon to lunch? Celebrate our deal."

"Talk about an offer I can't refuse," Boucher said.

"Great. You two enjoy the afternoon. By the way, John and I will be out of the office tomorrow, so there's no need for you to come in then either. Friday we'll show you our lab."

Cantrell gave him a good ol' boy slap on the back, which Boucher detested, and returned to his office. Dawn stuck her head in the door.

"Did I overhear him saying that we've got the afternoon off?"

"That's what he said. What's your pleasure?"

"Lunch wherever you like, then dinner and a movie; my place."

Boucher looked at his watch. "I've got to pick up a couple things," he fibbed. "Why don't you meet me in front of the building in half an hour? I drive a gray Ford pickup truck."

She smiled. "I'll be waiting."

He quickly left the office tower. His phone rang as he walked to the parking lot.

"I'm wondering what kind of testing they're going to show you," Palmetto said. "Might be our chance to see what they've come up with on their own."

"I'm not going just to satisfy your curiosity," Boucher said.

"I know. It's just that . . . oh, never mind. So you've got a hot date? A little 'afternoon delight'? Just remember to ask her some intelligent questions."

"I'm going to try. But it's only lunch, not a sworn deposition."

Dawn was waiting for him in front of the building, attracting the attention of every man walking by. He pulled to the curb and several men stole sideways glances as she folded her long legs into the cab of the truck. She ignored them and closed the door.

"A man's choice of transportation says a lot about him," she said as they pulled away.

"What does a used pickup say?"

"Well, first off, a Ford F-150 is not just a pickup. Anyone knows that. It says you look for performance and you want your money's worth. This is a popular model and has good resale value. But a pickup as your personal vehicle also says you are utilitarian. This is not just transportation. It serves other purposes. I'm trying to guess what use a federal judge with an historic home in the French Quarter would have for a truck. Do you have a garden?"

"Vestiges of one," he said. "At one time the house was known for its garden. It's mostly courtyard now, and I have someone who takes care of it. I just decided that I don't need a backseat and I do sometimes need to haul stuff around. Pretty simple, really; I don't think it reveals much about me."

"Give a girl a break. I'm trying to get to know you and I can't ask about the law or being a judge because you'd lose me in a minute."

"I've got an idea," Boucher said. "It's a little early for lunch. Let's go to my place first, have some coffee in the courtyard, then walk to a restaurant. You have to promise me, though, whatever you think my home reveals about my character, you have to share it. There's a piece of folk art that I can't figure out why I bought. Maybe it says something about me."

Her laugh fluttered in the compartment they shared, a perfect counterpart to the smooth jazz selection playing on the radio. The sun was out and warming the cab enough to invite lowering windows and letting the fullness of the delta air roll over them. In minutes, they were pulling into the driveway of Boucher's home. Dawn got out and stared.

"I've known this house since I was a little girl. This is one of the most beautiful homes in the Quarter." She turned to face him. "Jock, it's precious."

"Precious? What does that say about me?" He smiled and walked from the driver's side to stand next to her. He saw a familiar car driving slowly past, as Dawn stared at the home's façade. He walked her up to the porch and was not surprised to hear the phone ringing inside.

"Let me get that," he said, leaving her standing on the porch.

"How's it going?" Fitch asked. "Pretty well would be my guess. I didn't want to call you over to the car and get her curiosity up. It might have spoiled the mood. Considerate of me, don't you think?"

"Things are fine," Boucher said, his tone of voice indicating the timing of this phone call was not the best.

"I couldn't remember if I told you," Fitch said. "It was so damned obvious that everybody ignored it, me included. It might be nothing, but it's about that first lawyer's murder."

That was the inciting incident that had led to where he was now in every respect. "What is it?" he asked.

"The killer was left-handed," Fitch said. "I know from the angle of the gun pressed against the victim's skull."

"Why are you telling me this now?" Boucher asked.

"Because you're in the snake pit up to your neck, that's why. I want you to keep your eyes open, and you seem to be pretty observant about things like this. This is the second time this issue has come up. Remember, you pointed out to me that Ruth Kalin was *not* left-handed. Look, just be aware, that's all I'm saying, and watch out for lefties. Sorry to interrupt your afternoon."

Dawn was still staring at the colonnaded front porch. She commented on the unique period architecture, obviously well versed on the subject. He complimented her on this.

"New Orleans is my home," she said. "Anyone who lives here and does not become intimately acquainted with her history, especially her architecture, is missing so much. Are you going to show me inside, sir?"

"It would be my pleasure, ma'am." He offered his arm and she placed her hand in the crook of his elbow.

Boucher gave her the tour of his home. The folk art piece he'd spoken of was a carved sculpture made from mangrove roots. It stood four feet high and resembled black snakes twisting and writhing in agony, but on closer look one could see heads carved to reflect different creatures: an owl, a cat, and others. To most eyes it was hideous. He asked her opinion.

"It's your youth," Dawn said. "You grew up on the bayou; you loved it and felt at home there. If this piece of folk art didn't come from your own small town, it came from nearby or could have. It's a connection with your past. And, if it makes any difference, I like it.

I've always been attracted to Louisiana's bayous and the people who live there."

He saw the piece in a new light. "My dad did some carving. I never made the connection. I thought I was being daring since it is such a departure from everything else I've collected. Would you like some coffee?" he offered.

"Let's have it out back, please. I'm really looking forward to seeing your courtyard."

Boucher enjoyed her company. As the minutes passed, her beauty—of which he was most conscious—ceased to become a bar to the simple and enjoyable art of conversation. She even opened the door to a corner of his soul he had kept locked from the world, even from Malika. He spoke of the conflict he felt as a black man owning a home where slaves had lived. He had not even ventured into the slave quarters that looked down on the courtyard since he had bought the property.

"I sit down here, look up there, and all I can do is pray that they were treated well, that they lived decent lives," he said.

She took his hand in hers. "When you pray," she said, "give thanks for the changes in the world since those days. We are not responsible for the sufferings caused or endured by our ancestors. We are responsible for seeing those errors are not repeated—not here, not anywhere."

The hand she held, she brought to her lips, kissed it gently, then softly said, "I'm hungry."

"For anything in particular?"

"I have a sudden craving for oysters Rockefeller."

In New Orleans, when one has a yen for this famous dish, one goes to where it was invented.

Though it had been cool two days earlier, on this afternoon the sun was high and hot for late October, this being the time of year when any of the four seasons could be felt in a single day, sometimes more than one, from morning to evening. They walked from Boucher's house to St. Louis Street, to the oldest family-run restaurant in the entire country.

Established in 1840, Antoine's could reasonably claim to have served a member of all but the earliest of America's generations. For aficionados of New Orleans history, a better restaurant would have been hard to find. The lunchtime maître d' recognized Judge Boucher and hurried to greet him.

"Your Honor, it's good to see you." He recognized the judge's guest as well and greeted her even more formally, in keeping with customs established in this restaurant almost two centuries ago.

"Marcel," Boucher asked, "is the Mystery Room available?"

Antoine's contained fifteen dining rooms that seated from small groups to hundreds. The Mystery Room was the most intimate, having received its name during Prohibition days, when select clients would enter the room through a secret door and return to their tables with coffee cups full of hooch. When asked the source, they would reply, "It's a mystery to me." Hence the name. Boucher knew he did not need to regale Dawn with this anecdote. It was an urban legend she doubtless already knew.

"For you, Judge, I will open it personally."

"Thank you, Marcel. I have another request. We will be having oysters Rockefeller. Do you have time to walk us through the wine cellar and help us make an appropriate selection?"

"Of course, Your Honor."

Marcel was a sommelier and relished the chance to exhibit his expertise. The wine cellar was dark and dank—a good thing. Over twenty-five thousand bottles were stored in this treasure trove, but it didn't take long for a choice to be made.

"I'll think you'll like this," he said.

Boucher read the label: Didier Dagueneau Pouilly-Fumé, 2004. "This will be fine."

"Let me show you to your table."

The kiss came after the oysters, before the second glass of wine—which was of course a perfect accompaniment to the meal—the kiss *and* the wine. Great restaurants around the world offer private dining rooms and behind closed doors passions, like champagne, have been known to become uncorked, but this did not happen at Antoine's on this autumn afternoon. Conversation picked up where it had left off after the brief display of affection.

"Something's on your mind," Dawn said. "I can see it."

"You're perceptive. I was asking myself who kissed who just then."

"Does it matter?"

"If I kissed you, then I need to explain—"

She put a finger to his lips. "There's nothing to explain. It was just a kiss. If it makes you feel better, I think *I* kissed *you*. I know I wanted to."

"It's just that I've been seeing someone—" Again she hushed him. She looked around their private dining room, then at him.

"I don't see her in here. I don't see her in your eyes."

For the first time he noticed the color of Dawn's eyes: amber with flecks of gold. They were haunting, not unlike those of a wolf but radiating tenderness, not hunger. They were not threatening.

"I called her last night after I took you home," Boucher said.

"And what did you talk about?"

"That's just it. We didn't talk. She's in California, Napa Valley; working on a movie, or so she says. She was too busy to talk to me."

"Have you thought about letting go?"

Boucher leaned toward her. This time there was no doubt who kissed whom.

"I think I just did," he said.

There was a long silence, then glasses were raised, a silent toast to things living and dead.

"Do you trust your first impressions?" Boucher asked.

"I do, almost without exception. Why?"

"I'm battling with one."

"Since we've just met, can I assume this first impression has something to do with me?"

He nodded and refilled her wineglass. "I know I'm basing this on a very short period of time, but it seems to me that as a multilingual graduate of Wharton School of Business—"

"What am I doing serving coffee to executives, right?"

"I was going to say that you seem to be overqualified for your job—but I know my appearing on the scene has probably upset office routines. You told me you did . . . what was it?"

"I said I was responsible for SEC compliance. We are a publicly traded company and that involves a lot of work, but . . ." She sighed. "I do feel I'm overqualified for what I do. Mostly I fill out the same old forms." She sipped her wine. "But at least I'm overcompensated too. I am paid an obscene amount of money."

"I suppose overcompensation . . . compensates."

"I sold my soul a long time ago. I made my deal with the devil and I have to live with it. But it won't be forever. I'll have enough to retire early, move to the tropics, and take up painting."

"You would leave New Orleans?"

"Not necessarily. My dream is to have two homes in two different climates and flit between them as my mood and the weather dictate. Have you ever been to Puerto Vallarta?"

"Mexico?"

"Yes. Someday I'll have a home there. And should it come to that, yes, I would leave New Orleans. I think my days at Rexcon are numbered. I won't miss it."

The wine finished, Boucher called for the check and they left the restaurant.

Wine midday was something Boucher was definitely not accustomed to, and to walk it off they strolled to Jackson Square, made the perimeter, then sauntered back to his house.

"That was a wonderful lunch. Thank you," Dawn said. "Now I'm in charge of the rest of the day and it's going to be basic. First, we're going to my place and take a nap. For dinner I'm going to order a pizza and we'll watch a movie, *d'accord*?"

"*D'accord*."

When they were inside her home, she motioned him to the sofa. "It's more comfortable than it looks. I'm sure I don't need to tell you to take your shoes off."

"Yes, ma'am. I mean, no, ma'am."

Dawn excused herself and went to her own bedroom. After a few seconds she called to him.

"Jock, could you come here, please?"

She was standing in front of an open wall safe, fidgeting behind her with the clasp on her South Sea pearl necklace.

"Could you undo this? Be careful, it's very old."

He managed to unfasten it easily enough. She put her jewelry in the safe. "The combination is my birthday," Dawn said, "should you ever decide to become a cat burglar."

He chuckled, then excused himself. The bedroom door closed behind him as he walked to the living room and the couch assigned for his nap. Though his stockinged feet dangled over the edge, the sofa was comfortable and he dropped right off.

When he woke, late afternoon shadows were falling. In this temperate zone, seasonal temperatures varied, but the days grew short this time of year as they did everywhere in the Northern Hemisphere. He sat up and put on his shoes. Dawn stepped into the living area looking like a college coed. She wore what looked like black silk capri pants and a blue cotton oxford button-down shirt hanging loose, just like the one Boucher happened to be wearing. She wore brown penny loafers without socks. Little or no makeup, no jewelry; ready for an evening in.

"You stay here and make yourself at home. I'm going out and pick up some snacks." And she was gone.

With the house to himself, he stripped to his undershorts, pumped out a hundred push-ups and an equal number of sit-ups on the Persian carpet, then helped himself to a shower. He was fresh and clean and dry—and dressed—when she returned, a brown paper sack of groceries in her arm.

"I could have helped you with that," he said.

"It's just popcorn, and some Diet Cokes for me. I'll order the pizza when we're ready to eat." She went into the kitchen and yelled back, "I've got us a Denzel Washington movie. There's beer in the fridge."

He joined her in the kitchen and got himself a beer. "When do I get the tour?"

"How about right now? If you're not hungry, you will be after this excursion. This place is enormous."

That it was: seven thousand square feet of high-ceilinged rooms with detailed plaster and woodwork. The number of antiques—and their worth—was almost beyond calculation. The gardens outside were immaculate, with ornate cast-iron work throughout. As Dawn promised, covering the entire house and grounds did work up an appetite.

Little was said during dinner, and nothing during the movie. They both enjoyed it, but Dawn seemed pensive, distracted. She sat on the sofa with her legs folded under her in the lotus position, cradling a bowl of popcorn, which she ate methodically, one popped kernel at a time. Boucher was amazed she could maintain the position for the whole movie, but when it was over, she got up with ease. She took the empty popcorn bowls to the kitchen and returned. She stood before him and said, "If you'd like to stay the night, you're welcome to the guest room."

"How about breakfast tomorrow? We have the day off, remember?"

"Okay. Where?"

"Right here. I accept your offer. I'll take the guest room." He kissed her cheek and whispered good night.

He closed the bedroom door behind him and undressed. Spending the night under her roof might not be the smartest move, but he'd decided to go with his gut. There was something about her, something that got next to him and just sort of burrowed in. He felt she had something she wanted to say, and was weighing very carefully whether she should or not.

He pulled down the duvet and climbed between the sheets, turning off the bedside lamp. The door opened. He lay on the bed tense and rigid. If he was wrong about her, he was about to find out. Footsteps trod lightly on the hardwood floor; there was the rustle of sheets beside him. He flicked on the bedside lamp. Dawn stood naked at his bedside. He stared at her.

"I'm not the enemy," she whispered.

He turned down the cover and switched off the light. She slipped into bed. Her hand reached across his chest. He turned on his side and moved his head closer to the sound of her breathing till their lips met. His tongue pushed her teeth apart and she sucked it down her throat as if trying to consume him from the inside out. Their hands explored each other's bodies. She pulled him on top of her, raising her knees, kicking his buttocks with her heels as he entered her, nails digging deep into his back. Gasping for breath, she seemed to be suffocating, and he lifted his head. She pulled it back to hers, crushing his lips. His thrusts were deep and arrhythmic, accompanied by the percussion of her heels kicking him like a rider spurring a horse, urging him faster, faster. Then she sighed and collapsed beneath him. He was not finished, and his motions became more measured. He continued, speeding up slowly, and she began to move again with him. They ascended once more, now both gasping as the height of passion was reached. Exhausted, spent, he was dead weight on top of her for a long time before rolling off. Lying on his back, he felt her hand again caress his chest. He brought it to his mouth and kissed her fingertips. They fell asleep.

CHAPTER 25

T HE SUN STREAMING THROUGH the open slats of wooden shutters woke him and he reached over. Dawn was already up. He showered and shaved, pleased to find a full complement of toiletries for his morning ritual. Drawn by the fragrance of coffee and chicory, he found her in the kitchen, preparing breakfast with a no-nonsense focus on the task. He kissed her cheek. She motioned him to sit. The plate she served him was scrambled eggs with what looked like orange jelly beans on top.

"What's this?" he asked.

"Ikura. Salmon roe. Japanese caviar. It's better on the eggs than salt."

She brought a French press coffeepot and served them both. For herself, she spread the salmon roe on a piece of toast. He tasted his eggs and nodded his approval, sipped the coffee and pronounced it delicious.

"Now," she said, "we're over the preliminaries. Tell me what you're doing at Rexcon. There's something funny about this picture."

"You can't tell me they haven't briefed you about me," Boucher said.

"I was told to observe and report. That's all."

"You're not going to report everything, I hope."

"Cute." She bit a half-moon out of her toast. "Please answer me, Jock."

"I am providing some technical information that came into my possession, that's all—and getting handsomely paid for it."

She studied him. "I don't see that in you. There's something you're not telling me. That's okay. Just know that I know." She sipped her coffee, then said, "So, will you tell me why you aren't being a judge right now?"

"I will," he said. "I may be disillusioned, I may be unfit. I decided to take some time off to decide for myself. That is the truth."

"Good enough for me," she said, then stood up and walked to the refrigerator. "Do you like blueberries?"

After breakfast, as Dawn showered and dressed, he walked the gardens. When he got to the farthest corner he turned on his cell phone. Palmetto's smiling face was on the small screen.

"So, what's new?" Palmetto asked.

"I thought you might have something new for me. No, wait, I talked with Detective Fitch yesterday. He said that Dexter Jessup's murderer was left-handed."

"Jesus, it took the cops twenty years to discover that?"

"Don't blame him. It wasn't his case."

"So we're down to only ten percent of the world's population as suspects. We've eliminated ninety percent. That's something, I guess."

"It also eliminates Judge Epson. He was right-handed."

Palmetto paused. "You know what that means," he said.

"Yeah, the killer is still out there. We already knew that."

"That's right. What's on your program for today?"

"Nothing. I have the day off. Tomorrow they're giving me the tour of their lab."

"I'll be with you every step of the way on that trip. Well, I leave you in good hands. By the way, she just called her boss from her cell. She told him you were 'conflicted' about being a judge. You tell her that?"

"Don't tell me you can eavesdrop on her with this thing while you're talking to me."

"Isn't science grand? You have a fun day. I assume you'll be home tonight. Please keep your phone with you. Don't forget to charge it."

He put the phone in his pocket and returned to the house. Dawn stood in the kitchen waiting for him. She was brushing her hair, dressed only in a terry-cloth robe.

"There's something important I want to tell you," she said. "Not now, but in my own time."

"I'm a good listener," he said. "It's what judges do best."

They stayed together till late afternoon: making love, making conversation, and making grilled cheese sandwiches. When he pulled into his own drive Boucher imagined Malika, as she had stood on the porch waiting for him, but then he remembered her breathlessness the last time he'd spoken with her; when she was with her "client" and he could picture so clearly what they'd been doing. He banished her from his thoughts as he opened his front door.

That evening Boucher received what Palmetto told him was the last meaningful information he would be sending him. Future information transfers would contain less valuable data. Boucher would have to find what he was looking for soon. He studied the material for lack of anything better to do, knowing that the technical information would work on him better than a sleeping pill. He was right. Before nine-thirty he was in bed asleep.

Perry and Cantrell were not asleep. They were holed up in Perry's office like wolves in a cave, the solitary lamp on his desk casting more shadows than light. They were ranting against their number one nemesis and favorite target—governmental regulatory agencies.

"One of these days, they'll be *begging* me to take their fuckin' leases and I'm going to tell them to stick it. Who needs them?" Perry motioned an obscenity with one hand, slamming a flat palm on his desk with the other.

"How are you going to do it?" he asked.

"The judge? You don't want to know," Cantrell answered.

"You're right. I don't."

Then silence.

"She signs her name 'C.D.,'" Perry said.

"What?"

"C.D. Stands for Carla Dawn. She doesn't like Carla. C. D. Fallon."

"Big deal."

"C.D. stands for something else, I'm afraid."

"What's that?"

"Collateral damage."

Cantrell looked at him. "You sure you want that?"

Perry shrugged. "She likes the guy. He disappears, she might get curious."

"She's been a good scout," Cantrell said.

"C.D. Collateral damage. Take her with you."

Cantrell shrugged. "Doesn't matter to me."

CHAPTER 26

ARLY TO BED, EARLY to rise. Boucher woke before dawn and got in almost an hour of calisthenics before going to the office. He beat Dawn; he even beat the receptionist. He walked the halls of the executive warren, poking his head first into Cantrell's office, then Perry's. Nobody home. He walked to his own office. Somebody had moved his desk back to its original position. He wouldn't complain about it. This little act would soon be over anyway. He sat down. An image came to mind and he froze, eyes wide open like saucers. He stood up and ran from his office down the plush carpeted hallway back to Cantrell's office. Hanging on his ego wall were pictures of him accepting various awards for distinction in his field, awards going back decades. Earlier photos showed a younger man with darker, fuller hair. But though the subject aged, one characteristic remained unchanged: the manner in which he accepted these honors bestowed upon him. Bert Cantrell was left-handed.

Boucher ran from the office through the double doors that led to the reception area and the elevator bank. He pressed the call button and waited, and waited. Finally it arrived and it was like being pushed back by a tidal wave. It seemed that everyone who worked on this floor had arrived at the same moment and had taken the same elevator up. Dawn and the receptionist got out first, followed by two men he did not know, and last came Perry and Cantrell. Boucher's escape to make his phone call was impossible. Perry shook his hand and slapped him on the back. Cantrell threw an unwanted arm around his shoulder.

"Wait till you see what I'm going to show you today," Cantrell said. "You too, Dawn. Come along with us. I'm going to show you both our laboratory. You're going to see a glimpse of what is going to fuel this country's growth for the next two hundred years."

He herded Boucher back to his office and ordered Dawn to bring coffee as if she were a waitress in a cheap diner, calling her "hon." He sat down heavily behind his desk. His look was menacing for so early in the morning. Then he caught himself and his expression softened.

"I hate waste," he said.

Where the hell is this going? Boucher wondered.

"I hate to see our position as the best damn country in the world wasting away. I hate to see a resource that could ensure our energy independence wasted. And I hate that fucking bureaucrats are keeping us from exploiting the biggest hydrocarbon resource in the world. But they'll be sorry. Just you wait and see. There weren't any fuckin' regulators at Spindletop. We're gonna have a Spindletop all over again. You know what Spindletop is, right?"

"It was the first big strike in the East Texas oil fields, in 1902, I believe."

"It was 1901; beginning of the modern oil industry. Well, it's time for a new beginning. Today you're going to be one of the first to see what the future holds for this country and the world."

Dawn arrived with coffee.

"You too," Cantrell said, a little too loud. "You're both going to see the *fucking future!*"

"Did you get any sleep last night, Mr. Cantrell?" Dawn asked. "You look exhausted."

"I slept just fine. Let me just finish this coffee, then we'll go."

"I've had mine," Boucher said. "Excuse me for a minute. I'll be right back."

He went to the men's room, waited for someone to wash his hands and leave, then made a call despite what Palmetto had told him about not making calls within the building. No answer. Voice mail. He left a brief message. "Tell Fitch. Bert Cantrell, senior VP and chief geologist of Rexcon, is left-handed." The door opened and he slipped the phone in his shirt pocket. It was Cantrell. Boucher stepped to the sink and turned on the faucet as the senior vice president took a leak.

"Say, why don't we all grab a meal together when we're done at the lab?" Cantrell asked. "Anyplace you like. It'll be my treat."

"That's fine with me, if you're feeling up to it," Boucher said.

"I'm okay. John and I spent most of last night cussing the damn government. Woke up with a bit of a hangover."

As he watched him, Boucher realized that Cantrell had shot Dexter Jessup. He had shot Ruth Kalin and had put the gun in her left hand because, left-handed himself, he'd not thought twice about it. It was his normal.

Dawn offered to drive. A Cadillac rolling on an open four-lane can lull both infants and energy titans to sleep before you can say "hush-a-bye." Cantrell snored loudly and took up the entire backseat. Boucher rode shotgun. They were heading west.

"Where are we going?" Boucher asked, keeping his voice down.

"Sleeping beauty told me to wake him ten miles from Morgan City," Dawn said. "Gateway to the Gulf for the shrimp and oil industries."

"Good place for a lab, I guess."

"As good as any. Do you have any idea what they're going to show us?"

"It will have something to do with methane hydrate, but beyond that I'm guessing."

Cantrell woke with a snort and told Dawn to pull over. He got out, then got behind the wheel.

They passed an empty marina. Every single shrimp boat was out in the Gulf. Numerous oil field equipment manufacturing and service companies dotted the side of the road. On the outskirts of the small town Cantrell turned onto a secondary road leading through swampland, finally coming to a single-story structure bearing the company's name. There was one other car in the parking lot.

"Where is everybody?" Dawn asked.

"We gave them the day off to celebrate," Cantrell said. "These folks are going to be working overtime now that we're beginning our offshore program."

"You're starting your offshore program?" Boucher asked.

Cantrell ignored him. He parked the Cadillac and led them into the building. A man in a white coat came up to greet them. He looked like a scientist, if one associated clammy handshakes and pasty white skin that never saw the sun with the profession.

The lab had looked smaller from outside. It was huge, almost the size of a football field, with glassed-in cubicles of various sizes around the entire perimeter. In many of them equipment could be seen, their functions a mystery to the uninitiated. Cantrell called a lab technician over to him and the two conversed outside the hearing of Boucher and Dawn. Boucher turned his back to them all and took out his phone. He checked his text messages. The first was from Fitch. Boucher's observation was confirmed: *Cantrell. Gun permit 1988. S&W .38 Model 10. Modified for LH.* The second message was from Palmetto. *Weak signal. Where are you?*

In deep shit, that's where I am, Boucher thought.

Cantrell approached them, a big smile on his face.

"Are you ready for your tour?"

He led them first to a pressurized unit, a sign outside identifying it. It had a double entry. The first door, when one entered, closed and sealed automatically. Only then could one access the second door. They entered through it and were hit with a temperature below freezing.

"We'll just be here a few minutes. There are lab coats hanging on the wall if you want one."

Was he kidding? Dawn and Boucher each grabbed one immediately and put them on, though the coats didn't help much. Cantrell opened a huge stainless steel door and a gray smokelike mist escaped from a laboratory refrigerator in this already freezing compartment. He came out with a chunk of ice the size of a baseball, which he set on a counter. From his pocket he pulled a cigarette lighter. He set the ice ablaze. It was enshrouded in a wavy blue flame that seemed to induce a hypnotic trance the longer one stared. Boucher had seen this display and had to feign amazement. Dawn's astonishment was real.

"Ice on fire," she whispered.

"Yes, dear," Cantrell said. "That's what it is. The future of energy. That small clump will burn for hours."

"Can we watch it burn from outside?" Boucher asked, his teeth chattering.

Cantrell gave him a dismissive look, then led them out of the pressurized unit.

"Don't think I'm not impressed," Boucher said. "It's just that I have a low tolerance for extreme cold."

Cantrell smiled. It was an option he hadn't considered. That was the beauty of an industrial laboratory, one had so many choices.

CHAPTER 27

FITCH HAD ALWAYS HATED the New Orleans police evidence room on Magnolia Street, even before Katrina. But after the hurricane, with the storage facility underwater for eighteen days, he knew it was a lost cause and despised it even more. Now here he was, asking a poor beleaguered flunky in the twilight of his years about a twenty-year-old piece of evidence that might never have been found in the first place. He felt sorry for the guy. The hurricane wasn't his fault and the place had always been a mess. Now legislators were kicking up a fuss, demanding an audit and trying to pin the blame for the chaotic conditions anywhere but on themselves and their misplaced budget priorities. The drug cases were hopeless. Cocaine underwater for three weeks? Yeah, take that bag of glue to the courtroom. But a bullet doesn't turn to glue when soaked. Maybe even covered with rust the rifling can be saved and a bullet matched with the gun that fired it. A needle in a haystack was nothing compared to the task he'd set for himself. But here he was.

"Jesus, Detective, I'd like to help you, but look at this." The custodian held up a handful of requisitions. "Everybody wants everything yesterday and I don't know where to even begin to look for most of the stuff they want. This place is fucked. It's just fucked."

"Calm down," Fitch said. "I'm not here to bust your balls. I know it's a long shot. Would you mind if I looked for myself?"

"Mind? Hell, no, I wouldn't mind. But if you find anything, don't touch it. Call me. I've got both prosecutors and defense lawyers trying to hang my butt screaming that I screwed up chain-of-custody records." He opened the chain metal door and let him into the criminal evidence storage area. "You gotta wear this," he said, handing Fitch a surgical face mask. "We got some nasty shit growing back there."

"Where should I start?" Fitch asked.

"On a case twenty years old? Over there." He pointed vaguely to the right rear corner of the facility. "At least that's where I would have looked ten years ago."

The first thing Fitch noticed was the variety of fungi growing everywhere, on everything: on plastic, on metal. Cardboard boxes, the preferred container, were decomposing on every shelf. First the adhesive dissolved, then the sides fell and hung limp, the layers separating and rotting. Plastic, he read somewhere, took a hundred years to decay. Well, whoever said that should see this place. Even plastic containers were dissolving. And money: cash confiscated in the commission of a crime was often crucial evidence. If any was stored here, it was now dust and mold spores. After two hours he had to get out. He could hardly breathe. He walked back to the custodian.

"I need air," he said. "How do you stand it in here?"

"Six more weeks, then full pension," the man said. "I'm going to fish every goddamned day for the rest of my life."

"Brother, you've earned it."

Fitch stepped outside and, before even taking a breath of air, lit up a cigarette and drew deeply. He figured tobacco smoke had a better chance of killing any fungus in his lungs than a gulp of fresh air did. He smoked it down to the filter, then for good measure lit a second and smoked it before going back in.

He was going to find that bullet or satisfy himself that it did not exist.

Fascinating as it was, Boucher was getting tired of staring at the blue flame and the ice fire. Also, he noticed that the lab technician was nowhere in sight. He took off the lab coat he'd grabbed on the way in and Dawn did the same.

"If that's what we came to see, I say thank you for the tour and let's get on back home."

"Well," Cantrell said, "I was going to show you what we've been able to construct with carbon fiber, but you're right, it's time we moved along." He yelled, "How's it going in there?"

"We're all set." The lab technician's voice came from one of the peripheral cubicles.

"Let's go," Cantrell said, turning to face Dawn and Boucher. In his left hand he held a Smith & Wesson Model 10 Military and Police revolver. Pointed at them.

"Bert," Dawn gasped, "have you gone mad?"

"Sorry," he said. "Including you on this little picnic was Perry's idea. I can't even claim credit for the manner in which you are about to die. I have to admit I'm surprised it turned out to be so damned easy. Turn around and walk over to Mr. Quillen. He's not exactly a scientist, but he's very proficient at his specialty. I understand he's prepared something unique for you."

The lab Cantrell ushered them into was kept at normal temperature. The room was empty except for two folding metal chairs and a large stainless steel vat in its center. Beside the vat stood the man wearing the lab coat. Whatever was in the vat was fuming and gave off a familiar, suffocating odor.

"The king of chemicals," Cantrell said, "sulfuric acid. This batch is concentrated; very efficient. You know the beauty of using sulfuric acid? It has the broadest industrial use of any chemical; that's why they call it the king. It's perfectly natural for a company like ours to keep it in large quantities. It won't arouse the slightest suspicion. And there won't be the slightest trace of you left. It's almost humane. You'll dissolve in no time. This was Mr. Quillen's idea. I must say, he's far more creative than I am. A shot to the head is about the limit of my imagination."

"Like with Dexter Jessup and Ruth Kalin," Boucher said.

Cantrell shrugged.

"I suppose he was responsible for Judge Epson's death." Boucher nodded to the man in the white coat.

Cantrell shrugged again, a slight smile on his lips. "Okay, twenty questions is over."

Boucher said, "Why her?"

"Because she's fulfilled her purpose," Cantrell said. "Well, almost. I plan to have a little fun myself before we dump her in the pot. You go first, Judge. Just step on one of those chairs and climb in. If you don't, I'll shoot you and dump you in myself. But death will be immediate if you dive in headfirst. Don't worry about the lady, she'll be following you soon enough."

Boucher realized that a well-placed shot could bring death quickly as well, but Cantrell had shown no abilities as a marksman. His kills were contact shots. A bad shot could just mess him up and they'd still dump him in.

"Can I have a moment with Dawn?"

"Aw, isn't that sweet? No. Get on that chair."

Boucher walked to the chair and picked it up by its back to move it closer to the vat. As he did this, his cell phone beeped its warning that the battery was low.

"Give me that," Cantrell said. "I want to know who you've been talking to."

Boucher handed Cantrell his phone, holding it in both his hands, raising them till they were parallel with Cantrell's—one reaching, the other holding the gun. Boucher whipped his hands apart as he dropped the phone, spreading his arms, striking Cantrell on both wrists, then bringing his left around into a roundhouse punch, landing a glancing blow to Cantrell's chin as Cantrell got off a wild shot. Boucher grabbed the nearest chair, raised it, and slammed it down on Cantrell's head. Cantrell collapsed to the floor unconscious. Quillen rushed toward Boucher, his arms spread out from his sides like a wrestler. Boucher reached down, picked up the cell phone, and threw it, striking Quillen in the forehead, just above the bridge of his nose, knowing that there is a more ample blood supply in the face than any other part of the body. Blood gushed from the wound and filled Quillen's eyes. Dawn pounced on the bleeding man like a leopard, pulling his hands from his face, then digging her long nails deep into his eye sockets. Quillen screamed with the pain and terror of sudden blindness. Cantrell was coming to, his gun in his hand.

"*Run!*" Boucher yelled to Dawn. She bolted for the exit and he followed. Cantrell was groggy, but rising to his feet. He got off a shot as Boucher was out the door, slamming it shut behind him.

Dawn was standing in the parking lot waiting for him, the look on her face wild with fright. Boucher ran toward her and grabbed her hand. They ran to the road and crossed it, running across the field on the other side. Beyond the field was swamp. They kept running. Cantrell was behind them. He fired again. Reaching the first line of mangroves, Boucher jumped into the brackish chocolate-brown water. He sank to his knees. Dawn stood hesitating on the bank, wondering which was the better way to die. To be shot? To die of a poisonous snakebite—or as a gator's supper? She stood there weighing uniformly unpleasant options as Boucher held out his hand.

"Come on," he said. "I was born on the bayou. We'll be okay."

Dawn leapt and landed with a splash. They began to plod the muddy bottom, and of course she lost her shoes with the first two steps.

"Climb onto my back," Boucher said, and he carried her piggyback.

They had disappeared in the mangroves before Cantrell reached the point where they had jumped. He wasn't about to do the same. He yelled out, "You won't get far. You'll die in the swamp, but you're sure as hell going to die."

"No, we're not," Boucher whispered. "This is a walk in the park for me."

They slogged through the bayou. The water was mostly waist-deep but sometimes up to Boucher's chest. He stopped and stood still. "Shhh," he said, but Dawn could see nothing.

"Why are you shushing?" she asked.

"Water moccasin," he said, and she saw the tip of its head and the S wake on the water's surface. An hour or more passed. Afternoon shadows were lengthening. As frightening as it was earlier, the bayou's terror increased as darkness descended. Boucher stopped again, under a large mangrove tree.

"We need to get out of the water. Can you reach that branch?"

"If you can lift me up."

"Climb onto my shoulders."

He steadied her. She stepped onto his shoulders and grabbed the branch.

"I've got you. Now pull yourself up and swing your legs over. That's it. Good. Now sit there. No, don't slide towards the trunk. I'm going to climb there."

Boucher tree-walked, climbing, pulling himself up the trunk to the branch where Dawn sat. He positioned himself with his back to the trunk and spread his legs on both sides of the branch.

"Now slide yourself over here and very carefully turn around. I want you to rest your back against my chest and relax. We're going to be here awhile."

She did as instructed and Boucher wrapped his arms around her. Dawn caressed his arm and began to cry.

"It's all right." He kissed the back of her head. "We're safe here."

"I was thinking about where we might have been."

CHAPTER 28

FITCH BEGAN A FIT of coughing he couldn't stop. Four hours in the fungus, mold, and slime of the evidence room was beyond his endurance. He bent over with the wracking cough. That's when he saw it. In a gray plastic tray like restaurants used to carry dirty dishes, he saw a tag that read 1990. He recognized the case file number. There was a clear plastic bag that contained the remains of bloodied clothing, rotten with mildew. And a smaller one that held an object that looked like a brown pebble. He picked up the bag and examined it. It was the bullet.

He called out. "Hey! Come on back here."

The custodian joined him. "Find something?"

"Yeah. Can you put this tray someplace where it won't get lost and just sign out this single bag to me?"

"Sure, Detective. I just have to remind you to keep it secured. Chain of custody and all that."

"Don't worry. It's going straight to the lab."

"Glad you found what you were looking for. You're one of the few."

"Sometimes you get lucky," he said.

The evidence was signed out to him and, as promised, Fitch took it directly to the lab. He smoked three cigarettes in transit and bought himself a fresh pack before returning to his office. It was going to take a lot of smoke to drive out all the crud he'd breathed in today. He was accosted as soon as he entered.

"Got some wild man been calling for you," the duty sergeant said. "His name's Palmetto. Something about Judge Boucher."

Fitch ran to his office. He called the number given, not recognizing the area code. Palmetto answered on the first ring and identified himself and his connection to Boucher. Fitch knew who he was.

"I can't reach Boucher," Palmetto said. "I think he's in trouble."

"I'll look into it right away," Fitch said.

The dispatcher's office had the GPS receiver. The signal was clear.

"Where the hell is it coming from?" Fitch asked the dispatcher.

"Somewhere near Morgan City; actually, somewhere in the swamp near Morgan City. It's been stationary for some time. If your man's in the bayou and he ain't moving, I'd say he's got a problem."

"I want a chopper," Fitch said. "Now."

They were too scared to sleep, so there was little worry about nodding off and falling into the water. Boucher could feel Dawn trembling and tried to comfort her.

"Did you know the first Tarzan movie was made in this very swamp? Shot in 1918, starring Elmo Lincoln. Elmo was one of the early stars of the silent screen."

"You're a font of local lore," she said. "You wouldn't happen to know where the nearest bus stop is, would you?" Dawn didn't need to ask if they were really safer precariously propped in a tree; the chomping of jaws and splashing of tails in the dark convinced her.

"They sound like they're having a feeding frenzy," she whispered.

"They're fighting over something," Boucher said; then, "Shhh, listen."

It was the sound of a high-pitched motor. Beams of light were splayed on the water's surface and into the mangroves.

"Airboat," he said.

"Good guys or bad guys?"

"I think it's the bad guys."

"Jock, I want to turn around. I'd rather be facing you if they're coming for us."

"Actually," he said, "that's not a bad idea. Less light reflecting from your back than from your face."

He held her by the waist as she swung one leg over, then the other. They were inches apart. She stared into his eyes. Then she buried her face in his neck and sobbed.

"Those horrible men," she murmured.

The engine of the airboat continued its whine. It was moving slowly, getting closer. Searchlights could be seen: one from the bow of the boat, another from portside, fanning the trees. If he could see the lights through the branches, the lights could find them. A beam splayed on a nearby tree, then inched closer till it rested on them. They heard men yelling. And something else: the unmistakable sound of the rotary blades of a helicopter chopping through the air. Another searchlight split the night. The copter was approaching rapidly. An airboat *and* a copter? He and Dawn didn't have a chance. But the airboat's motor began revving up. It was backing away. Men were shouting. There was a single shot as they departed.

The helicopter was soon overhead, its intense searchlight burning pockets of bright light into the dark swamp. A voice called out over an amplifier.

"Boucher, this is Fitch. We chased them away and have teams down there looking for you. One will be by in a few minutes. Stay where you are."

The cavalry had arrived. He held Dawn to him and whispered, "We're safe now. Everything's going to be all right."

She didn't move, her face still buried in his shoulder. He lifted her head. "Dawn?"

Her eyes were closed, her breath shallow. Near the center of her back he felt warm liquid oozing between his fingers. "Oh God, no."

The police airboat arrived minutes later. He called out and they came to him.

"She's been shot," he said as he lowered Dawn down to outstretched arms. "Get that helicopter back here with a doctor on board."

He jumped onto the flat deck. The airboat backed up, then sped away as quickly as uncertain waters and the dark of night would permit. Overhead the copter was looking for a place to land. It was flying low and the wash from its props whipped up the surface of the bayou, soaking the passengers in the airboat. Boucher leaned over Dawn, protecting her from the spray. The chopper found an open spot and settled to earth. The airboat nosed to the bank. An officer jumped ashore and the woman's limp body was handed to him. No stretcher, he cradled her in his arms. Boucher jumped ashore and ran beside them, holding her hand.

Fitch was waiting in the helicopter. "We've got a doctor waiting in Morgan City," he hollered above the wind from the rotary blades. "We'll pick him up and get her to the closest trauma center."

Dawn was lifted in, Boucher jumped aboard, and they were away. The small clinic was near the docks where dozens of shrimp boats were moored, it being a few more hours before they would begin their day. The doctor was waiting in the empty parking lot. He was a big man, at least two hundred and fifty pounds. Somehow at this hour he had managed to commandeer several cars whose headlights illuminated a landing space for the chopper.

"You and me are going to have to get off here," Fitch yelled in Boucher's ear as the copter landed. "This bird won't hold all of us."

Reluctantly, Boucher jumped off. Both he and Fitch helped the large man board, and it was a job. He waved, then went to work. The helicopter lifted off. Boucher watched it fly away till there was no more sight or sound.

"You want to talk about it?" Fitch asked.

"No. Find out where they're taking her and get me there."

The Morgan City Police Department assigned them a car and driver to drive them back to New Orleans. Dawn was taken to the Spirit of Charity Level 1 Trauma Center at the Interim LSU Public Hospital on Perdido Street. She was still in surgery when they arrived, and though various members of the emergency team exited and entered the operating theater, their intense expressions made it clear they had no time for questions and answers. Finally a surgeon walked from the theater and approached them.

"Are you family?"

"I'm Detective Fitch, NOPD, and this is Federal District Judge Boucher. We're friends."

"Does she have family?"

"No," Boucher said. "Her parents are deceased and her brother was killed in Iraq. How is she?"

"Her condition is extremely serious." The doctor wrinkled his nose. The federal judge standing in front of him smelled like a sewer and looked like he'd been living in one. "Are you all right, sir?"

"I'm fine. I'll clean up later. I don't want to leave her."

The doctor nodded. "We'll keep you informed of her status. I'll see to it personally." He started to walk away, then turned back around. "Is your name Jock?"

"Yes."

"She kept asking for you. Look, clean up and get into surgical gear. You should be prepared to see her. If it comes to that."

"I will. Thank you, Doctor."

Boucher was shown to a room where he stripped off his slimy clothes and showered away layers of filth. A surgical gown, gloves, sterile foot covers, and mask were laid out for him. He put them on and waited. And waited.

The doctor who'd spoken to him earlier burst into the room. "Come on," he said, "quickly." They rushed into the operating theater.

Dawn lay on her stomach. A spotlight hung from a spiral cord above her, now turned off. The doctor nudged him to the head of the bed and he knelt down to be at her eye level. He wanted to touch her. He brushed her cheek with a finger encased in the sterile glove. She opened her eyes. They were two slits, but she saw and recognized him. There was a tear in one eye, only one. Then her eyes closed. Forever.

"I'm sorry," the doctor said. He wanted to say more. He wanted to say that the wound was too severe; that she had lost too much blood; that it took too long to get her here. But all he could say was, "I'm sorry."

Boucher stood up. The doctor put a hand on his shoulder. "She said some things as we prepped her for surgery," he said. "I don't know what she meant, maybe you will. She said, 'Get him.' I assume she was talking about whoever shot her, and she kept trying to spell something but couldn't get beyond the first three letters. She kept saying over and over, 'D-o-b.' Did she know someone whose name began with those letters?"

"I don't know," Boucher said.

Wearing borrowed scrubs, he retrieved his wallet and keys from his filthy clothes, then called for a cab to take him home. As he reached the Quarter, in the sky was the first hint of morning.

CHAPTER 29

FITCH CALLED HIM AT noon. It was as much time for grieving as he could give, being a cop with a new homicide.

"You up for it?" he asked.

"As long as you do the driving."

"Not after the night I had. We've got a driver."

They sat in the backseat of the patrol car, on the same route Boucher had taken just one day earlier. Fitch, in the one gesture of respect he could grant, asked no questions as they drove. They came to Rexcon's lab, the parking lot empty.

"Where is everybody?" Boucher asked, certain they had not been given another day off.

"Thing is, this place really isn't operational," Fitch said. "There's a security guard—he'd been given the day off yesterday—and when he came in today he told us they just bought this place a few months ago and from what he understood the company was just beginning to hire staff for a new project."

They walked inside, ducking under the yellow crime scene tape.

"Cantrell got away," Boucher said; impossible to tell if he was asking a question or making a statement.

"We'll get him."

"There was another guy here, a real sicko, name's Quillen. He had the idea to give us an acid bath. Dawn jumped him as I decked Cantrell. I think she may have scratched his eyes out. He was blinded and bleeding last I saw him."

"Plucky lady."

"Yes, she was."

Fitch sighed. "We got the bullet that killed her. It was a 30.06, common rifle caliber."

"Too much to hope that it was a .38."

"They wouldn't have used a pistol at that range. But that reminds me. I found the bullet that killed Dexter Jessup twenty years ago. Of course, finding the gun that shot it is probably impossible after so long."

Boucher stared at him. "But if you could find another bullet fired from the same gun . . ."

"Well, yeah, but . . ."

"Cantrell fired two shots in here. I hit him with the chair and he got off a wild shot, then another shot at me as I ran outside." He looked around. "They're somewhere in the walls or ceiling."

Fitch pulled out his cell phone and made a call, setting an investigatory team in motion.

"Has anyone called Perry?" Boucher asked.

"I called his office this morning. His assistant said he was out of town. I told her to have him call me the minute he gets back. You can bet he'll have alibis up the ass. He's probably meeting with lawyers right now."

"Where could Quillen have gone?" Boucher asked. "He was blind, this place is isolated."

Fitch walked to the vat and called to Boucher. "Come here." One of the metal folding chairs was placed next to it and was bloodstained.

Fitch climbed up on the chair and peered into the reeking cauldron, nearly choking from the fumes. He stepped back down.

"There's blood on the side like he was feeling his way. There's blood on the chair like he was climbing up, and there's blood on the rim. If he was a contract killer and your friend scratched his eyes out, I'd say that didn't leave him much of a future to contemplate, wouldn't you?"

"You think he fell on his sword?"

"That's too noble an expression for a shit-heel like him. I think he took the only way out, the way he had prepared for you. If there's anything left of him in that gumbo, we'll find it."

Boucher paced the floor, looking down.

"What are you looking for?" Fitch asked.

"I threw my cell phone at Quillen. It struck him in the forehead, he bled. That's when Dawn jumped him. It's not here. They must have come back for it."

"Just for a cell phone?"

"It wasn't just a cell phone. Cantrell said he wanted to know who I'd been talking to. The phone has a record of all my calls. They're going to find out Palmetto's alive. I've got to warn him. I'd like to get back home if we're done here," Boucher said.

"Sure. Let's get you back."

"Can I borrow your phone?" Boucher asked as they stepped outside. Fitch handed it to him and he punched in the numbers.

"Palmetto? Jock Boucher. Dawn's dead. It was Cantrell and a psycho named Quillen. They've got my phone, Bob. That means they know you're alive and they can locate you. Call the police up there. Tell them if they have any questions . . ." He looked at Fitch. Fitch nodded. "Tell them to call Detective Fitch, Eighth District. I'm on my way back to my place." He shut the phone.

Though they'd not spoken on the way there, Fitch found the silence on their return uncomfortable.

"I'm sorry about your friend, but you've got to pull it together," he said. "This thing isn't over yet."

"I know that. I was just thinking about what she said. 'Get him.' And she was trying to spell something that started with the letters *d-o-b*."

"She was in shock, near death, and anesthetized. Forget what the doc thought he heard."

"What about Perry?"

"Unless Cantrell turns on him, he'll probably skate."

"Not while I'm alive," Boucher said.

The patrol car stopped in front of Boucher's house. As Boucher got out of the car, Fitch asked him, "You pay your taxes?"

"What kind of a question is that?"

"Because you're going to get your money's worth, starting today. I'm putting a twenty-four-hour stakeout on your place."

"I don't want them parked in front of my house."

"You won't see them, but they'll be close by."

Boucher gazed at his block for a suitable observation post.

"Don't worry," Fitch said, "I'll get the best, and I'll stand some of the duty myself."

Boucher clasped Fitch's hand between both of his. "Thanks."

"It's my job. You're the key witness. I want you to stay home, get plenty of rest. No restaurants. You want to order in, you call us and we'll pick it up."

"So I'm a prisoner in my own home."

"You're breaking my heart. You're more like a bird in a gilded cage, I'd say."

"How long?"

"Until we find Cantrell. I'll let you know."

"Visitors?"

"Clear them with me first."

"Just like prison."

"It's nothing like prison, and you know it."

The patrol car pulled away. Boucher climbed the steps to his front porch. It was like he was wearing lead shoes. He turned the key in the lock and opened the door. His antique collectibles, a décor and an ambience he had spent years trying to create. Fitch was right: this was no prison. This was his home and he was free to enjoy it. Closing the front door behind him, he faced an early-nineteenth-century Regency period rosewood sofa table, raised on lyre-shaped gadrooned end supports joined by a shaped stretcher and ending on scrolled legs with foliate carved block feet. He had memorized the description from the auction program when he first bought it and remembered it verbatim. It stood behind a George III–style camelback sofa with its original frame. A nineteenth-century American rosewood turtle top coffee table; a mahogany George III dining table and chairs; he could go on and on. Boucher had taken such pleasure and pride in restoring this house and furnishing it. He walked to the sofa, sat, leaned back, and the tears flowed.

The knock on the door was unexpected. He looked at his watch. His grief-stricken trance had lasted hours. Through the beveled smoked cut-glass inserts he could make out the shadows of two men. He walked to the door.

"Who is it?" he demanded.

"I'm Officer Peabo, NOPD," one voice said. "I've got this guy here with me. Detective Fitch said if you don't recognize him I'm to take him directly to jail."

Boucher opened the door. A disheveled Palmetto stood before him.

"I know him," Boucher said to the patrolman as he looked up and down the street to see if there were any observers standing around. He grabbed Palmetto's arm and pulled him inside. "Thank you, Officer.

"What are you doing here?" he asked.

"If Cantrell thinks I'm in New England, this will be the last place he'll expect to find me. I also thought I'd join your security detail. Another volunteer can't hurt. I hope you've got a place for me to stay."

"Sure. That's no problem. Actually, it's probably not a bad idea. There are guards posted somewhere on the block. I guess we're both about as safe here as anywhere. The guest bedroom is upstairs. You want to get some sleep? You look exhausted."

"I am. You kept half the folks at the Institute up last night. Let me go dump my things and I'll be right back."

Palmetto could barely lift his feet to the next stair as he climbed to the second floor and the guest bedroom. A toilet flushed, water ran, then he returned, his hands gripping the railing as he descended. He looked so frail, Boucher thought, but there was no weakness in his voice.

"How are you doing?" he asked when he got to the bottom of the stairs.

"Not great," Boucher said. "Dawn took a bullet that was meant for me. I shouldn't have let that happen."

"I know the feeling. Dexter murdered all those years ago, then Ruth Kalin. I carry the guilt of their deaths. We've got to put a stop to this bloody rampage." Palmetto held on to the banister for support, or perhaps it was to keep his hand from shaking. "I think Cantrell's close by. I don't think he's running and I don't think he's looking for me. He and I are both obsessed with the same thing and he's not going to let it go when he's this close. He's going to come after you again. You're still in his way."

"We both are."

"That's right. So I'm here to help."

"I guess I should thank you."

"You've got just as much reason to curse me. I'm sorry I got you into all this."

Palmetto stepped away from the stairs and into the living room. He ran his hand lightly over a few pieces of furniture before he sat down in front of the unlit fireplace and stared at two centuries of soot. His muttered words didn't carry.

"What did you say?" Boucher asked.

"I said it's not over. Not until they're dead."

CHAPTER 30

BOUCHER'S SLEEP WAS TROUBLED that night. His nightmare was of Dawn jumping the sadist and clawing his eyes out, her lithe, lovely legs wrapped around the man like they had wrapped around him during their lovemaking. One material item differed in his dream: the eyes she was clawing out were his. He sat up and wiped sweat off his forehead, then rose from the bed. He was thirsty and headed for the kitchen, then remembered his guest sleeping upstairs and put on a pair of undershorts. He walked to the kitchen, opened the fridge, and drank milk straight from the carton.

"That's very unsanitary."

"Christ, Bob, don't sneak up on me like that. What are you doing up?"

"Same as you, but I think I'll pass on the milk. You just transferred your saliva to the carton. Did you know there are more germs in your mouth than a dog's? And your refrigerator is probably between thirty-five and thirty-eight degrees Fahrenheit, which isn't enough to kill the germs, so they're breeding, right there inside your—"

"Would you like a glass of water? The glasses are in the cupboard on your right. I promise you I will never drink from a milk carton again."

"You will probably never have a scientist as a houseguest again either." Palmetto retrieved a glass and got some water from the tap. "I'm going back to bed."

Boucher also went back to bed, smiling through his grief, depression, and, yes, fear. Across the street were one, maybe two cops, doing their jobs, to be sure, but probably wishing they were someplace else. Upstairs someone else was concerned for his welfare—and his hygiene.

Fitch called the next morning, on Boucher's landline. How quaint it seemed to hear a phone ring, to actually pick it up, mindful of the limitations of a cord, and say, "Hello."

"This is Fitch. I've been granted an audience with His Royal Highness John Perry. You can't imagine how much I hate it when some smug 'executive assistant' calls and tells me the boss will see me at ten. The boss can suck my dick. Anyway, I'll be at your place about noon. Anything I can bring you?"

"How about a muffaletta?"

"I'll bring two. You got some beer? I can't eat a muffaletta without a beer."

"Better make it three. I've got a houseguest. And yes, I have some beer."

"So he's staying with you? Good."

Boucher fixed his coffee using his favorite coffeepot. It made him feel that life might one day return to normal.

"Hmm, that coffee smells good," Palmetto said.

Boucher spun around. "Damn. Will you quit sneaking up on me like that?"

"You want me to wear a bell? I can't help it; I tread lightly." He walked to the kitchen window and looked out toward the old slave quarters.

"What's in back of your property? Could they get in over there?"

"Behind the slave quarters there's another antebellum home. It backs up to my property. It's now a museum. The only access to it is from the streetfront and it closes at five. By the way, I just thought of something. With the first package you sent me, there was something like a matchbox with little things in it. Some looked like buttons, some looked like hearing aids. You never told me what they were for."

"I forgot about them. They were Mark's idea. The things that look like hearing aids, that's what they are, more or less. You have them handy?"

"I'll get them."

He gave the box to Palmetto, who lifted out plastic objects no bigger than a fingernail. "The red earbuds are amplifiers. They have a tiny on/off switch on top. See here?"

"Yes."

"They amplify sound and are only for use in limited situations where there is little or no ambient noise. You can hear a rat crawl across the floor in the next room, but if a fire truck races by with sirens blaring you'll go deaf, so you have to be careful with them. The white ones look just the same but they're suppressors; just fancy earplugs."

"What are these things that look like after-dinner mints?"

"Nitrocellulose. It's flash paper like magicians use, compressed into a little wafer."

"What good are they?"

"Actually, they're a failure. Remember when we lost power in the sub? Mark came up with the idea to have these things in our pockets so we'd have easy-to-reach illumination in total darkness. But they're too unstable to carry around and the flash is too brief. Also, in total darkness the light is momentarily blinding. Anyway, you break the wafer. It causes a spark and ignites the nitrocellulose. Just make sure you close your eyes when you do."

"So I've got to close my eyes, and when I open them the light is already gone?"

"Yeah, as an invention it's a dud. Not really Mark's invention anyway. Jules Verne used it in his novel *From the Earth to the Moon*. That's how long it's been around."

"I think I'll finish my coffee outside. Care to join me?"

"No, thanks. I'm going upstairs to shower and shave. I heard Fitch say he'd be here at noon."

A lightweight jacket was sufficient for a stroll through the back garden. Boucher walked the perimeter lost in thoughts, memories, and regrets. He walked beneath the overhanging slave quarters feeling the chill of the shadows, and returned to the sunny center of the courtyard. He noticed that the stairs to the second story needed paint. He recalled what Dawn had said about responsibility and ancestors, and vowed to attend to this overlooked part of his residence. Someday. His coffee was cold before he finished it and he returned to the house.

The morning hours passed with interminable slowness. He could have counted every tick of the clock on the mantel, but had no interest in knowing the time. The phone rang, a shrill reminder of a world outside his solitary confinement. It was Fitch. He was on his way over.

Fitch stormed in when the door was opened for him. "Perry's been woodshedded," he said. "Fucking lawyers. There were two of the weasels in the office with him. He said he had no idea where Cantrell was and he couldn't believe his involvement in attempted murder. He tried to accuse you of having worked for him to steal company secrets and that you probably dreamed up the story. Can you believe it?"

He walked into the kitchen with the sandwiches he'd brought in a paper bag, opened the refrigerator, and pulled out three beers. "Where's Palmetto?"

"He's right behind you. He treads lightly."

"Hello, Detective Fitch," Palmetto said.

Fitch stared at the emaciated man.

"I'm Bob Palmetto." He offered a handshake.

"You called me yesterday about the judge," Fitch said.

"That was me."

"And you're the guy who started this mess all those years ago."

"I started trying to save my ass all those years ago, if that's what you mean," Palmetto said.

"Then you deserve to know this too. Our lab confirmed that the bullet that killed Dexter Jessup and the one we found at Rexcon's lab in Morgan City were fired from the same gun. Judge Boucher is the only witness to Cantrell's possession and firing of the weapon."

Fitch doled out the sandwiches and beer and the three of them traded ideas, mostly about the whereabouts of Bert Cantrell.

"I think he's close by," Palmetto said. "Judge Boucher could sink their whole operation. I think he's watching and waiting from somewhere right in the neighborhood." He took another bite. "Man, this is good." Palmetto finished his muffaletta. He had eaten it in three bites. "I'm a Louisiana man," he said, "and it's good to be home."

Fitch had other business and left. Palmetto went up to his room to rest and Boucher went to his study to pass a few hours reading. His antique collecting was not limited to decorative pieces; he also had a passion for rare books. Though his books contributed as much to his home's atmosphere as his furniture, they were not just for looks; Jock Boucher actually read his rare manuscripts. As with all of his collectibles, he took as much joy in the hunt as in possession and was always on the lookout for online bargains. There were few greater joys than finding a masterpiece at a fraction of its value.

The study was also on the first floor and he adjusted the blinds to give him natural light for reading, then he perused the floor-to-ceiling shelves of volumes. He selected the first of a two-volume set of *The Count of Monte Cristo* by Alexandre Dumas, printed by Chapman and Hall, London, in 1846; English first edition, polished calf-leather binding, top edges gilt, illustrated with wood-engraved plates by Valentin. He enjoyed holding the leather in his hands, turning the heavy pages. He knew the story, of course, that was why he had chosen it. This was a novel about the thing most on his mind at that moment. Revenge.

He was well into the book when Fitch called again. "I've had two patrol cars tell me you're sitting right in front of a damn picture window at street level. Damn it, Judge, don't make it impossible for me to keep you alive. Close your drapes and go sit somewhere else in the house." He hung up without saying please.

Boucher closed his book, then closed the shades. There was little light left anyway. It was late afternoon. Darkness would soon be falling.

CHAPTER 31

BOUCHER TOSSED AND TURNED, then sat up straight in bed, thinking about what Palmetto had said. The weak point in his perimeter. The slave quarters at the back corner. With police posted up and down his block and patrol cars cruising past, of course no one was going to try a frontal assault. He got out of bed and walked to the kitchen without turning on any lights. He stood at the sink, staring out at his courtyard, while thoughts turned over in his brain like clothes in a dryer. He drew a deep breath, maybe the way a scientist would on making a world-changing discovery, or maybe like a rookie cop discovering his first body. No other sound; he didn't want to wake Palmetto. He backed out of the kitchen, returned to his bedroom, and dressed: black socks, no shoes, black slacks—a better quality than he would have wished for this mission—and a black sport shirt with a breast pocket. It was color-coordinated overkill, but necessary for where he planned to sit and wait in the darkness, and for what he planned to do.

After dressing, he went back to the kitchen. With great care not to make a sound, he unlocked and opened the kitchen door and stepped outside. He crossed the courtyard and climbed the stairs to the second level, the area of his home he'd avoided and ignored since he'd first bought it: the slave quarters. He picked the room that gave him the vantage point he sought, opened the door, and entered. These small rooms were unlocked, unused, and unkempt. He broke through a barricade of spiderwebs, sticky threads clinging to his face. He felt along the wall, disturbing dust that had not been touched in decades. A stifled sneeze felt like an explosion going off inside his head. He couldn't gasp for fear of a repeat reaction and focused on breath control till he had attained it. The door to one room of the quarters open wide, Boucher pressed his back against the wall just inside the open door frame. He lowered himself, not to a sitting position, but squatting on his haunches. Asian rice farmers could hold this position for hours. He hoped he'd be able to maintain it for the time necessary.

With no idea of the hour, he stared at the roof and gutter above the corner slave room. This roofline extended to his rear property boundary. Cantrell would approach from the back, Boucher had determined, probably using an accomplice to create a diversion for the cops, maybe even approaching them in stolen police uniforms. He reached into his shirt pocket in the darkness and pulled out the box with the custom hearing aids. Trial and error told him which ones he wanted. Amazing. He could hear the ticking of the clock on the mantel in his living room. It took a while to adjust and discern the nature and origin of the sounds he heard, but the earbuds were effective. He settled in for his surveillance, and shut his eyes for just a moment.

He heard muffled sobbing, a woman crying. "They took my Tom," she said. "Hannah, they took and sold off my man."

"That's all right, Becky, Ol' Hannah's here. Let's just pray he's gone to a better place. We all goin' to a better place by and by."

"But I'm with child, Hannah. How'm I gonna care for a child when I ain't got no man?"

"The good Lord gonna care for us all. Lemme fix you a little warm milk. You'll feel better with a little warm milk, and so will that baby inside you. I'm just goin' in the next room now. You set right here.

"Becky, you get away from that railing now. That wood's done gone rotten. Get away from there, Becky. BECKY, NO!"

Boucher grabbed the plugs from his ears and opened his eyes to the pitch-black. He felt a sensation he had never known, a fierce, raging hatred. People had suffered under this roof. His nostrils flared, his upper lip curled. He seethed with an anger born of man's mistreatment of his fellow man. It gave him strength beyond mortal limitations. He heard sounds nearby. He heard the scratching movements of vermin. Crawling on the roof were rats: two-legged rats. He remained in his crouch. He listened as they climbed down the roof and dropped onto the second-floor walkway, six feet away: first one, then the other. They stopped, looked, cross-checked, took one slow step, then another. When Boucher could reach out and touch them, he stood. He closed his eyes and snapped one of the nitrocellulose wafers, momentarily blinding them both. Boucher opened his eyes just after the flash of light and threw a right cross, hitting his first opponent's chin dead on with enough force to snap his jaw. This was followed by an uppercut that lifted the man off his feet. Boucher lowered his head and butted the first victim into the second, knocking the latter off balance. The second man took two tottering steps backward and fell against the rotting wood railing. It splintered and they both fell to the ground below. Boucher jumped down, landing on top of them, feeling their bones snap as he used their bodies to break his fall. He stood up. One was still conscious and trying to move. He bent over him and delivered the most basic of boxing combinations, a right hook to the jaw followed by a jab with the left fist to the opponent's head with a power he had never known: the raw power of pure hate. The man was out. They both were.

Boucher flicked on his outside lights, all of them, and stood over the two. He stared at a lacerated face and eyes, hideous but superficial wounds inflicted by Dawn. Obviously, she'd not done as much damage as they had thought. Matt Quillen lay in a pool of blood, the dark stain expanding beneath him. Boucher kicked him over onto his back. Quillen had fallen on the hunting knife he had brought for the occasion, its lethal blade buried in his body to the hilt. The shit-heel had indeed fallen on his sword. Cantrell lay next to him, his eyes open wide, his broken jaw giving him a most curious smile. The odd position of his head showed that his neck was broken, by the punch or the fall, Boucher didn't know. He hoped it was the former. He hoped he'd killed the bastard with his own bare hands.

"They deserved to die."

This time Palmetto hadn't startled him. The two men looked down at the bodies on the ground.

"You killed them, Judge. And that is justice."

Boucher turned away from the bodies and walked toward his house, down the driveway to the front yard, and hollered for help.

There might as well have been klieg lights on his front lawn for all the cop cars, ambulances, and paparazzi that congregated around his place. Fitch had ordered a cordon of officers to keep the curious at bay. Boucher had heard an inebriated passerby with a particularly loud voice ask if they were making a movie. There were enough cameras present that this wasn't that wild a guess.

Fitch was considerate enough not to smoke in the house, but, ignoring his doctor's dictate, he'd already gone through a pack securing the courtyard as a crime scene. At least he was thoughtful enough to extinguish his cigarettes on the sole of his shoe and put the butts in his jacket pocket, which he emptied in the trash can. The odor embedded in his clothing, however, accompanied him into Boucher's fine salon. He scratched behind his ear before making his confession.

"Two guys in uniform relieved the sentries we had on duty; obviously hired by Perry and Cantrell. They were good; my guys believed them and left their posts. Either that or my guys took any cash that was offered them. It wouldn't be the first time. Anyway, the imposters probably split as soon as our guys were gone. So Cantrell and Quillen were able to enter by way of the back property with no problem."

Boucher said nothing, nodding at the people milling about within earshot. Fitch understood and ordered everyone to clear out.

"I want to know one thing from the autopsy," Boucher said. "I want to know the exact cause of Cantrell's death."

"Why?" Fitch asked.

Boucher flexed the fingers of his right hand and balled them into a fist. "I just want to know," he said.

The sun was up before the circus folded its tent. Boucher stood at the kitchen window once again, looking over his courtyard as he sipped a cup of coffee. Fitch and Palmetto sat at the breakfast table.

"Where are we now?" Boucher said. "Cantrell and the contract killer are dead. We know Cantrell killed Dexter and Ruth Kalin. Your lawyer's poor assistant all those years ago? Probably murdered by

Quillen, probably in very much the same way he killed Judge Epson. I know Cantrell shot Dawn, I heard his voice on the bayou when the shot was fired. The killers are dead."

"But their boss still lives," Palmetto said. "It's time to close the books on John Perry and Rexcon Energy."

CHAPTER 32

"**A**NY IDEAS ON HOW we get Perry?" Palmetto asked.

He and Boucher were seated in the courtyard at the glass-topped wrought-iron garden table. Chalk silhouettes in the corner marked where Cantrell and Quillen had fallen to their deaths. The chalk marks looked like graffiti, cartoonlike except for the dark stains in the center of one of the outlines. From these stains drying in the late afternoon sun could be heard the low buzzing of flies.

"Bob, I think I've had enough," Boucher said. "I think it's time to let those charged with enforcement of the law do their jobs: the police, the FBI."

"The police? Like those policemen who were supposed to protect you and walked off their posts, maybe with cash in their pockets? The FBI? Like those who investigated Judge Epson's bribery, then turned over their findings to him? Those guys? You expect them to go after Perry, a man who plays governmental agencies like hole cards in a poker hand? They won't touch Perry and he will not only get away with ordering the deaths of innocent people, he's going to be free to get away with something much, much bigger.

"Remember, I told you that the data I sent for you to use in stringing them along was incomplete. What I left out is fundamental to the safe extraction of methane hydrate. They didn't have this essential information. They didn't miss it and have no idea of its importance. We know Perry is exploring in international waters. If he goes forward without regulatory oversight he could be responsible for a cataclysm beyond our worst nightmare. That's why it is crucial that we stop him.

"Jock, with this fuel source our country can regain energy independence. We can have all we need for hundreds of years, energy that will be far superior to any source we use now. But its development must be done right. We can either begin to reduce global warming or we can dramatically increase it. We can safely mine this resource from the ocean floor or we can create chaos that will destroy the coastal areas of some of the most populous areas on the planet. If the greed of hollow men goes unchecked, if caution does not prevail, the result may not be a bang, but the whimpering will come too late to reverse the damage done." Palmetto was animated as he spoke, his hands flailing the air.

Boucher smiled. "You remind me of something Abraham Lincoln said. 'When I hear a man preach, I like to see him act as if he were fighting bees.' That's what you look like: like you're fighting bees. And you do sound like a preacher."

"I would hope, after all you've seen, that I'm preaching to the choir. I'm fighting a man as dangerous as anyone on earth," Palmetto said, "and it's not a job I'm prepared to delegate. You know, from that first minute I walked into your court, I decided to trust you. I felt your courage."

"Wasn't my court; it was Epson's."

"I knew that. I heard about his heart attack on the radio that morning. That's when I decided to turn myself in."

"I thought so."

"You treated me with respect. I appreciated that. Can I tell you something, a personal observation?"

Boucher nodded.

"I think you have too much compassion to be a judge."

"I didn't show Cantrell much compassion. I killed him with my bare hands."

"He got what he deserved."

"I'm not going back on the bench anyway," Boucher said. "I killed two men and I'm glad I did. I can't sit in judgment of others."

They were talking to each other, but were staring at flies as they massed on the blood drying in the final rays of the day's sun.

"Perry," Palmetto said.

"Yes," Boucher said. "Let's get him."

He stood up from the table as shadows fell on the courtyard. "Sun's over the yardarm. Ready for a drink?" Boucher asked.

Offer accepted, he went into the house as Palmetto followed. He fixed two glasses of bourbon and water.

"Cheers." They clicked glasses. Boucher was pensive. "I keep thinking about what the doctor said were Dawn's last words before she died. 'Get him,' and something starting with the letters d-o-b."

"Could it refer to something you did together?"

"I don't know. We didn't have time to do much together."

"It was an intense couple of days. You were hardly apart."

"She was supposed to keep an eye on me. I felt the same as you at first. I didn't believe our meeting was chance. I don't care if she had been to an art gallery like she said, or that the Columns was her neighborhood bar, and that she did own a home in the neighborhood. It was too much of a coincidence."

"Coincidences do happen, especially when all the factors you just cited line up. Anyway, of course she was told to keep an eye on you. That was just prudence."

Boucher shook his head. "I think she sought me out because she wanted to tell me something. She said she would, in her own time. She didn't get the time."

"Sounds like something was bothering her; maybe something about her job."

"Perhaps. Anyway, we'll never know."

It's not found in any manual, but there is a rule adhered to by all owners of fine antiques: After two drinks, get off the good furniture. Boucher moved the bourbon into the kitchen and they continued talking, much of the conversation recounting their near-death experience on the bottom of the ocean. After reviewing their nautical adventure, with several glasses poured in the process, both were pretty much hammered. Palmetto's laugh became a high-pitched giggle.

"Mae told us she woke up with you rubbing her ass."

"I said I was sorry."

"And Mark got out of his wheelchair yesterday. He's able to get around on crutches." He hiccupped loudly. "How 'bout them apples?" Then his chin fell to his chest and did not rise. Just like that, Bob Palmetto was out.

"Hey." Boucher nudged him. "You don't expect me to carry you up the damn stairs to your bedroom, do you? Hey."

But there was no response. Bob Palmetto had left the building. Boucher, who had left his own sobriety in a neighboring county, lifted him from the kitchen chair, astounded that an adult male could weigh so little. He carried him about as far as he was able with judgment and reason being so impaired and dropped him. It had probably been over a hundred years since anyone had actually slept on the nineteenth-century period sofa, but that night Bob Palmetto did.

Of course, the devil had his due the next morning.

Boucher had not bothered to get undressed and had just fallen on the top of his bed. When he woke, high-pitched whines were going off inside his head like clockwork, *zing, zing, zing,* the sound of his elevated blood pressure ringing in his ears. He went to the bathroom and threw cold water on his face, then to the kitchen for some coffee. Aghast, he spotted Palmetto sprawled on his antique sofa. He looked dead. He rushed over and prodded him.

"Get up, get up. You can't sleep on that."

Palmetto snorted, then rolled over on his side. And fell off the sofa. Boucher left him there. No patience for his French press coffeepot this morning, he fixed instant, heating the water by microwave. He went to the fridge for milk, cursing, furious with himself for drinking so much and getting so fucked up. He pulled too hard on the refrigerator door and the fridge slid forward. The safe. It's a pretty damn good piece of security that's installed where even the owner forgets about it. He pulled the fridge out farther, reached behind, opened the safe, and retrieved the file Ruth Kalin had given him. He put it on the counter and finished his coffee.

On the hardwood floor in the living room, his fall cushioned by a vintage handwoven Tabriz carpet, Palmetto snored like thunder.

Ten o'clock, the phone rang, jarring both to an unwanted state of cognition. It was Fitch.

"Just checking to make sure you're both okay," he said.

"We're both okay," Boucher said. "Thanks for calling."

Having been around that particular block more than once or twice himself, Fitch recognized the condition of the party on the other end of the line, and decided it was best to leave him alone. He had planned to caution them both about going out without letting him know, but from the tone of Boucher's voice there was little imminent chance of that. He'd call him later.

On the Tabriz carpet in the salon, there was movement.

"Oh, my God," Palmetto said, walking into the kitchen, where Boucher stared into a cup of stale, cold instant coffee. "What did you put in that bourbon?"

"Which one, the first or the tenth?"

The components for instant coffee were all in plain sight and Palmetto began fixing his own. He spotted the file on the counter.

"What's this?"

"File Ruth Kalin stuck in my truck. I put it in my safe and almost forgot about it."

Palmetto fixed his coffee and sat at the table. He focused his bleary eyes on the pages in front of him, turning them over slowly.

"Judge," he said softly, ominously.

Boucher looked up.

"Have you read this?" He stuck his index finger on the file.

"Ruth Kalin's file: it has charts and graphs of stock movements. I may be just an old scientist, but I did own a corporation once. I know what she was doing. She was tracking stock sales. Securities and Exchange Commission was Dawn's area of responsibility. Maybe what Dawn said she wanted to tell you had something to do with that."

"Stock fraud?" Boucher said.

"We've got a greedy CEO who will stop at nothing, not even murder. Do you think a little stock manipulation for personal gain might not be in his bag of tricks? Do you think that two women who knew of such criminal activity might not be exterminated as threats?"

Boucher looked around, at the walls, up at the ceiling, then into the eyes of Bob Palmetto.

"We've got to find out for sure," he said.

Palmetto sipped his coffee. "Gotta get past this hangover first."

Fitch paid a personal call midafternoon. He entered Boucher's living room, refusing a seat when offered. He stood before them as a priest facing penitents.

"Gentlemen," he said, "I want to tell you about the dangers of alcohol. One is especially vulnerable when one has suffered an emotional loss or crisis."

Boucher threw a pillow at him and Palmetto quickly followed. Fitch dodged the first, got caught in the face with the second. Both men told him to sit down and shut up. They had something to tell him. They had work to do. They needed his help.

CHAPTER 33

WHEN I FIRST RECEIVED the file," Boucher said, "I just stuck it in my safe. I forgot about it."

"If you weren't a damned judge I'd have you arrested for withholding evidence and obstructing justice," Fitch said, "but after spending a day in our evidence room, I've got to say I probably would have done the same thing."

"Also," Boucher said, "this was Dawn's area of responsibility. She was working up the nerve to make a confession to me about her work, I'm sure of it."

The three men sat in silence and stared at the open file on the kitchen table. The page to which it was opened showed a line graph with sharp peaks and troughs.

"Can you explain to me once again what this represents?" Fitch asked.

"Ruth Kalin wrote a report that explains everything in layman's terms," Palmetto said. "What this graph shows is how much money can be illegally made by backdating stock options." He saw Fitch's befuddled expression. "Backdating is just what it says: it's marking a document with a date that precedes its real date. A stock option is the right to buy or sell a company's stock at a fixed price at a fixed date."

Boucher offered his analysis. "Backdating an option is falsely altering an option to reflect a date that's before the date the company gave the option."

"I smell a rat," Fitch said, "but I'm still lost."

"The exercise price of the option is set to equal the market price of the stock on the grant date. The option value is higher if the exercise price is lower, so executives want to be granted options when the stock is at its lowest. If the executive can choose a date when the market price of the stock was low, he increases the value of his option."

"It's going to take me some time to get my head around this," Fitch said.

"It's supposed to be complicated," Palmetto said. "They get rich off our ignorance."

Boucher spoke. "Ruth Kalin made a study of the market swings in Rexcon stock every year for nearly twenty years and compared them with the company's annual reports, where option information is disclosed. What she says here is that she found evidence of Perry backdating his stock options over two decades. She claims he received over two hundred million dollars in undisclosed compensation."

"So, go nail the bastard," Fitch said.

"We feel that with his history—" Boucher began.

Palmetto interrupted him. "If Perry's been getting away with his stock fraud for two decades, don't you think he's been paying bribes to somebody for his ride? We announce to the SEC—the guys that he's probably had in his pocket all this time—they'll slam the door in our face, and Perry will bury the evidence we need to hang him."

"So what do you plan to do?" Fitch asked.

"I believe you call it B and E," Palmetto said.

Fitch laughed so hard, tears formed. He wiped his eyes with his sleeve.

"I've been on the force almost thirty years. I'm sitting here with a federal district judge and a noted scientist telling a police detective that they are conspiring to commit a felony. There's hard time involved with breaking and entering. I could turn you both in right now."

"Then Perry walks," Palmetto said. "A hundred other Perrys walk too, and they get to keep poisoning the well from which the rest of us must drink. Think of your hometown, Detective. Katrina slammed us to the mat and we've fought like hell to get back on our feet. There's not enough money for the investment we need. Our economy has been perverted by the Perrys of the world. They buy judges, politicians, regulators—and that's just to manipulate our financial system. I'm telling you, this guy's also about to do things with a unique but complicated energy resource that could cause unbelievable damage.

"I saw with my own eyes that he blasted a protective layer off a source of subsea methane hydrate. That could have caused a release of gas in such a quantity that it could have initiated irreversible climate change. He could have caused an earthquake and tsunami that could have flooded the East Coast. I'm tired of pissing in the wind. I want to get evidence so strong that no amount of money will be able to save him."

Fitch sighed. "What do you want me to do?"

"Simple. Just keep your boys away while I do what I have to do."

"You?" Boucher said. "Why you? I'm the one who knows the layout of the executive suites."

"And I was with you every step of the way with that cell phone you had in your pocket, remember? I've already got the floor plan. Right here." He tapped his right temple. "Besides, they'll recognize you. . . . What's wrong?"

Boucher looked like he'd swallowed a stone. "I just remembered. Dawn said her job was filling out forms. What is one of the most common entries on forms? *D-o-b*: date of birth. She was telling me to remember her birthday."

"No disrespect intended," Palmetto said, "but it's too late to order a cake."

"I know what she meant," Boucher said.

Palmetto definitely had the down-and-out look that fit the stereotype of a janitorial services worker. That evening he walked three times past the lobby of the Rexcon Tower until he saw a man polishing the street-level lobby's marble floor, the services company's logo on his overalls. By the next evening his counterfeit uniform was ready.

The plan was simple. Get in the building when employees were leaving, find a place to hide, then just meld in with the late-night cleaning crew and get up to the executive suites—specifically, to Dawn Fallon's desk and files. It wasn't foolproof. It was an act of faith.

He entered the building without problem, went to the basement, and found a storage closet filled with mops and brooms. He'd been told ad nauseam that he was as skinny as one, so it seemed logical to hide out with like company. He decided eleven o'clock was a good hour; late workers would have left by now, the last of the cleaning crews would still be working in the building. He changed into his uniform and got on a service elevator from his basement level. It went only to the lobby. From there he had to take another to the executive offices. In the lobby he pressed the button and waited. The security guard looked at him, then rose from his desk. He was walking toward him, staring at him.

"Hey," the security guard said, waving an unlit cigarette in one hand, "got a match?"

"I don't smoke," Palmetto said. "It's an appetite suppressant."

"Yeah, whatever." The guard returned to his desk.

Palmetto inhaled a deep breath as an elevator arrived. He stepped in and pushed the correct floor number. The executive lobby he recognized immediately. He even knew the number of steps from the elevator bank to the huge double doors that led to the executive office suites. He opened the doors and stepped inside. Dawn's office was to his left. The hallway was dark. To his right at the end of the hall, light seeped from under a closed office door, the office of CEO John Perry. Unable to resist the temptation, Palmetto walked toward the office of his nemesis like a moth to the flame.

Listening outside the closed door, Palmetto heard the sound of heavy breathing. There were piglike snorts that he recognized from his own errant ways. He was listening to the fitful sleep of an inebriate. He opened the door. Stuck his head in. Saw the man who had ruined his life sprawled out drunk on a sofa too short for his frame, empty glass and bottle on the rug beside him. Didn't he have a home to go to? Palmetto stepped inside. He walked over to Perry and stood right over him, casting a shadow on his face. He raised and looked at his own hands with their long, bony fingers; fingers that could so easily wrap around that neck and squeeze, squeeze the life out of the man. Palmetto brought his hands together as if in prayer, and bowed his head, his lips moving but no sound coming forth:

I will not take your life, but the life I leave you will not be worth living. You will lose your wealth and power: your identity. Those who once loved you will disappear. You will be alone and damned. You will long for death, but even this you will be denied. You will come to doubt whether the privileges you once enjoyed were ever real. You will retain just enough sanity to know one thing: you are living in hell.

He dropped his hands to his sides, turned, and walked out of the office, closing the door behind him.

It was a long, dark walk to Dawn's office. His cell phone had a flashlight and cast a pencil-thin ray to guide him. The door to her office was open. It was an inner office with no windows. He closed the door and turned on the light. Her desk was French provincial with a leather top. On her desktop was an antique silver blotter and inkwell. An old pen had a gold nib and a piece of carved ivory in the shape of a feather—all items purely decorative. He tried the drawer. It was locked. In a malachite pen holder containing cheap ballpoints he found a paper clip. The desk was a fine piece of furniture, but the lock was crap, a common five-pin mechanism. From his pocket he pulled a small pocketknife with a screwdriver, which he inserted into the lock with slight pressure. He straightened the paper clip and stuck it in and out slowly, gently pressing up on the base pins until all five were up and even with the shear line. He pulled open the drawer. It had taken him less than ten seconds.

The center desk drawer contained odds and ends and personal items. He moved to the larger side drawers; again with the screw-driver and paper clip. Bingo. The file was marked PERRY STOCK OPTIONS and was the first one he saw, as if it had been placed there for him to find. He stuffed it inside his overalls without even opening it, then went through the other files, finding nothing more of interest, but the first one was enough. He turned off the light and walked from the office. He again opened the double doors to the lobby. The lights were on, brightly blazing. A large black woman was pushing a metal wheeled trolley with mop, broom, and cleaning supplies. She was startled.

"What you doin' here? They ain't downsizin' again, are they? Damn it, every time I see a new white face on my floor, next day I get notice. I need this job."

"Hold on, sister. I'm not taking your spot," Palmetto said. "They asked me to find you to warn you that the boss is drunk again and for you not to wake him up. Just stay out of his office. That way we'll all keep our jobs."

She frowned. "That's all? You here to warn me?"

"Fact is, if it was me, I'd get on to your next floor altogether. Disturb him when he's out like he is now and he gets mean. He's a nasty drunk."

"Well, shit, don't have to be told twice." She turned her trolley back toward the elevator. "You comin'?"

"I'll catch the next one. You go on." And she was gone. Palmetto was right behind her.

Boucher had set himself a different task. He was committing no crime—Dawn had given him a key to her home—but it still felt like invasion. In the dark of night, it also felt plain scary.

The wrought-iron gate creaked as he opened it. That alone could have brought out the neighbors and their firearms. He walked the gravel-covered path to the front porch and the wooden stairs groaned as he stepped up between Corinthian columns. Beneath the leaded beveled glass inserts in the heavy oak door he inserted his key into the lock. It swung open of its own weight. He stood there, getting up courage to enter. Courage wasn't coming, but a car was, so he stepped inside and shut the door behind him. Dawn's unmistakable scent was heavy in the air, as if she were standing next to him. The perfume she had worn was subtle on her person, but as he stood in her home it was intense. He stifled the urge to call her name, its presence was so strong. It was enough to make him weep.

He recalled the afternoon. He'd been standing by the sofa in front of the fireplace when she'd called to him for help unfastening her necklace. Now he walked in the dark to the sofa, stood there as if waiting for the sound of her voice, and swore he heard it. Not as before, this time it was a whisper, but calling to him, calling for help. He walked toward her bedroom, wanting to find her there. The bedroom door was closed. He reached for the crystal glass doorknob and turned it slowly. Again the door swung open as if pulled from the other side.

Her authentic antebellum pieces, the solid walnut mansion bed, armoire, and dresser, all glowed with the light of the streetlamp outside. He stepped in. There was just enough light to see his reflection in her full-length dressing mirror.

He'd brought a Mini Maglite, and pointed it at the wall. He carefully removed the painting that covered the wall safe, a watercolor landscape from the antebellum Picturesque movement, and laid it on the bed. He addressed the combination lock: one complete turn left to the first number, a complete turn right past the first to the second, then direct to the third—month, day, year. He pulled. Nothing. He tried the combination again, same result. He couldn't have been wrong. He'd gotten her birth date from her Web bio and was sure he remembered it correctly. He could picture her standing in this room telling him what he needed if he ever decided to become a cat burglar. He was sure she had meant for him to know. Then he remembered. In Europe the order is different—day, month, year—and she had studied abroad. He tried the European order and the door opened. He shone the light inside the safe. There was jewelry, some cash, a will bound in blue-back legal paper, and a manila office file folder. It stood apart from her personal items. He took it out, stuck the Mini

Mag in his mouth, and read. He closed the file, the safe, and replaced the watercolor. He was done here.

Boucher was sitting at the kitchen table when Palmetto returned. He called out, "Any luck?"

"Well, I got in and got out. That was lucky. But this wasn't." He opened the file in his hands. The few pages held little information.

"I'm afraid Perry got there before I did. I would have broken into the safe in his office, but he was there, passed out on his sofa. How did you do?"

Boucher opened a similar file on the table in front of him. "Read this."

Palmetto stood behind him and looked over his shoulder. The script was feminine, the signature was Dawn's. It said:

If you're reading this, I'm either in Puerto Vallarta or I'm dead. I have a strong preference for the former. My role in John Perry's stock fraud was at first unwitting, but I should have known better and have no excuse. He was doing it long before I came on board. Then I became a witness and a party to his backdating of stock options, working with him to select the optimum dates and the various ways of covering up. It was too easy. I was too frightened to reveal what I knew, so to ease my conscience I began this record. I hope whoever is reading this knows what to do with this information. Get John Perry. He's guilty of stock fraud, and if I'm dead, he's responsible. Anyway, I hope I'm in Puerto Vallarta.
Sincerely,
Dawn Fallon

"I'm calling Fitch." Boucher grabbed his phone.

Fitch came running; he was there in ten minutes.

He did not touch the paper, but read it carefully. "I suggest you both get yourself good lawyers," he said.

"Us? Why?" Palmetto asked.

"To cover your asses. I don't want anything to corrupt this evidence and keep it out of court. You've done a good deed and I don't want it to blow up in your faces. Remember, Perry still has deep pockets. He can buy a lot of influence."

"You're right," Boucher said. "But I'm not worried. I did not break into Dawn Fallon's home. She gave me a key and she told me the combination of her safe. I'll swear to that and no one can dispute me. But we should get lawyers, just in case. I'll pay for them."

"And I didn't even find anything," Palmetto said.

"When you've got counsel, I'll call the FBI."

"No," Palmetto said, "not them. I've done that dance. Never again."

Fitch raised his hand. "You've got to trust me on this. They're the government's largest investigative body, with the broadest mandate. Fraud relating to executive compensation is one of their top priorities right now. This will have their undivided attention, I guarantee it. Now I'm calling my good buddy Detective Frank Hebert of the New Orleans Police Department. With Dawn's note we can book Perry on conspiracy to commit murder at the very least." He made the call, then looked at his watch.

"Detective Hebert will be walking into John Perry's office in about fifteen minutes to arrest him on a charge of conspiracy to commit murder. I would have loved to have done it myself, but it's better to hand this one off, for obvious reasons. I told my guys to make sure his mug shot is good enough for *The Tonight Show*. But definitely, get yourself some copies of the morning papers. Now get some sleep, both of you. You've earned it."

Boucher and Palmetto did get a good night's sleep but were up with the sun printing copies of Ruth Kalin's reports and the file found in Dawn's safe. Boucher refused to give the two FBI agents the originals when they came calling. They tried to play tough, making threats till Boucher said something he'd wanted to say for years: "Don't fuck with me; I'm a judge."

They took copies with them and left.

"I think we are due some decent coffee," Boucher said, getting out his French press.

"With chicory?"

"*Mais oui.*"

They took their cups out to the courtyard. Boucher surveyed the slave quarters and the broken railing.

"I was up there waiting," he said, "with those ear things on, and, God, what I heard."

"I told you that you could hear a rat crawling in the next room."

"It wasn't that, I was listening to slaves two hundred years ago."

"You fell asleep. Good thing you woke up."

Boucher stared at the broken railing. "It sure didn't feel like I was asleep."

"Then it was spirits," Palmetto said with no emotion or surprise whatsoever. "I felt them the other night. Somebody sure didn't like me sleeping on your antique sofa. He pushed me on the floor."

"Listen to us," Boucher said, "two educated men talking like this. I pushed you off the sofa."

"Maybe, but don't doubt spirits," Palmetto said, "they're with us. There's no doubt there was misery up there"—he pointed to the slave quarters—"and you've got to live with it because the Historical Society won't let you tear it down, but I think the spirits helped you up there. Maybe it was the spirits of slaves, maybe it was the spirits of those taken before their time, like Dexter, Ruth, and Dawn. Think about it. Two of them, one of you, and they were armed. I think you were a damned fool to do what you did, but I think you had help. I'll go to my grave believing that we both had help."

"If there are spirits up there, I think I'd better fix the place up a little."

"They'll appreciate that," Palmetto said. "Oh, by the way, you might want to put the battery back in your old cell phone. I think there's a lady who'd like to talk. She's been trying to call you."

"How did you know that?"

Palmetto just smiled.

CHAPTER 34

YOU'LL PROBABLY NEED TO charge your cell phone before calling her," Palmetto said. "That seems to be a constant failing of yours." Then he changed the subject. "I don't mean to denigrate your hospitality, Your Honor, but since I've been your guest in this fine historic home, I've had little more to eat than a muffaletta. You can't imagine the nights I've spent on the road, dreaming of standing in line on the sidewalk of Bourbon Street, maybe a U.S. senator in front of me, maybe Mayor Landrieu himself, all of us equal because it's first come, first served, all of us hungry and waiting for a table at Galatoire's.

"They take reservations now," Boucher said.

"You're kidding."

"Only for the second-floor dining room. The first floor is the same as always, and people still line up on the street to get in. On their one hundredth anniversary, they tried for a world record: longest line. Didn't make it, but it was still quite an event." Boucher looked at his watch. "It's eleven forty-five. They opened for lunch fifteen minutes ago. There shouldn't be too long a line if we hurry."

"No," Palmetto said. "No hurrying. I don't even want to walk, I want to *amble*, maybe *stroll* on over to Bourbon Street, take my place in line and wait patiently till I'm seated and served. I am going to be especially cordial to the waiter and let him know that if his pace is slow and measured, the amount of his tip will be in direct proportion to his time spent with us. I'm going to tell him as I sip my Sazerac that if he should care to regale us with anecdotes from his long history with that fine establishment, that too will be appreciated. From now on, in my vocabulary, when it has anything to do with my manner of living, the word *time* will be proceeded by the word *leisure*."

Boucher chuckled. "You don't amble, Bob, and you don't stroll. You lurk, sneaking up on people the way you do. Anyway, to celebrate your homecoming, when you're ready for lunch, just let me know and we'll lurk on over to Galatoire's."

A few minutes later Palmetto announced he was ready and they left. Stepping onto the front porch, they both stopped and inhaled deeply. The scent from the river was strong, but on its heavy air it carried the perfume of the Quarter: the scent of pastries freshly baked—beignets from the nearby French Market—the seafood and meats being prepared in numerous restaurants in a myriad of manners but all with the characteristic and unmistakable spices of Cajun cuisine. With so many places to eat preparing midday meals in such proximity, the air was an olfactory symphony, each breath a teasing appetizer.

They eased on over to Saint Philips Street and turned toward Bourbon. A Sysco truck was stopped on the corner for a delivery at Irene's, whose charbroiled oysters Boucher would not have been able to pass by, but the restaurant was open for dinner only.

"If I lived in your neighborhood, I'd weigh three hundred pounds," Palmetto said.

"Where do you plan to live, Bob, and what do you plan to do now?"

"I haven't had time to give it much thought. I've always assumed I'd do something with the private sector, but I wouldn't exclude government. I'd like to find out just what they are planning for methane hydrate."

"I hope you'll keep me informed."

"Of course I will. I owe you that."

They took a few steps further and were passing the delivery truck. There was no other pedestrian traffic on the block. Palmetto walked looking down, his hands thrust deep in his trouser pockets. He pitched forward as if he had tripped. Boucher reached out to break his fall, then was himself struck on the back of the head and knocked unconscious. The rubber heels of his shoes left parallel lines as he was dragged backward along the sidewalk, then thrown from the curb into the open back of the Sysco food services delivery truck. Palmetto was given the same treatment. At that precise moment, less than a hundred yards away, the phone was ringing in the home Boucher and Palmetto had just departed. There being no reply, a message was left.

"Judge Boucher, this is Fitch. Damn, I hope you haven't left the house. Listen. Perry wasn't in his office when Detective Hebert got there last night. He only just called and told me. He got caught up in some other nighttime fun stuff. Anyway, we've got an APB out on Perry. I don't want you or Palmetto going anywhere for the time being. I'll have men watching the house, though he'd be a fool to come anywhere near you. Anyway, call me when you get this message and I'll be over to see you as soon as I can get out of the office. You guys keep your eyes open."

The loading doors slammed shut. A man got in the cab of the truck, started the engine, and pulled away, driving slowly at first but speeding up when out of the French Quarter.

* * *

Boucher regained consciousness. "Bob?" he whispered.

"Right here," Palmetto answered. "What happened?"

"We've been abducted."

"Do you have your cell phone with you?"

"It's home charging, like you told me to do."

"Damn. Who's doing this? Fitch sent someone to arrest Perry last night."

"Maybe he was gone when they got there."

"My head hurts."

"Mine too, but I think that might be the least of our problems," Boucher said.

There was silence for nearly an hour before Palmetto spoke again.

"I don't know where we're going," he said, "but if we ever need to find our way back there, I might be able to help."

"What are you talking about?"

"Road surfacing. We were traveling on a highway constructed of joint-reinforced concrete pavements, I'm guessing about fifteen feet between the joints, and I counted just over thirty thousand joints. That's about eighty-five miles. Twenty minutes ago we turned onto a rubberized asphalt surface. That composite greatly reduces noise levels. It was much quieter than the plain asphalt surface we're traveling on now. I'm guessing it's a single lane because I've heard branches brushing against both sides of the truck simultaneously. We can get the State Highway Department to give us a map showing the different composition of state roads, we might be able to figure out our route. I don't know how long I was out, but I figure we're about a hundred and fifty miles from New Orleans."

"That's brilliant, but if Perry is our abductor, I think he's planning on this being a one-way trip."

"Well, we'll just have to change his plans. We've been pretty good at doing that so far."

"I salute your optimism," Boucher said.

They were slowing down, and even Boucher could tell they'd turned onto a dirt road, its consistency muddy. The transmission whined as wheels spun, tires unable to gain purchase. Finally, the truck stopped. The motor was shut off, they heard the cab door open and close, and heard footsteps to the back of the truck. The outside latch was slid back and the loading door was opened.

"Get out," John Perry said.

Whatever angels of a better nature might once have existed in this man, they had been disposed of by the demons in his soul. Evil shone through his hooded eyes. His eyelids were swollen and droopy, his hair matted and disheveled. He held his mouth open with his tongue resting on his lower lip, biting down lightly on its tip, as if causing himself pain was an inducement to inflict it on others. His upper lip was curled in a grimace. Given a top hat and a handlebar mustache, he would have been a cartoon of the archvillain, but this was no caricature. In his hand was a .44 Magnum.

"You first." He pointed the barrel at Palmetto. "Slowly."

"You're in enough trouble already, John," Boucher said. "Don't make things worse."

"Oh, I don't plan on making things worse. In fact, I plan on improving my position considerably. The two of you are going to help me solve all my problems. Now, get down, Palmetto. Keep your hands up. Jump. The ground's soft, don't worry."

Palmetto jumped down, the landing soft as promised. Boucher was ordered to do the same.

"Now, gentlemen, I am not going to bind your hands, but if you don't recognize it, this a .44 Magnum. You remember Clint Eastwood in *Dirty Harry*? Nobody ever put it better. Ask yourselves if you feel lucky. Just remember what Harry did to the punk."

Palmetto's calculation based on road composition was sheer genius, but Boucher knew where they were from his first breath. The scent of pine told him they were somewhere in the vicinity of the Kisatchie National Forest. Palmetto's estimate of distance supported this supposition. They were surrounded by dense growth. There had been some heavy rains; the ground beneath their feet was moist. Perry pointed his massive firearm, but only at one target: Boucher.

"If one of you moves an inch, the judge gets the first bullet. At this range I won't miss. Now, turn around and walk," Perry ordered.

The hood of the truck was pointed toward a house that was not visible until one was practically on its front porch. It was certainly not a shack, its solid construction obvious. There was a screened porch spanning the front of the building with several large wooden armchairs and tables spread about. From the roof a large brick chimney was visible, indicating a grand fireplace inside.

"It's been a hunting lodge and a corporate retreat," Perry said. "We're quite remote. You feel like whining about your ill treatment, go right ahead. There's nobody for miles and miles who's going to hear you. Go on, step up. The door's open."

They did as ordered and entered the house, stepping into a large living and dining area with, as suspected, a huge fireplace right in the middle.

"This was kind of impromptu," Perry said, "so there's no waitstaff and I'm afraid there are no refreshments."

"What do you want with us, John?" Boucher asked.

"Well, let's all sit down and I'll tell you. Over there, by the fireplace."

The chairs were massive, with thick red leather–covered cushions, a loud whoosh of air escaping from them as the three men sat. Perry rested his gun on the arm of his chair, not taking his hand off it. He leaned back.

"You boys have pretty much ruined something I've been working on for a long, long time."

"Something you stole from me," Palmetto said. "Innocent people died because of your greed and ambition."

"Ambition I'll admit to, but not greed," Perry said. "Money's not my motivation. You of all people should understand that, Mr. Palmetto. We both wanted energy independence for this great country of ours. I was a patriot, but because of your meddling, I'm now a wanted criminal."

"You're delusional," Boucher said. "In this 'great country of ours,' we don't permit the murder of innocents to further one's dreams, no matter how grand."

"Now who's delusional," Perry said. "Lives are sacrificed for the greater good every day. Sometimes they're called accidents, but people die when they get in the way of progress, Judge Boucher. People die."

"I'd like to repeat an earlier question," Palmetto said. "What do you want with us?"

"The real question is, what do I want with you?" Perry addressed Palmetto. "The judge is just here as a bystander—well, almost."

"All right then, what do you want with me?" Palmetto asked.

"I want it all," Perry said. "I want everything you have on methane hydrate. Everything. What you sent in Judge Boucher's little scheme wasn't nearly all you've got. Cantrell thought he could fill in the gaps. Well, Cantrell's gone. I want it all."

Now Palmetto leaned back in his chair. "I don't have it," he said smugly. "I don't carry it in my shirt pocket, you know."

"I asked myself about that," Perry said. "I couldn't see you traveling like a vagrant all over the country, carrying a computer, even if they have become very portable over the years. When I found out you weren't dead, I knew you had sent files to Boucher. I figured you were using cloud computing. It's in the cloud, isn't it?"

Palmetto's expression was his answer. His shoulders sagged. He slumped in his chair.

"I thought so," Perry said. "You are going to give me the key to your cloud."

"You won't be able to use it. You're going to jail for murder. And stock manipulation."

"I'm not going to jail. I'm going to follow a suggestion Judge Boucher gave me early in our relationship. He said if I wouldn't buy the information he was selling, he would take it to India. That's what I plan to do. I'm going to India. If the U.S. isn't ready to invest in this resource, I know who will. If not India, there are other options. Far from these shores, far from extradition treaties."

"I'm not going to do it," Palmetto said.

"I think you will."

"What are you going to do, torture me?"

"No," Perry said. "Him." He pointed the gun at Boucher.

Perry marched them through the house to the backyard, talking as they went.

"I'm guessing you sent me what, twenty percent of your work product? Thirty percent? It was enough to give me an idea of what you had been up to all these years, but not enough to duplicate it. I think Cantrell would have gotten there, but I think he underestimated the time it would have taken."

"But you were still going hell bent for leather into something you didn't understand. Your actions were reckless and dangerous."

"Energy is a dangerous business. Sometimes we have to make mistakes to learn."

They had stepped out into the backyard. A large barbecue grill was over to one side, on the other, what appeared to be a water well, abandoned before completion. Several pieces of rebar jutted out from the brick wall surrounding the shaft. Perry directed them toward the well, picking up a length of rope from one of the outdoor tables.

"Okay, stop," he said as they stood at the well.

"I know you both share the same love for this state as I do. That's one thing we have in common. Here in Louisiana we enjoy a more abundant variety of wildlife than anywhere else on this whole continent. We've got gators, we've got bears, birds of every description, and forty-six varieties of snakes, seven of which are venomous. A neighbor is a herpetologist. He showed me his collection once. I borrowed it, or at least part of it. The interesting part."

"No," Palmetto said. "You're not going to . . ."

"I'm not going to do a thing. You are. Take this rope and slip it over the judge's head." Palmetto hesitated. "Do it," Perry ordered, "or I'll blow a hole in him your skinny ass could crawl through."

Boucher stood with his arms hanging down at his sides, his fists tight in impotent anger. The barrel of the pistol pointed at him looked like a small cave.

"Slide the rope down to his feet and tighten it around his ankles," Perry said. Palmetto did. "Good. Now, you see that piece of rebar sticking up from the wall? Tie the rope to it, about four of your arm lengths from the end. I'm going to need about twelve feet of play. I suggest you make it your very best knot."

Palmetto measured, then tied off the rope as ordered.

Boucher was as taut as a bowstring. His arms unbound, he prayed for a chance to use them. "Shit," he said. "Why don't you just shoot me?"

"Not a bad idea," Perry said. He stepped forward. Boucher clenched his fists. Perry took another step. He was within arm's reach. Boucher tensed, ready to strike. Then Perry raised his gun and fired. Right next to Boucher's head. The concussion from the shot nearly knocked him out. His ears rang like cathedral bells as he stood there dazed and wobbling. Perry raised his left hand and pushed him over the edge like he was flicking a flea. Boucher fell down the shaft. The rope snapped taut, nearly ripping his legs from his body. Perry aimed his pistol at Palmetto, admonishing him to stand fast. He then leaned over.

"You hear me down there, Judge?"

"Fuck you," Boucher said through clenched teeth.

"There's no water down there," Perry said. "This was a dry hole. So you don't need to worry about drowning. Also, you are not alone. I have managed to get one each of the magnificent seven. They're all slithering together on the bottom. Judge Boucher, meet your new playmates."

Perry walked to where Palmetto stood and motioned him to step back. He set his gun down and checked the rope, retying it, watching Palmetto all the while.

"You move a muscle and I'll dump him down there with some of the deadliest critters on earth. Now, watch and learn something. This knot is a variation of the sheepshank," he said, "called a kamikaze. It's used in rappelling, and I've added my own little adaptation to fit the circumstances." His fingers danced. He didn't even need to look at the rope. He finished, picked up the gun, and leaned over the shaft.

"You have nothing to worry about, Judge," Perry said. "The striking distance of each one of those bad boys is no greater than its body length. I, uh, didn't measure them precisely, but I don't think there's one down there longer than six feet, and several are much shorter. I think the shaft was dug to twenty feet before we quit. You're about six feet tall, so you've got maybe eight feet of margin. Of course that margin is going to be decreasing if your pal Palmetto doesn't cooperate with me. I'll just keep lowering you down a notch. Like this." He adjusted the knot, then called down.

"Judge Boucher, let me tell you a little bit about those critters down there. First you've got a canebrake rattlesnake. He's close to six feet long. Scientific name is *Crotalus horridus*. I love that name, don't you? Despite his name, he's a bit of a pansy. He'll do a lot of rattling to scare you away before striking. He releases a lot of venom, though. It's a neurotoxin that induces paralysis. Death to humans is rare, but no picnic either.

"Next is your average copperhead. The one down there is about four feet long. His bite causes intense pain, swelling, and respiratory distress—which I imagine will be compounded by the fact that you're hanging upside down. Then you've got a cottonmouth. You can die from his bite; his venom has tissue-destroying enzymes. You'll probably be able to see him in the dim light down there. He'll throw back his head and open his mouth wide. It's white. Looks scary as shit in the shadows.

"Then I've got something special for you, an eastern diamondback rattler, the most venomous snake in North America. Death can occur within minutes. Intense pain, lots of bleeding, cardiac arrest. The rest are lightweights. You've got a harlequin coral snake, a pygmy rattlesnake, and a Texas coral snake. I'm not saying they won't give you a world of hurt, but they rarely kill folks. Can you see any of them? Judge Boucher?"

Boucher refused to answer.

"Okay. You hang out there and think about things. Palmetto and I are going into the house and hopefully do a little cloud computing. I'll be back in a while and tell you how it's going. You know something, Judge? You just might be able to answer a fascinating scientific question. Just how long does it take a man to die of bites from each and every venomous snake in the great state of Louisiana?"

"Don't do it, Bob," Boucher yelled from the depths of the shaft, his voice reverberating in his ears. "He's going to kill us anyway. Don't do it."

But Palmetto was walking away, Perry's gun digging into his side.

CHAPTER 35

BOUCHER LISTENED FOR THE sounds of stirring beneath him, but there was nothing at first. Then he heard a rattle, like dried peas in a pod. A warning, but to him or was one of the snakes warning off another? Some of them did eat other snakes. The rattling stopped. He spread his arms to try to gauge the width of the shaft. He was hanging with his back against one side. He pushed away from the wall with his arms. The width was more than an arm's length, but was it wide enough? He raised his head, his headache from the blow to his head increased by the pressure of hanging upside down. This in itself was dangerous enough. Blood could pool in his brain and cause a stroke. It could fill his lungs and cause him to suffocate. The venomous creatures below weren't his only problem.

He rested his back flush against the brick wall and tried to press the backs of his legs against it. He raised his torso. It was like an extreme sit-up. He had done thousands of them with his feet raised forty-five degrees, but at this angle? He reached out his hands. Maybe if he could grab his trousers at the knees. He reached up, looking at the light in the sky above the shaft. His fingers clutched only air. He lowered his back, took a breath, and tried again. Nothing. Did he reach any farther on the second effort? The pain in his abdomen was certainly greater on the second try. He rested for thirty seconds, if you could call it resting when straining every muscle in your neck and upper back just trying to raise your head to a horizontal position. He finally lowered his head and it hit the wall, his muscles already tiring. There was a shadow overhead.

"Sorry to tell you, Judge, but your pal Palmetto is not cooperating. Here. Have a word with him. Tell him how it's going down there. Oh, but first, let me do this."

Boucher free-fell several feet. The rope snapped taut and he again felt as if his ankles were being ripped from his legs. He cried out. Palmetto leaned over the well.

"I'm going to give him what he wants," he said. "Even if he is going to kill us, that's no way to die."

"Bob, these snakes haven't done a thing. They're more scared of me than I am of them."

"Oh?" Now Perry was leaning over the shaft. "Then let's just get you in range."

Again he was dropped. Again the excruciating pain in his ankles. And there was a whoosh of a reptile striking. It missed, but he could feel the air caused by the sudden motion. He was in the range of one of them.

"Afraid we must leave you again," Perry said. "Mr. Palmetto is expressing a wish to oblige. Perhaps we can offer you a more suitable fate. We'll see. Be back in a few. Hang loose down there."

Now there were several rattles, and Boucher thought he could hear the sound of scales slithering over the bottom of the pit. He turned his head and out of the corner of an eye could see the white mouth of the cottonmouth, open wide. There was another whoosh, as a strike just missed the top of his head. Boucher gritted his teeth and bent at the waist, lifting his upper body, reaching out, fingers extended. Fingertips touched fabric. He bent further upward. His right hand grabbed at his knee, then his left, grabbing fistfuls of chino. He pulled himself up, using the muscles of his hands, wrists, forearms, then biceps; walking his hands up his legs to his ankles. He grabbed his ankles. If the muscles in his lower back could have screamed their pain, the noise would have been deafening. He was a closed jackknife, his forehead resting against his knees. But it wasn't enough. There was still an impossible task. He felt the rope around his ankles, then stretched his arms as if he were trying to remove them from the shoulder joints. He felt around his heels till he could get one hand on the rope, then the other. He had the rope in both hands. So what? What could be done from this position? He was doubled over, his head pressed against his knees, his hands reaching above his feet. There was no movement from this position.

Yes, there was. Houdini did it. The artist's most exceptional escapes involved using musculature in ways that defied human physiology. Boucher began to reach up the rope and to push his legs away from his body, the jackknife opening. Finally, he was able to straighten out. He grabbed the rope between his knees. From this point it was rope climbing, just like in his high school gym. Just like in boot camp. He pulled himself up to the lip of the well shaft, loosened the rope from his ankles, climbed out, and fell on the soft ground, gasping for breath, staring at the blue sky above, the smell of pine replacing the smell of terror in his nostrils.

Palmetto and Perry were huddled over a notebook computer.

"So you've developed different carbon fiber composites for

decompression, separation of CO_2, and transmission of methane hydrate from the seabed," Perry said.

"Yes," Palmetto said. "The efficient use of carbon fiber composites allows for cost-efficient extraction."

"Makes sense. They're now making long-range passenger aircraft from the stuff because it's half the weight and twice the strength of the metals they had been using."

Boucher snuck up on them from behind. Perry's hands were in his lap; the gun was nowhere else to be seen. Boucher was two feet behind them, creeping forward, when Perry saw his reflection in the computer screen, stood, and fired. The shot went wild. Palmetto had also stood and knocked Perry's arm with his shoulder. Perry raised his hand for another shot, but Boucher's right cross was already on its way, one of the best punches he had ever thrown in his life. Perry's head snapped back and he fell to the floor unconscious. Boucher kicked the gun out of reach, and used the computer power cable to bind his hands behind his back. They stood over him.

"Is he dead?" Palmetto asked.

Boucher knelt down and felt his neck for a pulse. "No," he said.

"Good. Let's dump him in that snake pit in the interest of science. I would like to know how fast the poisonous vipers of Louisiana can kill a certified son of a bitch."

"It's tempting," Boucher said. "It's awful tempting."

EPILOGUE

TWO MONTHS LATER, JOCK Boucher had chartered the forty-eight-foot ketch because he liked the name, *Revenge*. She was sleek and swift under sail, a luxury vessel. For many the chance to sail such a craft at sunset across Banderas Bay on Mexico's Pacific coast, one of the world's loveliest bodies of water, was the pinnacle of luxurious living. He assumed that the ship's name was a reference to Oscar Wilde's famous quote, with which he agreed. Living well was the best revenge.

But neither living well nor revenge was on the agenda on this evening. His was a solitary and a solemn task. He was lucky his bag had not been opened by customs on arrival in Mexico; his suitcase contained jars with labels identifying their contents as crushed black pepper. He had not prepared a logical excuse for carrying such a quantity of the condiment if challenged, knowing only that if he had declared Dawn's ashes the red tape would have been endless. He was the only passenger on board the ketch. His mission was to grant her last wish. The gentle waves would carry her ashes to the shore and she would lie eternally on the sandy beaches of Puerto Vallarta.

*   *   *

"Did you catch anything?" Malika asked when he returned to the hotel.

He raised his empty hands. "That's why they call it fishing, not catching," he said. "Did you enjoy your day?"

"That's not hard to do here. I napped out by the pool, went into town to shop, found this great place on the beach where people go to watch the sunset. I missed you." She kissed his cheek.

"Thanks for understanding," he said. "Some things a man's got to do when he gets next to water."

"I know, I know, but that's all you get. No more solo adventures. Where would you like to have dinner tonight?"

"Someplace on the beach."

"Okay. Get yourself ready. Oh, by the way, I was watching CNN and there was something about a businessman from New Orleans. He was refused bail and is awaiting trial on a lot of charges. Sounds like an awful man. His name was John Perry. Did you know him?"

"I knew who he was," Boucher said. He walked to the bathroom and turned on the shower. "I knew who he was."

He turned the water on full force and hot—and heard the phone ringing. Malika answered it, then called out, "It's Bob Palmetto for you."

Muttering curses, he wrapped a towel around himself and walked to the phone.

"Perfect timing. I was in the shower."

"Ah, well, drip-dry, Judge," Palmetto said. "Did you hear the news about Perry?"

"Malika just told me."

"I wish him a long and miserable life. With him behind bars, I think we can say the case is closed."

"I think we can. How's the new job?"

"I don't know whether I can even discuss it over an international phone line. I tell you, I'm working for one of the most secretive government agencies in the world. You just whisper 'methane hydrate' and doors slam shut. They don't want *anyone* knowing about what they're really doing until they're good and ready. They treat me like I'm Einstein with plans for an atomic bomb in my head, but I'm not complaining. I think they mean well. More important, I think they're responsible people. They're treating this with the respect it deserves. You two having a good vacation?"

"We are. This place is beautiful."

"What's next? Have you decided whether you're going back on the bench?"

"No. I've got another month before I have to decide. Malika and I might go to India. I'll think about it on our trip."

"Well, happy trails. Give me a call when you get back."

"I'll do that, Bob. You take care." He hung up the phone.

"Was that the gentleman you helped?" Malika asked.

"We sort of helped each other," Boucher said.

She walked up to him and put her arms around his neck. "I should be angry with him. I thought for a while that whatever you were doing with him had taken you away from me."

He put his hands on her waist and looked into her eyes. "I thought whatever you were doing with your client had taken you away from me."

She shook her head. "We must learn to trust each other. Now get dressed. I'm starving."

There was a knock at the door. Malika went to open it as he stepped into the bathroom, closing the door.

"Jock, you'd better come here," she said.

"Malika, I'm wrapped in a towel."

"I still think you'd better come here."

He gave the towel a tighter wrap, then stepped out. A man in U.S. Air Force blues stood in the center of the room, a bird colonel. He removed his hat.

"Judge Boucher, I'm Colonel Lance Barrett. I have orders to transport you to Washington immediately."

"Orders from whom?"

"From the President of the United States, Your Honor."

"The President wants me? What for?"

"I wasn't told, sir. We need to get moving. There are several aircraft in holding patterns pending our departure. The President of Mexico granted us landing rights, but we have a tight window."

"What about my friend?" Boucher motioned toward Malika.

"I'm sorry. The F-15 Strike Eagle is a two-seater."

"That's a jet fighter. You flew a military aircraft into Mexico's sovereign airspace?"

"The President is anxious to see you, sir."

Boucher shook his head and turned to Malika. "I'm sorry, honey."

She smiled. "I'll be fine. You'd better get dressed before you drop that towel."

He walked to the bathroom, then turned to the officer. "Can you tell me one thing, Colonel?"

"What's that, sir?"

"Is the President pissed off at me?"

"I'll have to let him address that, Judge Boucher."

POSTSCRIPT

METHANE HYDRATE IS POISED to become a major worldwide energy resource. It is estimated that there is twice as much methane hydrate in the world as all other carbon-based fossil fuel sources combined.

Methane hydrate is found in marine sediments and Arctic regions. Consisting of gas molecules surrounded by a cage of water molecules, it resembles snow or clumps of crushed ice. A striking feature of this ice: when lit, it burns. It is stable in ocean depths of more than three hundred meters and can form layers several hundred meters thick. Mapping by the U.S. Geological Survey has shown an immense deposit of methane hydrate off the outer continental shelf of North and South Carolina. Other deposits have also been discovered in U.S. offshore areas. Other countries that are actively exploring and developing deposits of methane hydrate in their own territorial areas include Russia, China, India, and Japan. New Zealand has recently announced that it intends to be the first country to commercially produce fuel from methane hydrate. The U.S. government has announced its plans to begin large-scale production tests for methane hydrate in the Arctic in 2012.

Methane is clean-burning, and one source claims that replacement of current coal and petroleum with methane extracted from hydrate could reduce global carbon dioxide emissions by 50 percent.

On the downside, disturbance of subsea hydrate layers may destabilize the ocean floor and cause landslides on the outer continental slope, which may in turn cause tsunamis engulfing coastal population centers. Furthermore, excessive release of methane gas into the atmosphere may contribute to global warming.

In summary, a clean-burning, abundant energy resource exists that may last for centuries and lessen reliance on imported fuel sources for the United States and several other of the world's leading economic powers. The development of this resource may create entire new industries and the jobs that accompany them. It also presents challenges and risks that will require analysis and prudence, if not an abundance of caution.

But regardless of one's perspective, the term *methane hydrate* is about to assume a prominent position in the lexicon of global energy.